CW00520153

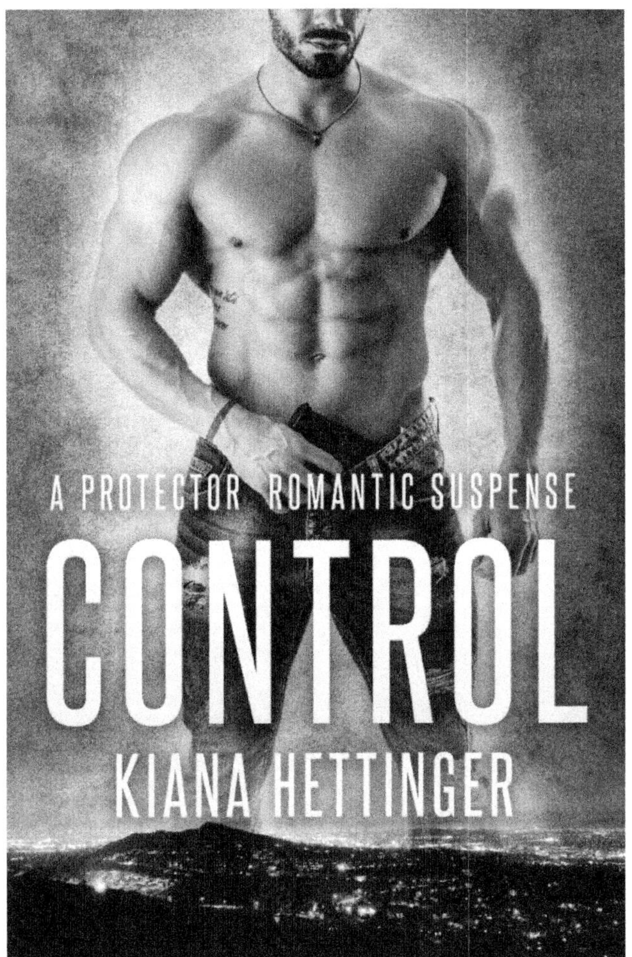
A PROTECTOR ROMANTIC SUSPENSE
CONTROL
KIANA HETTINGER

A Friends to Lovers Protector Romantic Suspense

By Kiana Hettinger

This book is an original production of Hardmoon Press.

ASIN:
ISBN: 9798594072824

Dedication

This book is dedicated to all my closeted kinksters
Come out and play
We have chocolate

More from Kiana

NOVELS

NOVELLAS

Coming Soon...

PNR ROMANCE

Light of Embre Series
The Hunt Trilogy
Alpha Elite Trilogy

DARK ROMANCE

Exotic
Captive
Carnal
Uncover

BILLIONAIRE

Billionaire Heartbreakers Club

Keep in Touch

Newsletter: www.sendfox.com/hardmoonpress1 free novellas and release updates

Facebook: @AuthorKianaHettinger

Twitter: @HettingerKiana

Please Consider Reviewing

Reviews go a long way in helping authors get noticed. If you have read any of my works, please consider leaving a review on Amazon, Goodreads, BookBub, or your own blog. I'd love to feature any reviews or comments.

Contents

Chapter One

Lafayette Street wasn't wide per se, but Evie always forgot how intimate it could feel until it was too late. Too much ornamentation crammed the sidewalk for it to be so narrow, cutting its labyrinthine way between Chinatown and Little Italy. Lafayette made neighbors out of strangers.

Evie, stranger turned neighbor herself, felt Lafayette was the quintessential city street, several running blocks spanning her entire world. There could be no other reason for why she focused the whole theme of her first art show on said street, or why she simply named them the street numbers of each block she painted. No other reason than she liked it and wanted to capture it.

Evie was about to learn a very important lesson on artistic inspiration. Namely that everyone expected there to be more to it than mere preference.

The first patron to corner her, babbling questions of 'why' and 'how' and 'what does it mean' drove Evie into the bathroom, anxiety coiling around her stomach in a tightening snake of panic. She didn't have answers. She didn't know what else to say aside from what she had already said. She did it that way because it felt right.

Other people are going to ask, she thought to herself, the flop sweat she feared more than anything lining her upper lip and catching the light like opals. *They'll all want to know.*

She wished Rachel was with her. Rachel didn't have an artistic bone in her body, so she never bothered Evie with questions like 'where do you get your inspiration?' Rachel accepted that Evie had this talent and was putting it to good use. Nothing more to the story. It was her clear-sighted straightforwardness that connected the two of them. Evie was bright-eyed and open to inspiration but loathed the idea of explaining it. Rachel was black and white and what Evie needed most right now.

"Just laugh and say something enigmatic," Evie told her reflection in that fancy gallery bathroom. It was all onyx and polished marble, gilded handles, and fixtures she could tell were hollow. She pressed the pad of one finger to the spotless mirror. "You're the artist. They're here to see you. Anything you say, they'll eat it up."

Her breathing had become shallow, and she tried to return its fullness. There were artists she had worked with or admired who managed to shrug, wave a hand, and shoot off something about the mystery of the process. Evie's own mother called it 'being a vessel receptive to genius' though admiration wasn't what she felt for that woman.

Evie gave the whole routine a practice run in the bathroom, studying each move in the mirror, trying to line the feel of the pose up with the intent of it. In the end, she felt it looked dumber coming from someone who was obviously playing the role.

"That's cool," she managed to laugh, dropping her arms at her sides. "Just be yourself. You're charming and whatnot. People will get a kick out of you."

She gave her reflection a once over then dropped her chin into her chest and heaved a ragged sigh. If only Rachel would have let her come to this thing in jeans. If only she wasn't teetering around in heels picked out for her by an eager shopgirl excited for the commission. She should have gone to Chinatown and bought knockoffs like she usually did. That had actually been her plan until Rachel got wind of it and dragged her somewhere filled with glass cases and the sharp alcohol scent of expensive perfume.

After deciding there was no time like the present and being utterly tired of staring at her own face, Evie headed back out to the main room of the gallery. To her excitement and horror, there were more people on the floor now, milling around in lazy, wine-drinking circles. She saw a cluster of heads turn to her, and her heart, which had been rapidly beating up 'til a second ago, screeched to a halt like a reckless city bus.

"The artist herself," the curator of the gallery said as Evie stepped out of the shadows of the alcove in which she was hoping to hide out until everyone was gone, "Genevieve Hansen."

She watched the cluster applaud her in a performative spectacle. One woman held her plastic cup of wine between her teeth in order to free both hands. Evie had to look away so as not to burst out laughing. The woman resembled a trained animal doing a clever trick, her flippers flapping against each other in a bid for her reward.

"You capture humanity very well," a small light-voiced man told her, putting a cold hand on her arm. "These people in your paintings...it's like I can see their souls."

"Thank you," Evie said, blushing with both genuine embarrassment and pride.

"How did you manage to get such a sense of urgency in this one?" the woman who put the cup between her teeth asked. "The runner passing the fishmongers working around the man dragging his food cart. It's so alive, I could swear it was about to start moving."

"I take photos first and then go through them and find ones I like." This was a question Evie could answer. More practical process inquiries, less waxing poetic about ideas and inspiration. "My photography isn't that great, but it doesn't need to be. The point is to have that moment frozen."

"Plus, some of us help her." Rachel appeared on Evie's left and bumped into her with her hip. She pouted, which Evie knew to read as a smile. Rachel's lips were heavy and full so even when she smiled, she looked pouty.

Evie hip-checked her friend back, though in reality her savior couldn't have come a moment too soon. "Every artist needs help at some point. I hesitate to use the word 'muse' but if ever I had one it would be –"

"Oh, enough with that malarkey," Rachel snorted. Her whole family had a habit of using goofy words that made them sound like they were a thousand years old. Few people could pull it off, and Rachel was one. "All I did was point at the runner and say, 'boy, is that guy built or what?'"

The cluster laughed politely, and Evie took the chance to pull Rachel away from the crowd and into a quiet corner. She knew there was a time limit anywhere she went. Even when they had only been sitting together for a moment, she could see people whispering to each other and motioning in her direction.

"Jesus God, it feels like high school," Evie muttered, noticing how Rachel cringed at her using the lord's name in vain. "Everyone pointing and gossiping together."

"Except now they're not saying, 'look at how weird Evie Hansen is.' Now, they're saying, 'look at that amazing artist. I'll bet she's weird.'"

Evie snickered and glanced over at Rachel with narrowed eyes. She wanted to tell her how happy she was to see her, how much more relaxed she felt now that Rachel was around. Instead, she leaned her head on Rachel's shoulder and exhaled as if she had been holding her breath all night.

"You're here to answer everyone's questions for me, right?" Evie asked, tugging on the side of Rachel's immaculately tailored dress. "Anytime someone asks about my inspiration, you can explain it to them."

It had only been half joking and they both knew it. Rachel always stepped in when Evie's anxiety got the best of her. The only place Evie felt calm was her studio, and she'd been forced out of her controlled environment for too long.

"Of course, boo-boo," Rachel replied in a tone that edged on mocking. She reached over to wind a finger through one of Evie's trademark curls then retracted her hand when she couldn't snare one. "Huh, it's like I forgot your hair was straightened. Isn't that funny? When I'm not looking at you directly, I can't even picture you with flat hair."

"Flat?!" Evie sat upright, arms crossed over her chest. "It's straightened. Not flat."

"You know what I mean," Rachel said, tossing her own hair away from her face. "I'm just not used to you without that halo of lovely curls."

Neither was Evie, if she was being honest. There had only been a handful of times in her life when she bothered to straighten her hair, and it took forever. This time, she had gotten it done professionally and it still took hours. But she had decided after turning her head side to side in the mirror, it was worth it. Her chin length curls had been crafted into a sleek 20s style wave, and since they hadn't quite lost their coppery summer glow, they shimmered with a blond-hinted auburn. Rachel had found Evie a dark brown dress, declaring it officially time for autumn colors, and made her put on makeup. In the end, Evie thought she looked okay but would have much preferred to be comfortable.

"We women are not here to be comfortable," Rachel had hissed as she zipped Evie into the sleek, shining dress. "We are here to kick ass and look fantastic."

Easy for Rachel to say; she always looked fantastic. Tanned and pouty with long dark hair, she turned heads constantly, which is saying something in a city like New York. Plenty of beautiful people strolling around, as Evie was always noticing in her attempts to capture moments of humanity. For someone like Evie, curly headed with bright green eyes behind round glasses, it was easy to feel like a face lost in a crowd of millions stacked on top of one another.

Jackson almost flaked on the art opening. He'd been tired all day and for a reason he couldn't figure out, his head was pounding. The aspirin he took did nothing except irritate his stomach. It was almost an hour before he realized he had taken them without food, then a few moments longer for him to remember he hadn't eaten all day.

Lapses of judgment like that had become commonplace for Jackson. His mind was still on that sweltering night several months ago when his whole life changed.

On the way to the gallery, he found a small dim sum place closing up shop and bought whatever dumplings they had left, eating them out of the oil-logged container as he power walked to the village.

Damn arty types making me go out of my way, he thought bitterly. Then he remembered it wasn't any 'ol art type. It was Evie's art opening, Rachel's best friend, and Rachel would murder him if he missed it. She had told him as much, though she'd tried to make it sound like a joke. Jackson knew his sister too well to fall for that.

When he entered the gallery, the headache which had slightly abated came roaring back. The lights alternated from too bright to too shadowy, and people moved in chaotic patterns he couldn't figure out. Just trying to cross the floor he crashed into two different couples. They each regarded him politely, if not particularly warmly, and he was thankful for the fact that Rachel had reminded him to dress nicely.

From across the room, in an almost darkened corner, he saw Rachel sitting next to a striking young lady in a chocolate brown dress. If he hadn't been going that way to see his sister, he would have been drawn in her direction anyway. Whoever the woman was, he couldn't stop staring.

"Rachel," he called as he got closer. He didn't raise his voice too much; just enough to get her attention. They had a bad family habit of shouting in quiet situations. Not because they meant to but because they were used to talking loudly over their big, noisy family. "I made it."

"So you did," Rachel said, getting to her feet. Her eyes went to his hair and she started to mention it, but he furrowed his brow.

His normally close-cropped hair had grown into a dark mess of waves. The sides almost touched his ears now. Completely unlike him. He knew she'd see it as a bad sign and he wasn't in the mood.

The woman next to Rachel stayed seated, her eyes furtively moving around the room.

Rachel stepped aside and asked, "What do you think of Evie's work?"

"I didn't get a chance to check it out yet."

"She's the main showcase. There are two other artists but honestly, no one's hounding them the way they're hounding her."

"I guess she's in hiding, huh?" Jackson craned his neck to survey the room searching for the bobbing head of dark curls and a flash of jeans covered in clay dust and paint. When he came back to Rachel, he noticed how the odd expression she and the young lady next to her were giving him. "What? Where is she?"

With bugged eyes and an incredulous snort, Rachel pointed down at Evie. The woman waved meekly then tugged at her dress, letting it snap back against her skin.

"I'm not usually dressed like this," she told him as if to promise there would be no hard feelings.

"I'll say." Jackson cleared his throat and shook his head. "I'm sorry, Evie. I... I don't think I've ever seen you done up so fancy."

Rachel gingerly touched a stray hair on Evie's head back into place. "I helped. Or, more accurately, I pointed her in the right direction."

"I should have guessed as much. Considering that you, my darling sister, are always so ravishing."

Rachel gave another snort at that, slapping Jackson's shoulder with the back of her hand. The two of them had grown up close and gotten closer as adults. In a big, loud family, allyship is as precious as attention or bathroom time, especially since they all had to share one of those.

Evie squirmed a little. She inched one side of her hips up then rested it back down. Jackson thought she looked like she was trying to adjust her underwear without anyone noticing but when she stood up, it was more obvious than he cared to admit that she wasn't wearing any.

"I can't wait 'til I'm famous enough that I can come to one of these in my normal clothes and everyone will just think I'm eccentric and delightfully quirky." Evie straightened her dress as well as she could. "I'm super thankful that all of this is happening and just thrilled that people like my work, but I'd rather be at home making more art. Hobnobbing isn't a skill they teach you at art school."

"They should," Rachel said, her eyes now locked on a man across the room. "That way at least they'd be teaching you something useful."

Now it was Jackson's turn to land a slap. Rachel brushed his hand off her shoulder and fluttered her fingers at him dismissively. "Evie knows I'm joking."

"You can go introduce yourself, Rachel," Evie told her, almost hushed and embarrassed to be noticing her friend's wandering eyes. "I should really face the masses and do another round myself."

"As long as you're ok with it," Rachel responded but she was already cutting through the crowd to the spot right next to a wealthy looking dark-haired man staring intently at one of Evie's small earth-colored sculptures.

Jackson extended his arm for Evie to take, and they re-entered the polite noise of art patrons sipping and whispering and crisping into the starchy snacks laid out for them. It wasn't the first time Jackson attended an art opening, but he struggled to think of another one he had been to. Growing up in the city, art was everywhere, and even though he himself never really sought it out, there were always friends with shows and college girlfriends doing performance pieces in some warehouse in Brooklyn. For his money, this was the first time he was sure the artist in question would be a huge success.

Evie stopped in front of the first piece of the Lafayette series. It was a frozen moment of two cops buying pastries from a Chinese bakery. The bakery was one of those long buildings with no doors on the front except a metal sheet that came down like a garage when it was time to close. The one cop was paused in a peal of laughter shared by the old couple working behind the counter. The other cop already had his purchase in his mouth and was balancing the wax paper bag in the same hand as his coffee.

"You did this?" Jackson asked, leaning in as far as he figured he was allowed to go. "Wow."

"Yeah, it was the first in this series. It made me realize I could do a million paintings of Lafayette street alone and never run out of interesting subjects."

Jackson studied the two cops in the painting, amazed at how specific yet ordinary they looked. He felt like he was staring at an image of himself and his late partner even though neither of them fit the descriptions of the men in the image. It occurred to him that there was more universality than he cared to admit; that a picture of cops laughing with a store owner while buying pastries and coffee could look exactly like people he knew solely because the action was so familiar.

A small shiver passed through him, nothing Evie noticed (at least he hoped), and he wanted more than anything to get away from that painting. He moved along to the next one, Evie's arm still connected by the crook of their elbows.

"I guess I never really got to see much of your work, Evie," Jackson said as he studied the next one, faking the intensity with which he had inspected the one with the cops. "Maybe, like, a sculpture or something from your student days but nothing on this level. It's really something else."

"Thanks, I worked really hard on it." She allowed herself an inspection of her own, but of Jackson's attire and freshly shaved jawline. "And thanks for dressing nice for the event. You clean up well."

Jackson did the same snort Rachel always did. "Right back at ya, kid." He smirked, glancing at her out of the corner of his eye. "I don't think I've ever seen you look like this."

"Like an adult?"

"Yeah, but more than that."

He ended his thought there. No need to tell her that he had literally never seen the shape of her body before; that he was surprised at how lean and toned her arms were and that he was fitting the lines together in his head as to what her slender torso looked like stretched out on a bed. His bed. Her bed with him in it.

Jackson cleared his throat, hoping the image in his mind would move along with the noise he made. It didn't work, and he silently hoped Evie couldn't read his thoughts. It would only lead to disaster.

Chapter Two

It was a relief to be pulling up to her familiar brownstone. Not only because she could soon slip out of her binding, albeit stunning dress and kick off those modest, as Rachel called them, heels but because the whole night had been overwhelming. Everyone wanted to talk to her. Everyone wanted a piece of her. She had never felt so flattered and so dehumanized all in a few hours.

Eventually, she had tugged on Jackson's arm and whispered for him to get her out of there. The night was winding down anyway, and the last score of patrons had crossed the threshold from appropriately tipsy to drunker than they realized.

One large man had cornered Evie to gush about her work in an intoxicatedly genuine way. She hated the overly familiar tone many of the guests took with her, but this time it was uncomfortable, embarrassing. He rambled drunkenly on about growing up in the city and feeling like it had lost its energy, its spirit.

"Your paintings brought it all back for me," he said, a burst of his hot breath exploding into Evie's face. She could smell the putrefying mixture of booze and gallery-bought cheese churning in his gut. "You reminded me of why I loved living here."

She wanted to say thank you and take the comment as a lovely compliment, but he had isolated her, gripping her arm tighter as he spoke.

When she made eye contact with Jackson from across the room, he sauntered over with his cop walk and extracted her with a simple, "Honey, I've been looking everywhere for you."

Since Jackson towered over both Evie and the creep with horrid whiskey breath, and had the broad shoulders of a linebacker, even her unwanted admirer got the hint. He stumbled off muttering something under his breath.

Jackson drove her home after the event. The gallery was close enough to her building, she could have walked, but something about the night made her apprehensive. She didn't want to be alone.

He'd asked her if she wanted him to walk her inside, but Evie tittered lightly, tilting her head to the side. "I've entered my empty apartment by myself millions of times," she had told him. "Thank you, but I think I'm fine."

"Hey, I dunno. Maybe you're worried about your number one fan being there to tell you more sad stories about his childhood."

"But the city, it has no more spirit!" Evie rested a hand against her forehead in a melodramatic pantomime. "Whatever shall we do?!"

"Don't get the vapors, my darling," Jackson joked, fanning her rapidly. "Stay strong for me. Promise me you'll stay strong."

Evie bit her lip as a spurt of laughter choked out through her nose. She dropped her hand, happy to see Jackson smiling again.

He had always been warm and easygoing, a perfect nature for law enforcement, Evie had decided when she heard he was going to be a cop. By his size alone, which had become even more impressive these past few months, Evie thought Jackson could subdue the hardened city singlehandedly.

Evie's unorthodox childhood didn't lend itself to the fondest image of authority, especially the police, but she remembered Rachel telling her about him getting into the academy and thought that if more of the cops were like Jackson, people might actually trust them. He was fast to calm situations down, to de-escalate tension with his charming smile or well-timed joke, not that many criminals would be dumb enough to try him.

"Thank you for the ride home," Evie said as she fumbled for the car's door handle in the dark. She found herself thinking 'less than innocent' thoughts about her best friend's big brother and needed to get out of there quick.

"It was my pleasure, but you know, you could take a cab instead of walking. When it's late like this."

"It's not that late."

Evie looked at the numbers on Jackson's dashboard clock. They were the color of toxic waste, and in the moderate darkness of a city night, since cities rarely ever go completely dark, they seemed to pulse.

"You're about to be a rich and famous artist," Jackson told her. "Spend a few bucks on a cab so I don't have to worry about you."

"Yeah, yeah, yeah."

Evie got out of the car then closed the door and leaned into the open window. Her hair had fallen out of shape slightly, and pieces of it were rebelling against the ozone layer of hair spray and product used by the woman at the salon.

In that moment, with the halo of stoop lighting behind her, Jackson saw a flash of the Evie he remembered, the goofy skinny kid who had to wrinkle her nose to keep her glasses in place.

"I'm glad I came out tonight," Jackson said. "I didn't want to but Rach... well, you know how she can be."

"I do." A long beat as Evie gave a slow smile. "I'm glad you came too." She removed herself from the window and waved over her shoulder as she started toward her building. "Get home safe!"

Jackson waited until the front door clicked shut and he could see Evie walking through the shabby lobby of faded colors to the stairs.

He put his car into gear and started the drive out to Queens. No man's land, Rachel called it when he moved there even though he lived only a few blocks from a subway stop. Rachel and Evie were both true city creatures, but Jackson liked the idea of being able to have a car, a yard, all the things they never appreciated as children.

He had always said that when he had enough seniority to put in for a transfer, he would ask to be sent to Long Island. Find a town out east with less than ten thousand people, buy an old house on a bunch of acres, hear silence and see darkness. All that seemed further away than ever now.

He didn't mind being on leave, even though he was dying to get back to work. There were projects to do around the house like the barbeque pit he had managed to finish just in time for summer to end. Some friends from the force came over for a Labor Day party, none of them razing him about how nobody starts building a barbeque pit in August. He had expected a few comments, some good-natured jokes, but there was nothing. The absence of them only made him feel worse; people were being too nice to him because they didn't know what he could handle.

Jackson's partner had been one of the better cops at the precinct. He had grown up in Rockaway Beach, the first person to turn Jackson on to the charm of Queens. Marcus had seen the way the cops treated him and all the other black kids in the neighborhood. Jackson was surprised that this would inspire him toward law enforcement, but he often told Jackson that you can't change the system from the outside.

"I knew if I was going to make this place better, I had to be the one wearing the badge," he had said. "I want to be a force for good around here."

Then one day a few months ago, they'd come across a perp holding two customers and a cashier hostage at a liquor store. The perp had already been convinced to let everyone go and was about to give himself up when an alarm somehow triggered and in a panic, he started firing. A stray bullet caught Marcus square in the neck.

The sight of him staggering backward with his hand pressed against his throat, preternaturally placid as if nothing was wrong, then collapsing to the sticky asphalt of the New York summer streets haunted Jackson's dreams to this day. And sometimes when he was awake. And sometimes when he was trying to read or garden or focus on anything but that horrible image.

The ride to Queens was not a long one but now it felt longer and longer each time Jackson made it. He pulled into the driveway at a quarter to midnight, laughing to himself that Evie was right.

"It's not that late," he said then he threw the car in reverse and continued going east out toward Long Island and the beaches that flanked both its shores. He lived in a city that never sleeps, so why should he?

Chapter Three

Evie was exhausted the next day as she wandered around the gallery watching her pieces being packed up and readied for shipping. She hadn't slept very well, but she had no clue why. It wasn't that she hadn't been tired because she was drained in literally every way possible. No matter how long she lay there with her eyes closed, she couldn't get her brain to stop ticking.

Plus, she had gotten a call hours after she got home. The call was nothing but scratchy, weird breathing that Evie mistook for static. After hanging up, she found herself too jumpy to fall asleep. The idea of not moving for hours on end seemed impossible.

She figured she'd gotten too excited and overwhelmed by the night, finally caving and taking a few milligrams of melatonin. That was about the hardest drug she did. Evie didn't even drink that much, though she was known for being able to put away coffee like a college student cramming for finals.

Her mother had been a heavy drinker, flighty and brilliant; a complete nightmare. Young Evie would come home from school to find her in any variety of moods. Or, if lucky, completely passed out and slumped against her canvas. The first few times Evie saw her like this, she'd been understandably upset. Eventually, 'out cold' came to be her favorite mood of her mother's. At least when she was out, Evie could do some cleaning, make dinner, and get her homework done without banshee wailing rattling the windows.

When her mother was low, she drank and popped pills to knock herself out. When her mother was up, she did the same thing to level herself out. As an adult, Evie could see the pattern and wondered if her mother was undiagnosed bi-polar, as often was the case with women in most previous generations. The one time she dared to bring it up, her mother flew into a rage and screamed that no one would dare call a man sick in the head if he was behaving this way.

Evie didn't argue back, though she was tempted to land the jab, "Of course they would." Instead, she just left, and decided her attempts to be a good daughter were over. She didn't need to see this woman again if she didn't want to.

All that being said, the specter of what she might become haunted Evie. Every time she had a few beers with friends or smoked a joint out someone's window or accepted a sleeping pill when she couldn't get her mind to stop working, she saw her mother's face yelling at her. Angry and lined, ruddy from malnutrition, sallow from dehydration. Evie vowed to do better, though Rachel had to order her to eat sometimes, and she peed dark yellow from drinking coffee and no water.

You're not your mother, she reminded herself, yawning as the movers gilded one of her pieces with bubble wrap. *You just need a wife to make sure you don't miss too many meals.* She and Rachel joked about getting married so Rachel could take care of her but they both knew Rachel's motherly instincts only went so far. It was up to Evie to take care of Evie.

The gallery door opened but no one paid much attention. During installation and dismantling, people went in and out all day. A half-alert security guard usually posted near the front to make sure no one came in off the street and wandered away with the art, but he was currently in the bathroom.

Evie, like everyone else in the gallery, didn't notice anyone coming in so when Jackson appeared at her elbow, she startled and jumped away.

"Oh, so that's the reception I get when I don't shave?" he laughed, running a hand over the stubble on his face.

Evie stammered then pressed her lips together to focus before speaking. "I was just in my own little world. I didn't even hear you come in."

She watched the movers take down the painting of the runner passing the fishmonger. Her expression fell as they wrapped it and prepared to leave.

"What's the matter?" Jackson asked.

"Nothing. I just... it's hard to let these things go. I worked on them for so long and now..." she threw her hands up, "they're gone."

"You sound like my mom each time one of us went off to college."

At the word mom, Evie flinched. To her chagrin, Jackson noticed it, and asked again what was wrong.

"I think my mother called me last night," she admitted after a moment of thought. If not her mother, she didn't know who it could be, and that was scarier. "It was this weird call where something just sighed into the phone."

"A heavy breather?"

"A what?"

"It's just what we'd call it. Usually a guy calling a woman, ya know? Gets her on the phone and makes all these noises." He mimicked the sound of panting and heaving. "Supposed to sound like sex or something, I guess."

The sound of Jackson's sex moans made Evie's mouth go dry and a tingle formed at the base of her spine. She played off the strange sensation by saying, "Man, isn't there anywhere we can get away from you creeps?"

Jackson smiled and extended a hand. "How about I buy you lunch? That way you'll only have to deal with one creep bothering you."

"I should really be here for this," Evie replied, motioning to the almost empty gallery. "Most of the stuff is being sold but there's a few sculptures and one painting left over."

"Which reminds me." Jackson dug into his pocket and pulled out a greeting card with the word Congratulations printed across the front. He handed it to Evie. "From my parents. They wanted me to tell you how proud of you they are."

Inside was a blank check with her name on it. Evie frowned, her nose wrinkling up the way it used to when her hand-me-down glasses were too big for her face.

"What's this?" she asked, holding it up between two fingers.

"They want to buy a piece. Whatever's left. They weren't sure how much it was going to cost so they told me to tell you to just fill it in."

"I can't do that. They haven't even seen anything of mine. What if they hate it?" Evie's skin clammed up and her breathing became shallow. She hated being put on the spot. And the thought of Rachel and Jackson's parents being so kind to her, especially right after reliving some of her worst moments with her own mother, Evie couldn't deal with it all.

Jackson narrowed his eyes and tilted his head to the side the way Evie did when she was being inquisitive. "They'll love anything you make. Besides, those two have plenty of money, and they want to support you."

"Well, I can send them photos of what's left and they can pick from that." She paused, check still clenched between her fingers. She tried to hand it back to him but he wouldn't take it. She shoved the check forward and added, "I'll give it to them as a gift."

"Evie, do you know what obstinate means?" Jackson asked, stepping away from the check.

"Vaguely. Stubborn, right?" she said, playing dumb. She fell easily into the role of 'kid sister's weird friend' when Jackson came around.

"Exactly. You're being obstinate."

Evie planted a hand on her hip, a gesture that meant a lecture was coming, but right then something crashed, and she nearly jumped out of her skin. They both turned to see one of the movers cleaning up a floor lamp that had been pushed into a corner to be out of the way. The other movers were lightly scolding him, calling him a bull in a china shop and other more colorful things.

"Yeah, you're like a mover in an art gallery!" the foreman yelled, flailing his arms around to demonstrate. "Careful ya don't cut yaself but get that cleaned up."

"Scared you, huh?" Jackson asked as she turned away from the commotion. "You really are jumpy today."

"I also didn't sleep well last night," she said, pushing her hands under her glasses to rub her eyes.

"Let me buy you that lunch. You don't need to be here for this, and you know it."

Evie looked at the guys delicately sweeping glass into a dustpan. The security guard had returned to his usual post by the door.

She knew Jackson was right and nodded. "Ok. Where should we go?"

"I know a place around the corner. It's good. Nothing fancy."

"Well, after last night, that sounds just my speed."

On the walk to the diner around the corner, Jackson realized Evie's gait was back to normal. Dressed to the nines and weaving through her adoring fans, she had taken on a slinky, sleek walk as opposed to how she usually moved. Ordinarily, she strode very squarely like she walked from her shoulders like a man, not her hips like most women. She didn't keep her chest out and her head high the way Rachel did, extending one long leg then dragging the body up behind it. When Evie walked, she walked all at once, everything moving forward with no performance or focus on how she might appear to people watching her.

For the first time since he'd known her, Jackson found this square, hurried gait supremely enticing.

They got a booth with windows facing west. Not that it mattered which direction they were facing. Jackson knew it was west because of the spill of sunlight starting to penetrate the aluminum slats of the blinds.

Evie leaned against the red vinyl lining and exhaled loudly. "I just realized I'm actually starving."

"Told ya."

The server came by with menus, but Evie didn't take hers. Instead, she ordered a burger and fries with plenty of mayo on the side. Jackson shrugged and said the same, changing the mayo to ranch so he had something to dip his fries in.

"I never liked ketchup," he said as their server walked off, scribbling their orders on his notepad. "The smell of it makes me sick. Ranch is the superior dip for fries."

"I mix ketchup into the mayo then dip my fries in that." When Jackson grimaced, Evie laughed. "Do I disgust you, Jackson?"

"Only most of the time."

Evie stretched her arms overhead, the spears of light from the window catching the green in her eyes, the tint of gold in her hair. She looked tired and lovely. Jackson had seen a beautiful woman at the airport one time who was telling the person next to her she was flying in from Singapore and had been awake for over a day. Her natural beauty was evident, the circles under her eyes and the lopsided bun her hair had been in highlighting rather than detracting.

That was what Evie looked like now. She didn't have her normal sparkly expression, the wide-eyed wonder that led her to seek a life in the arts. Where else could she have put her childlike ideas and probing eyesight to good use? Still, she was beautiful, drained, and lightly grinning in that tacky red booth.

"Amazing," Jackson said suddenly. There was no silence to break since noise came from all angles in a city, but between them, nothing had been said for a minute.

"What is?"

"Amazing that the gorgeous woman I escorted home last night could be the same person as this scrappy little artist wearing men's clothes."

Evie tugged on the front of her button-down shirt. "Is a man wearing this right now?"

"No."

"Did a man buy this?"

"I don't know. TMI?"

"I bought it. I'm wearing it. So, it's not men's clothes. It's Evie's clothes." She let the shirt drop, jutting her chin out at him with a weary but humored expression. "Besides, you're not nearly as pretty as you were last night either."

"Well, I was going to say that despite all that, I think you look quite lovely today."

Evie shrugged, brought her elbows down to the table, and rested her face in the palm of her hand. She wasn't looking in Jackson's direction anymore but rather around the diner at the clatter of silverware and chewing and human noises. Jackson wondered if she was having a moment of inspiration. He wanted to make another joke or keep the conversation going about how pretty she was, yet he stayed quiet.

"I hate getting dressed up like that," Evie said finally. "It's such a bore to pretend to care about my appearance. Those shoes, spending hours on my hair. All that makeup."

"Yeah, you don't even need makeup anyway. You're so pretty without it."

Evie shot him a weird look and sat up straight. She didn't seem put off by what Jackson said, just surprised. They hadn't been close the past few years. Life got in the way, as it did to most old friends. She probably hadn't expected to see him again after the night before. Her eyes were focused elsewhere when Jackson cleared his throat, a nervous tic he'd had since he was a kid.

"I'm glad we got out of the gallery for a bit," Evie told him, toying with a sugar packet she'd pulled out of its miniature glass container. "I think the walls were starting to close in around me."

"You seemed a little—" Jackson held his hands up and shook them. "Maybe you're just on edge from the call."

"No, no, that's not it." Her response was too abrupt, like she wanted to breeze right over anything having to do with the night before. "You know what I think it was? A few years ago, I had a few pieces in this rinky-dink place on the Lower East Side. Someone barged in when we were taking everything down and tried to steal something. In the struggle to stop him, one of my sculptures got knocked over."

"And you were thinking about it today when the lamp broke?" Jackson tried not to sound incredulous but it didn't work.

Evie smacked her lips together then set them in a straight, firm line. "I was, yes. Isn't timing a funny thing?"

"Very," Jackson replied as the server returned with their orders and they ate in relative and comfortable silence. He made a mental note to give her a good tip, since she no doubt saved him from himself. Who knew what he might have said next?

Chapter Four

More than anything, Evie wanted to get back to work. She was right in the middle of the largest sculpture she had ever done and didn't want to spend any more time watching heavy-gutted men struggle with bubble wrap or fend off questions from Jackson about if she was feeling safe. Or not safe.

Her work called to her from her studio, the room in her apartment that would have been her living room had she been a normal person. It was the only space big enough for wide canvases and massive lumps of clay. Her bedroom was small, her bathroom tiny. Her kitchen didn't even have a full-size stove. The only reason she had jumped at the place when she had seen it for the first time years ago was that big living room with the massive windows letting in more light than she could ever need.

Evie loved light. She knew lots of artists who were willing to stay in basement apartments in exchange for enviously cheap rent, but she saw their faces when they came over to her place. Aside from being well-lit, it was spotless. Other artists lived in dust and clutter; Evie had trouble focusing if there was anything out of place.

"Control issues stemming from a chaotic childhood," Rachel said once when Evie snapped at her for moving a pallet out of its proper place.

"Spare me your diagnosis and just don't touch my stuff."

Naturally, Rachel would move methodically around the room, placing a single finger on every item until Evie either got angry enough to kick her out or started laughing about how absurd they were both behaving. Either way, it ended with Rachel convincing Evie to have a glass of wine and relax for a bit.

When she got back to her apartment that afternoon, she locked the door behind her and felt normal for the first time all day. Jackson had wanted her to tell him more about the weird call she got as he thought it was someone harassing her. Evie, under the impression that it was most likely her mother, told him it was far worse than a horny creep.

"At least a psycho's just going to murder me," she deadpanned as he walked her home. "My mother's going to want a favor."

Jackson laughed despite her dark humor, which he'd never found amusing before. Then Evie suddenly remembered that his partner had been shot dead in front of his face only months earlier. She wanted to apologize but felt it would make the moment worse. The whole day was an off-putting wash, and she was dying to be in her own space, in her own apartment, with nothing else to do but scrape away at layer after layer of clay.

The slow, methodical work of sculpting was Evie's favorite part of the process. Painting was more energetic, even when it was painstaking. There was movement and color, ways to fix mistakes or build new ideas on top of them. Sculpting had to be approached with more intention, with a fully realized vision in mind.

A scratching noise at the back door made Evie jump but she knew it was the cat who wandered the neighborhood and like hanging out in her apartment. She opened the door to let the stray in. An appropriately named catwalk led down to where the garbage cans were, which made it pretty easy for this strutting bit of fur to get to Evie's any time she wanted.

Evie had taken to calling the cat Cagney, after a TV policewoman she and Rachel had watched as kids. Besides, the cat looked like a

Cagney. She was cute but strong with orange fur and tufted ears. Despite living on the street, Cagney always looked neat and taken care of, though she was getting too skinny. Evie saw a flash of herself in the cat; a creature living amongst chaos and coming out clean.

"How are you today, my dearest?" Evie asked, dumping a handful of dry food on the ground by the door. She watched the cat move in a circle to come back around for the offering. "Did you happen to call me last night?"

Cagney made a listless meow as she started eating. Evie had given her wet food one time, and ever since, Cagney was not impressed with the dry stuff.

"But it's cheap and can sit there for hours," Evie told her, aware of the fact that she was arguing with a cat. "This way you can graze all you want."

She went back to the block of clay in her living room, imagining the curves and details she was going to put into it. A man, tall and well-built, with armor like a Grecian soldier and the soft, pretty eyes of a boy bander. She could already see it in her mind's eye, then laughed as she realized she was fantasizing about him.

"Boy, kitty, I need to get laid."

She went to work, drab clay stuck under her nails almost immediately. The sound of crunching from the door was steady like a metronome; she used it to keep herself paced. When the cat was done eating, she circled Evie's workspace, studying her with the sharp eyes of someone who spent her life on the street.

Evie often imagined conversations between her and Cagney, how Cagney would ask what it was like to sleep in a bed. To be warm and safe and loved. Evie wouldn't have the answers she wanted to hear, and Cagney would vomit a pile of dry food at Evie's feet in rebuttal.

"Do you like it so far?" she asked. She was on a stepladder to shape the head. The cat had decided the step closest to the ground was hers to sit on, and she curled there with her tail dancing in front of her face. "I'm not sure what I'm going to call it. Naming pieces is my least favorite part of being an artist."

Cagney made a commiserating noise then dropped her tail and closed her eyes.

In a few hours, when it would start to get dark, she'd spring to her little kitty feet and prance out the back door as if she was done visiting and suddenly remembered she had lots and lots of errands to run. For now, she stayed curled under Evie who tried to get lost in her work and to shake the funny feeling that someone was watching her.

"Someone sent me flowers, Rach," Evie said. She sat on her tiny couch, which she had gotten as to not take up any more floor space than necessary, with her legs crossed beneath her. "No card, nothing. I was just wondering if maybe they were from you."

"Oh my God, no. When I spend money on presents, I want everyone to know about it."

Evie heard Rachel take a sip of something. Still mid-afternoon, what she was imbibing was anyone's guess. Then with the sigh as she swallowed, Evie knew it was a cocktail.

"Are you drinking already?" Evie asked.

The answer came in the form of a snort.

"You are, aren't you?"

"What're you? The head nun? I've had a busy week. It's the first day in a month where I don't have anything to do. I wanted a vodka soda as I talked to my best friend, sue me."

"Alright, alright. I rescind my comment." Evie touched the petals of the flowers. She didn't have a dining room table so they were centered on the teeny end table she had gotten to put next to her tiny couch. "They're lovely. So, if you did send them, thank you very much."

"You're welcome but I didn't. Maybe Jackson did."

"Jackson?"

"Yeah, he's been talking about you a lot lately. Super subtle stuff like, is Evie seeing anyone? I wanted to tell him I know what he's fishing for but it's so much fun to watch him fluster and squirm that I just act like I don't get it."

"You're evil," Evie said, meaning it more than she should have. "Just plain evil."

"Oh please. That asshole once stole my bra and paraded it around the cafeteria. Kevin Stephens paid to touch the inside of the cups! Buck fifty each. I made him split it with me."

"That was high school, Rach. You don't have to be so mean to him now."

Rachel got quiet save for another sip. Her lips smacked with that same sigh as she swallowed down her drink. In that moment, Evie knew what Rachel was thinking.

"Why are you suddenly on his side?" Rachel finally asked, suspiciously. "Something... happen between you two?"

"Happen? Like what?" Evie suddenly wished she had a drink to sip on, keep her hands and lips busy.

"I dunno like what. Maybe the flowers are from him, and you're trying to pretend you didn't put out."

"You're disgusting."

Rachel cackled.

Evie was glad her friend couldn't see her blushing through the phone. She was sure to figure it out anyway by her tone. Evie had never been great at hiding her emotions. The best she could do was keep them under control until she got someplace safe to explode. Still, in those cases, people knew she was covering, especially Rachel.

"Well, I didn't send you flowers, and I don't think Jack did either. I can't imagine he'd send them without a card."

"Why not?"

Rachel belched, the drink working its magic through her body. "Because he knows it's creepy. He's seen too many cases of dudes sending some woman they saw on the street flowers and thinking it was cute and romantic."

"Yeah, I guess this isn't his M.O." Evie wondered if Rachel noticed the disappointment in her voice. She was surprised to hear it, herself.

If Rachel picked up on it, she didn't let on. Instead, she asked, "Did you call the flower place?"

"Yeah, but they didn't have any information for me. Whoever did it paid in cash. Some generic man fitting a non-description. Medium height, brown hair, brown eyes."

"Jesus, it's like those amber alerts. Can bad guys have a crazy scar or an eye patch so we can at least pick them out of a crowd?"

"Well, maybe it was someone who knows the curator at the gallery. He might not have realized he didn't send a card."

"Sure, maybe."

"I've got to get back to work, anyway. Thanks for the chat. Oh, and Rach?" Evie let a moment hang, waiting for an answer so she was positive she had her friend's attention.

"Yeah?"

"Don't tell Jack about the flowers, ok? I don't want him to worry about me."

Chapter Five

Rachel lasted almost a week before telling Jackson about the flowers. She didn't intentionally set out to tell him anything, but he called her later than normal one night with a weird tinge of anxiety in his voice.

"Jack, you sound like you're freaking out about something," she said, staring longingly in the direction of her bed. She was not in the mood for some heavy conversation, but she also wasn't about to hang up on her brother. Considering the trauma he had gone through fairly recently, she hardly ever missed a call from him.

"It might be nothing. The last time I saw Evie she was sorta freaked out. Ya know? Jumpy in a not Evie way. At the slightest noise..."

Evie was not, by nature, a high-strung person. She liked things organized and clean but her artistic side smoothed down the jagged edges of what could otherwise be a compulsive and neurotic personality. Rachel knew what Jackson was saying; seeing Evie flinch at noise was not the norm.

"Maybe she was still on edge from the show," Rachel suggested. The flowers loomed in her mind again. "You haven't spoken to her since when?"

"Last week, I guess. Why? Something happened?"

"Depends. Did you send her flowers with no card?"

"No way. I would always attach a card. I've seen too many horror stories on the force about weirdo men who do that thinking it's romantic." He made a disgusted noise on the other end of the line.

"That's literally what I told her when she called and asked if you had sent them. Anything going on there?"

"Rach, you gonna give me her info or what? Time's up. I'll go knock on every door in her building until someone maces me."

Rachel repeated Evie's address and phone number, though she hesitated for a split second before she did. It always feels like a betrayal between women to let someone have that information. Her trusted brother couldn't possibly be a pervert creep out to harm Evie, but then again, why couldn't he be? Women were taught from childhood that everyone poses a threat to them. Even men who love them have the ability to hurt them.

"Don't freak her out though, alright?" Rachel told him right before they hung up. "She'll kill me if you wind up at her doorstep in the middle of the night holding up a boombox or something."

Jack snorted. "Exactly who do you think I am, darling sister? And what decade do you think we're in?"

"Shut up. And women never know who the men in our lives really are, dearest brother."

Jack snorted again and said goodbye. He heard nothing as Rachel hung up. It was too late at night for him to go bother Evie right then, even though he constantly worried about her. So, he decided to sleep on it and see how worried he was in the morning.

Very, very worried as it turned out.

Jackson woke up with the uncomfortable feeling of cooling sweat all over him. It was barely light out, but he couldn't get back to sleep or get his anxiety to shut up for one second. All he could think about was Evie alone in her apartment where some freak had sent her flowers, proving he knew where she lived and slept. Where she showered and walked around naked getting dressed. It was all he could do to wait until a reasonable hour to take the subway into the city and knock on her door.

Evie answered looking bright-eyed but sleep logged. Jackson knew he didn't wake her up, but she certainly wasn't prepared for visitors. He smelled the coffee brewing in the kitchen past her shoulder and the residual moisture of her morning shower on her neck and shoulders.

"Jackson? What the hell are you doing here?" Evie's brow furrowed. She squinted at him without her glasses on. "Did we have plans today?"

"No, nothing like that. I wanted to make sure you were ok. After the call and the flowers—"

"Ugh, Rachel!"

"She only told me after I called her and told her I was worried about you. So don't be too mad at her."

Evie groaned and swung the door open wide, beckoning for him to come in. "Want some coffee? It's fresh. Just made a pot."

"Yeah, alright. Thanks."

Jackson sat on the tiny couch and noticed a small pink papered package on the end table. There was no card or tag on it. Nothing to indicate where it came from. When Evie came back with his coffee, Jack pointed to the gift.

"Don't ask because I don't know," she said before a word left his mouth. "It showed up a few days ago. I'm assuming from the same person who sent the flowers."

"You sound pretty calm for someone who might have some whack-job obsessing over her."

"What else am I supposed to do? I can't go to the police with something like this."

"Sure you can!"

"And say what? I got flowers and a present? Someone might have made a prank phone call to me, but I also think that might be my loon of a mother trying to insert herself back into my life. There's real crimes in this city. They're not going to bother with me."

"I'll go with you," Jackson offered but Evie waved a hand in his face and changed the subject as quickly as she could. There was something in her manner that made him think she wanted him gone. Something about her quick, almost babbling talk, her fast moving eyes never landing on anything for more than a second. When there was another knock on the door, she jumped to her feet to answer it.

"Busier than Grand Central around here," she quipped, her hand on the knob. She peered over her shoulder at Jackson, her lips pressed tightly together. "Don't read too much into this, ok?"

"Read into what?" Jack asked, but as soon as the door opened, he knew what she meant.

A contractor in a blue jumpsuit with the words City Security printed on them stood in the alcove with a collection of wires and tools puddling at his feet. "Genevieve Hansen?"

His voice was thick with a New York accent. He moved his mouth after speaking in a way that made Jackson think he was chewing gum though he didn't seem to be. Evie welcomed him in, offering him the same coffee she had just offered Jackson.

"Let us know if we're in your way," she told the man then she tugged Jackson by the arm into her bedroom and partially closed the door.

"So, you're getting a security system put in, but you're not concerned about your safety? Do I have that right?"

"It was just time for an upgrade." Evie shrugged, chewed her bottom lip, then laughed brightly. "You know as well as I do that most crime is less about intention and more about opportunity."

"Uh huh."

"I told you not to read too much into this."

Jackson saw the kid he once knew for a second, pouting at an unfair call in a game or not being allowed to do what she wanted. The cop instinct he had been trying to silence for the past week came through even stronger. Evie, for all her intelligence and savvy, was still that girl. Still someone who needed to be protected.

"Let me take the package down to the station," he begged her. "I'll at least have someone dust it for prints. Even if there's five people's prints on it, it'll narrow it down from a pool of six million."

"Fine, take it. I don't care. I want it out of my house anyway." She waved a dismissive hand toward the front room.

Jackson didn't ask if the thought of keeping it frightened her. He knew the answer already. Marcus had told him about a case where a guy tormented a woman for months by leaving little presents for her. The whole point had been to remind her that he knew where she went, and he knew what she liked. This wasn't information she had readily offered him, yet he knew it all the same.

This sounded an awful lot like that to him.

Evie went out to the kitchen then came back with the package. It was unopened, and she didn't seem that keen on Jackson bothering with it. "Won't you get more prints on it?"

"My prints are on file. They won't confuse anyone in the crime lab."

He undid the paper, lifted the top of the box, and startled at the sight of sexy black lingerie.

Evie peeked also then averted her eyes, holding her hands up in front of her as if expecting to be struck.

"Gross. Now I'm happy you want to take it."

"Someone just dropped this off on your doorstep?"

"Not exactly."

"What does that mean?"

Evie brushed her hair back from her face with both hands and sighed. She released her curls, and they sprung to life around her head. "It was in the kitchen when I woke up."

"What?!" Jackson's grip tightened around the flimsy box, crushing it.

"Look, I know how frightening that sounds so that's why I've got the security system. That's why I'm trying to lock this place down a little." She clicked her tongue and pressed the heel of her palm into her forehead. "I'm trying not to come apart at the seams here, Jackson. Do me the favor of not tugging on any threads."

"Fine," he said, opening her bedroom door. "But if anything... anything... happens, you tell me immediately."

Evie promised to do so, all while ushering him out.

As Jackson left, the contractor was running a wire up along the molding of the door. He nodded to Jack as if assuming he lived there. Jackson stared back at him, hardly able to muster up a polite smile.

"Don't worry about a thing, bud," the contractor said as he wove the wire through the drywall. "We're the number one security company in the whole city. Our customer satisfaction rate is something insane like 99 percent."

"Mainly because the dissatisfied customers are the ones that got murdered in their bed," Evie croaked dryly, from her bedroom doorway.

Jackson shot her a dirty look but the contractor didn't seem to hear.

He went on for a few minutes about how happy everyone was with their system, and how much safer the city would be if everyone was smart enough to rig something like this up. Neither Jackson nor Evie paid him any mind.

They hadn't broken eye contact since his glare. Jackson tried to figure out what went on in that mind of hers, all while not letting on where his own mind had gone. Even with the stress of the situation, the fact that he'd been in her room hadn't gone unnoticed.

When Jackson stepped out into the hallway and Evie's door closed behind him, he was stuck with a very peculiar feeling he couldn't pinpoint. It was somewhere between butterflies in his stomach and agita clenching in his chest. He wasn't sure if he liked the feeling, hated it, or wanted to vomit right there in the hallway.

Darkness had never frightened Evie. Before waking up to mystery parcels sitting on her counter, the darkness had inspired her, allowed her imagination to move the straight lines of the world into whatever shape she wanted. She was angry at the person responsible for shattering her security; she was angry at the man who made her afraid of the dark.

For a night or two, she left the light in the main room on but with nothing but white walls and limited furniture, it blasted into her tiny bedroom more potently than she would have imagined. She finally went back to sleeping with everything turned off, thankful that no true blackness exists in a city night. Not in New York or Paris or anywhere else she had been.

She remembered Paris the way dreams are remembered by the one who had them. There was a certain physicality to her memories, but she had been so young when they lived there, they couldn't sustain themselves in her mind. Memories, like imagination, needed to be nurtured. Shared. Humans reminisced not just because they liked to discuss their pasts but because it preserved what they remembered. The moment they think of may become more and more tattered with each visit, but it still kept its place in the mind.

Evie remembered the dark, slippery water of the Seine and throwing scraps of a croissant to birds in the park. She remembered being so small and thinking all the structures around her were enormous. Bigger than anywhere in the world.

Arriving in New York alongside her mother right before Evie turned six had rattled her to her very core. If the buildings in Paris were big, then New York was a city made for giants.

And in a way, it was. Evie came to understand that before too long. New York had always been "the big time," the place where people flew or faltered. It would be untrue to say she loved it right off the bat. For the first couple of years, the city intimidated her. The fact that her mother was less than thrilled about leaving Paris and called New York a cesspool or an open wound more times than Evie could count didn't help matters.

"Zis city rots us from zee inside," she had told the tiny wide-eyed Evie as she sat cross-legged on the fire escape.

Evie'd had her eyes closed, listening to the sound of the cars moving, but her mother's desperate hacking cough broke her out of her trance.

"And zhis air is poison. I am sure it ez."

Her mother would take another drag of her cigarette without the slightest semblance of awareness. Evie watched her lips curl around the filter, the lines at the perfectly formed cupid's bow becoming angrier by the day. At barely ten years old, Evie knew her mother was aging.

Nothing could be done about how much her mother hated New York, though Evie was beginning to suspect that her mother enjoyed complaining more than doing something about her problems. There were never any plans made on her end to return to Paris once Evie was on her own.

With Evie's father out of the picture, and Evie busy at school, her mother spent most days alone. Plenty of time to think, to swallow pills, to make cocktails that paired well with imported cigarettes. There was never an explanation as to why they were suddenly in a city her mother hated except the vague notion of New York being where the art was. Where it really was.

A year or so later, right before summer vacation started, Evie's mother tore open the window next to the fire escape and stuck her head out.

Evie was there again, eyes closed, drifting in the noise of the city.

"What ez it that you are doing?" her mother asked in that dense, nasal French accent. People everywhere commented on how lovely she sounded but it made Evie's skin crawl.

"I'm listening to the cars," Evie answered, hugging her knees to her chest. "When they move steadily without braking or honking, it sounds like rushing water." She peered between the oxidized bars of the fire escape. "It's like we have a river next to us. A river of cars."

"A river of exhaust, you mean," her mother spat, and the next day she declared that Evie was going to be spending a month upstate at a camp.

"A camp?" Evie asked cautiously. "What kind of camp?"

"A camp, a camp! Et's out en nature, and zhere are real rivers and trees. Not zhe exhaust you love so well."

Evie had argued that there were trees in the city too, but her mother scowled and called them deformed, mutilated. All the trees in the park near them had been marked up by overzealous teenagers carving coupled names into the bark with the hubristic notion their love would last forever. It gave the trees character in Evie's mind, and she wondered if upstate trees would look naked to her. Clean and bare in their natural form without the decoration of arrogance, youth, and first love.

She didn't want to leave the city but staying away from her mother for a month sounded pretty good. She didn't fight it when her mother rented a car and dropped her off after an hour-long drive. The view outside her window had only started to look different when her mother announced that they had arrived. Despite the fact that the woman drove like a maniac let loose from the Grand Prix, it still didn't seem like that long of a trip.

"I thought I was going upstate," Evie said, frowning slightly at the moderate suburbia they had driven through.

"Zis ez upstate," her mother replied. "Zis ez Westchester." Her voice sounded so tired. Each word seemed to take more effort than she could spare.

Evie didn't say anything else as she got out of the car and inspected her new temporary home.

The rental car's taillights weren't even out of sight when a pretty girl with long brown hair approached Evie, studying her with an expression that made Evie wonder if this was actually a camp like her mother said and not a home for wayward children.

"This your first year, huh?" the girl said, crossing her arms over her chest. "I've never seen you before."

"My name's Evie, and yeah."

"Evie?" The girl's bright eyes scrunched.

"Genevieve but everyone calls me Evie."

"Who's everyone?"

"I guess just my mom and dad."

Thus far, making friends in New York had eluded the quiet, thoughtful little girl. Nobody bothered her, but also nobody asked her to have sleepovers or spend a Saturday chasing ducks around the park like she saw kids doing. Most of the other students at school didn't call her Evie because they didn't know she existed.

"Well, I'm Rachel. You can just call me Rachel. Or I guess Rach because what else do people call someone named Rachel? Either way, I'm Rachel."

The spurt of a speech came in such a fast stream of words that it knocked the wind out of Evie. She nodded as if she agreed, as if she absorbed anything that was just said to her. That was good enough for Rachel anyway.

"I don't know what bunk you're in but if you want me to ask the counselors, I bet they'll put you in mine." Rachel motioned with her whole hand for Evie to follow her. "I've been coming here since I was five."

"Oh, wow."

"You live in Westchester?"

"No, I live in the city."

Rachel screeched to a halt and turned toward Evie with newfound respect. "Like, the actual city?"

"Yeah."

There was a long pause as Rachel mulled this fact over. "I kinda thought kids weren't allowed to live there."

"Why not?" Evie found herself at once impressed and puzzled by this girl. She seemed equally experienced and naive the more they spoke. "Where else would they live if their parents live there?"

"Sure, yeah. I just never thought about it."

Evie let Rachel pull her along for the rest of the day, and silently thanked her later when the girl was lying in the bunk below hers in the true indigo dark of rural night. There was a small town not too far away so at the edge of the camp was bouncing glow of streetlights, but in their cabins, tucked back into the circle of woods, Evie saw nothing but black. Were it not for the reassuring whistle of Rachel's comical snoring, she wouldn't have gotten to sleep at all.

Good thing that's all changed, thought the adult that child grew into as she clutched her covers to her chest and listened for any noise out of the ordinary.

Cities ceased to exist without noise, but Evie knew which ones to listen for. She heard the sound of her next-door neighbor leaving to work the night shift at the hospital; the clanging orchestra of the pipes as the woman above her, a bartender, drew her semi-nightly bath. Outside it was trucks and cabs and occasionally people fighting over something petty and dumb. All these noises were welcomed, and in the same way that Rachel's snoring would become by the end of their first summer together, comforting.

If only Evie could concentrate on them and not the mysterious package from her own personal weirdo.

Chapter Six

Jackson couldn't help himself. He didn't want to freak out Evie any more than she already was (and despite her nonchalant act, he knew she was freaked out) but he had also seen more than his fair share of creeps when he was active on the force.

One guy stalked a woman he had never even spoken to but decided she liked him because this one time she had smiled at him while out for a run. In actuality, she was being polite considering he hadn't been paying attention to where he was going and almost plowed right into her. She gave a quick smile before she jogged off to avoid further confrontation. When watching didn't do it for him anymore, he followed her as she left her house one day to do her normal run. Her body turned up three days later.

"And that guy had to start from zero," Jack told his former boss, Captain Wheeler, who had offered to take him out to lunch and catch up. "He had to find where she lived and shit. This guy's two steps ahead of that; he knows where she lives and he knows how to get in."

"Does your friend have a firearm?" Wheeler asked. She was the one who wouldn't let Jackson return to duty until he passed a litany of psychological tests. He had resented her for the decision at first but then saw her point when he suffered countless panic attacks at simple things like backfiring cars.

Jackson gaped at her then closed his mouth firmly. "Civilians within the city limits of Kings County are not allowed to possess firearms." He took a bite of his sandwich. "Ma'am."

"Don't come at me with that boy scout routine. I know the law. That doesn't mean I necessarily agree with it. Not where a woman's safety is concerned."

"To answer your question, no. She doesn't."

His boss stuck her tongue out just enough to touch her top lip. Jack knew the gesture as her 'in the middle of a thought' face. After a moment, she said, "Get her mace or pepper spray. Tell her to leave a bat next to her bed. The security system isn't a bad idea but all that does is make sure we know where we're headed. It'll still take ten minutes unless there's a cruiser right nearby, and we've both seen what can happen in less than ten minutes."

Jackson tried not to think about the jogger's slime-covered body when they pulled it from its hiding place in the Gowanus canal. There were hand marks on her throat; it took minutes for the monster to choke the life out of her.

After lunch, though he'd hardly had an appetite, Jackson went directly to Evie's. Captain Wheeler had given him her pocket-sized pepper spray and said to get anything else he thought she needed to be safe. A stop at a sporting good's store netted a solid wood baseball bat and a can of bear mace.

He was nervous about knocking on Evie's door and intruding on her space in the middle of all of this. She was alone most of the time, and the sound of someone unexpected would probably make her whole body tense up. Even with this thought in mind, Jack headed her direction and pressed the intercom button for her apartment.

"Yes?" came a voice crackling through the ancient device. It didn't sound like Evie. The voice was female but too deep to be hers.

"Yeah, hi. I'm a friend of Evie's. My name is Jackson."

"Oh, Jack, hi." The voice lifted, and he recognized it instantly. "I can buzz you in. There's no one else around, right?"

"Nope, just me."

A loud screeching noise shrieked out as Evie hit the buzzer to let him in. When he got to her floor, she was standing in the doorway.

"I guess it worked," she said as he approached her.

"What worked?"

"Disguising my voice to sound like a man. You couldn't tell it was me."

Jackson laughed as his eyes lowered to meet hers. "Evie, kid. I didn't think it was you but I sure as hell didn't think it was a man."

Evie bristled. Clearly this was not the answer she wanted.

Jackson regretted saying it as he knew the feeling of grasping at straws to feel safe, to be whole again. On the other hand, he didn't want her to believe in a layer of security that wasn't there. Nobody, especially someone who had already been inside her place, would have thought the person who buzzed him in was a big, dangerous man.

"Well, it's just something I wanted to try out," Evie stammered. She was still standing in the doorway. She abruptly stepped back to let Jackson pass. "I'm trying to cover all my bases. Maybe if this psycho thinks I've got a man here—"

"I get it, I get it. But you should also know that it won't work." He extended his hands to show her his peace offerings. In one, he held the baseball bat by its neck. In the other, the pepper spray and bear mace.

"What is this stuff?" Evie asked without touching anything or taking the odd gifts from his hands.

"Protection. Maybe not the best but a good deal better than—" he lowered his voice to a comically deep baritone, "talking like this for the rest of your life."

"Says you," Evie retorted, yet she smiled and plucked the items from his fingers as if they were sacraments. "Thank you, Jack. This has been a... scary feels like too gentle of a word to use."

"Yeah, I know. Roller coasters are scary. Movies are scary. Stuff like this is—"

"Terrifying."

She couldn't look directly at him after she said it out loud. If he didn't know better, he would have thought she was embarrassed. She fidgeted with the bear mace, studying the can as if she had no idea what to do with it. It occurred to Jackson that she didn't really want to admit to being scared. Not that she was trying to act tough or show off about how she laughed in the face of danger.

Quite the opposite, as Jackson had learned in one of his first therapy sessions. Admitting to fear made it real, made it hard to deny and ignore. Her flippant comments when the contractor was installing the security system repeated in his head; the unsatisfied customers murdered in their beds.

"Do you want me to stay with you?" he asked, suddenly and without a natural segue. He had brought the fear into her reality; the least he could do was provide comfort against it.

"I don't think it's come to that yet," Evie said, her voice barely a whisper. She turned the can of bear mace over in her hand. "Besides, I've got this stuff to protect me."

Jackson nodded despite wanting to tell her she was crazy for not taking him up on the offer. He stared over her shoulder toward the huge lump of clay she was glacially modeling into a recognizable form.

"Ya got a lot of work to do on that thing, huh?"

Evie spun around as if unsure what he was referring to. "Oh, Adonis? Yeah. I want to have him ready for the winter show. I have to admit, I'm not as far along as I'd like to be."

"I'm sure it'll be amazing." Jackson forced a tight smile then stepped back out of the door. "Alright, well, be safe, and call me if you change your mind. Or call Rachel. Call anyone so long as you're not alone. Ok?"

"I'm not alone. I have Cagney."

Jackson's heart leapt.

Then, Evie finished with, "My cat."

Giving his pulse time to recover, Jackson peered around for evidence of this cat, as if that would have made some difference against a night stalker. When he saw nothing, he gave her the same tight-lipped smile.

"Well, I hope it's a big cat. A lion maybe."

"On loan from the Bronx zoo," Evie joked, and she closed the door behind him before he could say something, anything, to change her mind.

Rachel was getting tired of answering her brother's calls. She worried about Evie too, but she was starting to think his concern had gotten out of hand. There was never a moment, or at least not a lasting one, where she thought Jack might be the one following Evie's pretty little footsteps, no matter how obsessed he seemed. Rather, she was pretty sure he had focused his anxiety on this so he could avoid facing Marcus's death and the mountains of work he had left to do on himself.

"When was the last time you went to therapy?" Rachel asked before Jackson could get a word out.

"I dunno. Mid-summer, maybe. What's that got to do with anything?"

"Just wondering."

She waited for him to get to his point. Knowing Jackson the way she did, it wouldn't take long.

"Look, I don't want to freak Evie out so I'm coming to you."

"Coming to me about what?"

"I think someone needs to stay with her. Like a security detail."

Rachel groaned, dropped her head to her desk with a hollow thunk. "Jackson, I already invited her to stay with me, and she said she had too much work to do on her hunky man sculpture—"

"Adonis."

"Yeah, him. I offered to stay there, and she literally said there was no space for me to be comfortable. As if that matters!"

"You could have insisted on staying."

"Insisted?!"

"Told her you weren't gonna leave until you knew she was safe."

Rachel snorted. She knew Jackson was serious but she couldn't believe he didn't hear himself. "Why didn't you insist then?"

"Because it's different. She and I aren't close. Plus I'm—"

"A guy?"

"Well, yeah! I know a thing or two about gender dynamics. Especially when it comes to people being stalked." His voice cracked as if he was getting too upset to continue the conversation. "The whole world probably looks very scary to her right now. A man staying in her apartment might not be the comfort we assumed it would be."

"Yeah, yeah. You're right." Rachel ran her tongue over her teeth then clicked it against the roof of her mouth. "So, what's the purpose of this phone call?"

"I'm just asking that you keep me informed, alright? If Evie suddenly wants people staying with her 24/7, you let me know."

"Of course I would. I'd need you to take a few shifts anyway seeing as I'm the one between the two of us with a job."

Jackson didn't dare offer a comeback; that would only solidify Rachel's point.

Unlike everyone else in his life who had been treating him with kid gloves since his leave, Rachel kept poking him like the nuisance she always was. She knew he was grateful for one person not treating him delicately, no matter how much it annoyed him.

Truth was, if he had taken the leave on his own terms and there was nothing more looming over him, Rachel would have left him alone. But that wasn't the case. She knew he wanted to be back on the force, but they weren't letting him. She also knew it was because he wouldn't do his mandatory therapy.

"I called my old precinct before I called you," he told her, brushing over her comment about the jobs. "You remember my boss, Captain Wheeler, right?"

"The one who won't let you come back to work?" She got one last free jab in before deciding to chill.

"That's her. Anyway, I met her for lunch and she took everything I was saying about Evie very seriously. I told her if there's any news or calls from Evie's building, she had to let me know right away."

"Can't imagine she agreed to that considering she doesn't think you're fit for duty." Okay, maybe one more.

"This isn't duty," Jackson shot back. "This is a friend's safety. There's different, I dunno, rules about it, I guess."

"Sure, that makes sense."

Rachel switched the phone to the other ear and cradled it against her shoulder. She had been trying to get work done while she talked but the clicking of her computer keys was too noticeable. Jackson was the type to demand her full attention.

"You'll tell me if Evie tells you something too, right?"

"I swear on the souls of all our brothers and sisters. And our parents for good measure."

"What does that mean to anything?"

"It means they go to hell if I'm lying."

Now it was Jackson's turn to snort. "Leave mom and dad out of this. They might have a shot at a decent afterlife. As for the rest of the family, I'm not so sure they'd be spared hell even if you were telling the truth."

"I promise, but I'm sure you're overreacting." Rachel regretted the words the moment they were out of her mouth. Not one for superstition, she still had common sense and a respect for tempting fate.

Chapter Seven

The problem with waiting for dangerous noises in the night is that once the noise is made and close enough to be heard, it's too late. Evie wasn't sleeping well anyway, so every noise sounded like someone creeping around her apartment. Logically, she knew it was nothing more than the gears of the creaky old elevator or the expanding pipes. City nights were dark enough for an imagination already on edge.

And logic be damned after 2 a.m.

She tried not to think about how she turned down two different people's offers to stay with her, at least through those airless nighttime hours of filmstrip shadows on the wall and twitching noises half identified. But if Rachel was there, would she actually be any safer?

Or would she just feel safer next to someone who never flinched, so confident about her right to exist and make noise that she even made it boldly as she slept? Either way, Evie figured it'd be easier to close her eyes, lower her breathing, and let unconsciousness come over her.

The bat and various canisters Jackson had brought by were right next to her on the stool she used as a bedside table. She'd had a proper nightstand at some point, but it took up too much space and blocked the door just enough to be annoying. Crashing in an artistic rush back and forth between her studio and her bedroom she always caught her little toe on the corner, and after a few times of doing that, she got rid of it.

So many things getting in my way, she thought, holding her breath as she listened for more suspicious sounds in her apartment. I could be working on my Adonis tonight instead of biting my nails in the dark.

A clatter resonated from the living room, catching Evie in a moment of exhalation. *That was dumb of me.* She raised herself stealthily from the bed, her outstretched fingers closing around the baseball bat. *I should have known better than to exhale.* Her other hand rested on the can of bear mace, but she decided against it. Easier to get a good swing if she double gripped.

Evie stood as close to the door as she could, leaning out as little as possible in order to stay hidden while getting a look. The noise she heard had to have been made by someone close by. It didn't have the distant quality of pipes or gears; it had the human distinction of sounding like an accident. Like someone knocking plates together.

She peered around the molding and focused in the dim light. The studio and living room area were a bit brighter than her bedroom considering it had the big windows looking out onto the street. In the nighttime, in the dark, the space was a spider web of tree branches cast across the whitewashed walls.

Directly in the middle of that web, only feet from where Evie's eye first landed on her darling Adonis, was the hunched body of a man. She could see his shoulders moving as if she was working something in his hands. His back was bathed in a slash of yellow light; his head entirely in shadow.

Evie wasn't sure which approach would be better; slow and sneaky or quick and as quiet as possible when charging at an intruder with a baseball bat? Both ran the risk of him turning around, getting the weapon from her. God only knew what came next, the thought of which turned her blood to ice.

Everybody who grew up in New York saw and heard enough stories of how interrupting a petty crime could turn into a murder. She pictured poor Rachel's face when she would bust down the door only to find her best friend's broken body laid out under Adonis's gaze.

The next thing to cross her mind, which did nothing for the frigid state of her blood, was that whoever this was hadn't come here for any small crime. He wasn't here to steal her things or smash her sculptures. He wasn't here for anything that could be interrupted. This person, this headless muscled form feet from her Adonis, was here for a big crime.

Evie charged the intruder, bat raised over her head. She was swift and light enough to not make much noise, and she landed a solid hit against the man's upper back. If she had been able to see his head, she would have aimed there, but her imagination had run slightly away. She had almost convinced herself that this was a preternatural monster bent to a spiral in her studio; there was no head there for her to take a swing at.

The man slumped to the floor with a growl. He sounded a monster after all. His noises were throaty, guttural. He breathed too heavily as he stood to full height. And he moved fast, faster than Evie had anticipated. She thought he might be lumbering, strong but slow. Instead, he hit the floor, and got back to his feet just as Evie was bringing the bat down for another blow.

He caught it with his open palm, a wheezing whimper emerging as it made contact. Using the bat, he jerked Evie toward him and wrapped an arm around her shoulders. He pulled her against him, inhaling as he buried his face in her hair. Evie went rigid, suddenly very angry at herself for not bringing the bear mace.

She dropped to the floor. The man took a step away. His head was still in shadows and he moved soundlessly toward the door. Evie hadn't noticed that he'd been holding her slightly off the ground, that she had been petrified on her tiptoes as this beast sniffed her, catching her scent, making her easier to find. Now on the ground, she watched his form move out into the hallway, shutting the door behind him with a soft click.

"Don't ever say I'm not true to my word," Wheeler said when Jackson picked up the phone. "Your friend's building just had a B&E. I don't know whose apartment, but nobody was hurt. A young woman called it in."

"You're sure nobody was hurt?" Jackson hadn't been asleep anyway. He didn't even feel particularly tired. "Tell whoever's on site that I'm coming by."

The captain sighed through the phone, yet Jack knew she wouldn't let this happen. "Can you do me a favor first; call your friend and make sure it's her? I don't want you showing up to a startled victim who's never seen you before in her life."

Jackson agreed, and immediately dialed Evie's number. It rang a few times then a gruff male voice answered. "Who is this?"

"Is Evie there? It's Jackson."

"Does she want to speak with you?"

"Look, this is Jackson Adams. I'm not sure who this is but we might—"

The voice brightened. "Oh shit, Jackson, yeah. Sure, let me tell her you're on the phone." He heard the faraway conversation of his message being relayed. "Alright, she's here."

Evie's voice wasn't intimidating under normal circumstances. At the current moment, it sounded more lost and shaky than Jackson had ever heard it.

"Evie, what happened?" he asked.

"Did someone from the station call you? I'm fine, fortunately. It was... well, it wasn't nothing, but I'm not hurt."

"What happened?"

"What did they tell you happened?" Her voice got snappy for a second. Jackson heard her release her breath and swallow. "There was someone in my apartment. He... he didn't hurt me but he grabbed me."

"I'm coming over. I'll be on the road in two minutes."

He paused for a beat to give her a chance to say yes or no. The last thing he wanted to do in a time like this was impose on someone who wanted to be alone. He also knew they'd likely leave an officer or two parked outside the building until the sun came up, so Evie wasn't in more danger. He waited another second, hoping her voice wouldn't come back tired and sharp.

Her breathing came through again and then he heard, "Yeah, come over."

"Two minutes," he repeated, and threw on whatever clothes were closest on the floor.

His blood pumped faster than it had in months. Part of him was drawn to adrenaline, to seeking out danger. He hated that about himself, but it didn't stop it from being true. The first time he chased down and tackled a perp, he felt like howling at the moon, tearing off his clothes and sprinting naked through Central Park.

That's what he liked about Marcus; he didn't even notice adrenaline. To him, it was merely a necessary tool for survival. It was part of his job and his chemical makeup, but it wasn't there for him to enjoy.

"Fuck man," Jackson said once after receiving a lecture from his partner on how his adrenaline junkie ways were going to get him into trouble, "You sound like a nun talking about jerking off or something." He pinched his face together and went falsetto. "Your dirty parts are a natural part of propagation. They are not there for you to abuse."

"Hey, as cops, we've got to be extra careful," Marcus had said, relenting with a smile at Jackson's impression. "We've gotta be better than people expect. And one day, there's going to be someone who gets mad at the idea of you being buzzed off what happened to them." Marcus had stared out the windshield, expressionless, after that.

This is what he was talking about, Jackson thought as he flew down the BQE. His face was flushed; heat burned upward from his cheeks into his eyes and forehead. *Evie would kill me if she knew how I feel right now.*

Not far off, the city skyline cut the edge of the sky, creating a horizon all its own. Jackson, who was only lukewarm on cities as it was, would always love the consistent artificial nature of a place like New York. In a city, the people decided where the horizon is. In a city, the people decide when it's nighttime, when it's time for the world to be dark and beds to be filled.

When he eventually found himself living in nature, a goal he hoped wasn't that far off, he would yield to the idea of nature being the only one to make decisions. It would be dark when the sun went down; people would turn in once there was nothing left to do. The horizon would be a long, straight line, and everything living under it would accept its border as non-negotiable.

All he had to do was make it that long.

Chapter Eight

Outside her window, Evie saw the two cop cars pointing inward at each other on an angle. The cops in her apartment were taking pictures of things they thought might be useful. One of them stared at the Adonis curiously.

"This is a work in progress, right?" he asked, jabbing a finger in its direction. He noticed Evie tense up when he got too close, so he lowered his hand and took a step back. "You're an artist, huh?"

Evie nodded. She didn't turn all the way away from the window as she spoke to him. "I just finished up a show in a gallery, which was exciting."

"Been quite a month for you, huh?"

The cop was smiling too hard in a way that Evie found surprisingly disarming. He was trying to put her at ease, but she wouldn't turn away from the window because she wanted to see Jackson the minute he arrived. Even with two cops outside and three of them pacing through her living space, she felt safer at the idea of Jackson on his way.

"Jack Adams is on his way over," the cop who had answered the phone told the one who had gone down to the squad car to grab the camera. "He's friends with her."

"No shit," the camera cop said. He crouched down by a piece of paint splintered by a loose nail on the front doorjamb. "I think this might be a fabric fiber." He snapped a few pictures then whistled and asked one of the other cops for an evidence bag. "It might be nothing, but it looks like a piece of someone's sweatpants."

They all watched as the cop with the camera carefully loaded the almost invisible scrap of cloth into a plastic bag and sealed it. Evie even let herself turn all the way from the window, only looking back when she saw a car squeal into a spot across the street and kill its engine.

"Jackson's here," she announced.

He bolted out of the car and buzzed the intercom. The cop closest to it hit the door release.

"Well, this might not be exactly what you want to hear," the cop said, raising the evidence bag to the light, "but I don't think we've got a ton of physical evidence to work with."

"Don't say that to her," the other cop scolded.

"Look, I'm being honest. Besides, she already knows."

Evie shrugged for lack of any better reaction. She did know that. The intruder hadn't broken her lock or battered down her door. He hadn't clumsily cut himself or leave a trail of saliva like the beast he was. For someone who had committed a B&E, the breaking had been minimal. It was the entering that was the problem.

Jackson flew into the doorway, his face red in a way that Evie thought complimented him nicely. Almost like he was wearing blush on his high, crafted cheekbones. He and Rachel had similar bone structure, though Rachel's chin was more narrow, her jaw protruding more forward. Jackson's jaw was square. It was currently unshaven, another thing Evie noticed.

"Thank God you weren't hurt," he said as he crossed the room and pulled her into a hug. She didn't resist. "You didn't get a look at his face by any chance, did you?"

"No, they asked me that already."

She pulled away though their bodies were just touching. In an apartment in New York City, people wind up touching just because there's not enough space. So neither of them paid attention to how much contact they were making. Or at least they both acted like they weren't paying attention.

"We're gonna post up outside for a few hours," the cop with the camera told Jackson. "I assume you're sticking around for a bit."

"Yeah. I mean, I doubt this creep would come back twice in one night but if he does, I'd rather be here for it."

"You kinda hope he does, huh?" the other cop said, his over eager smile going wide, almost wicked. "Get a chance to catch this perv and get a buzz on."

"Oh, shut up," Jackson said, pushing them toward the door. Then he paused, smirked, and said, "Alright, maybe a little."

"Get a buzz on?" Evie asked as he came back in and closed the door. "Are you—do you want something to drink? I might have a beer in the fridge, but I don't know how old it is."

"What? No, that was nothing, don't listen to them." He gestured awkwardly as if he was still chasing his colleagues away. "Just shop talk. You get it."

"Sure," Evie answered.

Jackson shuffled his feet for a second as Evie glanced around her apartment. It had gone from empty to invasively full to back to empty in several short hours. "Now I kind of wish I did have something to drink. And eat. I'm usually working. I... I can forget to eat when I'm doing stuff."

"There's an all-night bodega a few blocks down. Let's go do a midnight snack run. My treat."

Evie wanted to laugh at the idea of her being safer out on the streets than in her own apartment, but it made a weird bit of sense. The stalker, the intruder, the hulking monster hunched and bisected by light, had come to her home to find her. At her home, she was the only person there, the only point of interest so to speak, a thought which thoroughly dehumanized her.

On the street, walking through the languid sprawling gaits of late-night city dwellers to the fluorescent lit store where everyone's face looked lined and haggard under the harsh lights, there were too many points of interest for him to focus on. Besides, she was safer on the street with Jackson and various witnesses, useless as they may be, than she was alone in those four walls.

"Let me grab a coat," Evie said.

Moments later they descended in the creaky elevator to the street, the level of the mere mortals.

They didn't talk much along the walk there. Evie put her hood up and strode along with her hands buried in her pockets. Jackson kept his head up and moving in all directions. That should have made Evie feel safer, that he was vigilant and ever ready, but instead it depressed her.

She didn't like the idea of having to be on guard every moment of the day. Most women living in cities were used to being wary and keeping their eyes peeled for danger but Evie had found, like many other women who lived in cities, that a thick skin gets built up and with that, intuition. She didn't need to be always alert, always watching, because she'd navigated enough sketchy situations to sense wrongness.

Danger had a distinct smell. Hard to describe, but one knew it when it came near. Jackson probably had a similar skill from his years on the force but right now, it was the last thing she wanted to talk about.

"I don't even know what I'm hungry for," she said as they stood in front of the deli section. An old man leaned against the glass case waiting for them to make up their minds. An old TV mounted in the corner showed a rerun of a sitcom Evie's mother had once referred to as 'boorish and utterly American.' The old man seemed to be enjoying it though, guffawing in an accent along with the canned laughter.

"I'll take a roast beef sandwich," Jackson told him. "Actually, give me two. I'm sure I'll be hungry by morning."

The old man grunted his confirmation of the order then waited until a commercial came on to get it started. Evie picked up a bag of chips, the faded menu of choices above the old man's head too daunting to pick through.

"This, and ya know what? Something to drink." Evie nodded to her own request, gazing at the beer selection lit like a work of art in a glass case. "I'm usually not a drinker but I feel like something alcoholic is the right move for tonight."

"And a sandwich," Jackson said. "Don't just eat chips and booze."

"Alright, alright. Uh...same as what you're getting."

The old man looked up, making eye contact with Jackson as he motioned for a third sandwich. He grunted again and went back to work.

"What kind of beer do you want?"

They stood together in front of the selection, and when Jackson pulled the door open, a pearly tumble of fog spilled out over their feet. Evie watched it as it moved then broke into shards before turning back into air.

"Have you ever been to San Francisco?" she asked as Jackson squatted down to take a look at the beer on the lower shelves.

"Nah. Haven't done much traveling on the west coast. Why?" He pulled two big bottles of a moderately expensive craft beer out and held them up for Evie to pursue. "See anything ya like?"

She shifted her eyes around his crouched form, swallowing the flood of drool she suddenly found pooling on her tongue. "Those work. They look delicious."

"So, what about San Francisco?" Jackson asked. They headed to the cash register as the old man was wrapping the last sandwich, and his show came back from commercial.

"Oh, it's got great fog." She laughed, aware of how ridiculous it sounded now without the visual aid. "When you opened the fridge, there was this fog that came out. Made me think of it."

"Ah, you artists. Never stop using your imagination."

Jackson paid, and they walked out into the night. He looked as if he were about to pop the bottles open. Evie imagined the two of them strolling arm and arm, toasting to the never-full city darkness. She shook the image from her mind at the same time he seemed to decide against it. It was probably for the best.

In case someone's watching, Evie told herself. Nothing to do with impure thoughts about your knight in shining armor.

Jackson pulled the chips out of the bag and tore into them.

"I guess you really were hungry," Evie said, then reached over and grabbed a handful. "I guess I am too."

She gorged on chips to silence her mind, letting the nervous energy give way to an oily, salty haze.

Rachel hadn't heard about the break-in until almost a day later. Jackson had wanted to call her the night of, but Evie insisted he not wake her up since things had turned out alright. The next day when he went to go call his sister and let her know, Evie said there was no reason if he was there.

"So you want me to stay through the night, too?" he asked. "Why don't you want me to tell Rachel? You think she's gonna be mad at you? She won't."

"I just…" Evie threw her arms wide. Jackson was struck by how long they were, like a wingspan for an ancient bird. "I feel like a total idiot."

"What for?"

"I... look, you and Rachel both offered me help and I turned it down even though I kind of really wanted to take you up on it, and then last night happened. I mean, I just kept thinking that if I didn't react, if I didn't give this freak the satisfaction, that he'd get bored and go away."

"Oh, Evie," Jackson sighed, trying not to sound patronizing. "You don't know how stalkers work, do you?"

"I know enough."

"They're not like bullies. They don't go away because you don't pay attention to them. There's plenty of situations where the person in question has literally never paid attention to the stalker because they never even met face to face. It doesn't deter them at all."

Evie collapsed on the tiny couch next to Jackson. She slumped down, one arm slung over her face. Their empty beer bottles were on the floor, and they had multiplied. At some point, Evie demanded more alcohol, and once it was delivered, she got a few hours of restless but necessary sleep. Jackson had stayed up to watch over her.

"I hate this," she muttered, not lifting her arm at all. "I just want to get back to work and not have to think about anything else."

"Anything but your muscle man," Jackson snarked. The shape of the Adonis was starting to come through nicely. Jackson could see it would be an enviable figure when it was done. "Is that your perfect man?"

"A big dumb lump of clay without a thought in his pretty head? Sure is." Evie sat up. They exchanged glances and laughed lightly. "I don't think I have a perfect man. I don't think any of you can be perfect." She rested her elbows on her knees, taking a masculine posture by accident.

Jackson didn't respond except to put his arm around her and squeezed her to him. There was a silence he didn't want to break, wherein Evie had left her vulnerability. It washed over him, turning his guts and spine to jelly. He wanted to tell her she looked very pretty, even though she was tired and scared, but everything sounded creepy in his head. Now wasn't the time.

"Let me call Rachel now," he said instead after the moment passed. "Let me tell her what happened last night."

Evie nodded, her curls brushing against his cheek. Jack released her and crossed the room to pick up the phone right as Evie bolted upright.

"The intruder," she said softly, slowly getting to her feet, "he pulled me to him and smelled my hair."

"Smelled your hair?"

"I think so at least. He buried his face into my hair and sniffed loudly." She shifted uncomfortably as if the pressure was still there in the curls, pushing into her neck. "Like an animal taking in another animal."

"Did you tell the officers about it?" Jackson knew sometimes victims have trouble piecing their memories together. Trauma had a tendency of making that difficult, something he had experienced firsthand. "Anything you remember, you can tell them. We can call them right now."

"I did, I did." Evie held her hands up, laughing stiffly. "I told them every single thing down to the fact that you bought me pepper spray and bear mace."

"Technically, the pepper spray was given to me by Captain Wheeler, and she's everyone's boss so that's allowed."

"It was just a weird moment and I meant to bring it up to you when we were talking. Ya know, after we picked up the food. But I lost it before I got the chance."

"Well, you were... ravenous," Jackson said, remembering how their hands had wrestled in the bottom of the chip bag, both fighting for the last crumbs. He could still smell the salty tang of her breath if he tried hard enough.

Evie must have had the same flashback because she inadvertently wiped her hands down her shirt as if they still had flakes on them. "I just... I'm surprised is all."

Jackson gave her a quizzical look, wondering what memory had unlocked itself in Evie's fragile mind.

"You and I have... We've been close today. A lot. You've pulled me..." She made a motion similar to how he'd enveloped her in his arms many times since the incident. His need to protect her had overridden his sense of propriety. Now, he feared, he'd gone too far.

"I'm sorry," he started, but she waved him off.

"It's fine. I'm fine. It's just... that's what he did. The same thing. But when you did it, it felt different. I guess I expected it to freak me out, trigger a flashback. Something. I don't know."

Jackson stepped toward her, wanting to wrap his arms around her again, but stopped himself. She looked like she might be in the middle of a flashback right now.

She wrapped her own arms around herself and lifted up on her tiptoes. "He sniffed me. I'm sure he did. And then..." She slumped down, hard, almost falling over. "He dropped me like I was nothing. Dead weight."

"This guy's a real piece of work," Jackson muttered, though he regretted saying it as soon as he saw the expression on Evie's face. "But, I mean, we're not gonna let anything—"

"How bad do you think it is?" Evie asked weakly.

"Honestly, I don't know. Either way, I'm glad nothing really bad happened this time around, and now we can keep a better eye on you."

Evie gave him a slow, meaningful smile.

Jackson cocked his head to the side. "What?"

"I forgot to tell you another thing."

Even though she'd been grinning, Jackson braced for the worst. "Yeah?"

"Last night, when I saw him, I whacked him with the baseball bat."

Chapter Nine

"So you're taking the first week then I'll start next week, and we can keep alternating if we need to." Rachel had her calendar out, marking schedules in a dying black pen. She shook it fiercely then stabbed the ballpoint tip into her tongue before trying again. "God damn it. Why do my pens always die?"

"Because you write like you're pissed at the paper," Jackson joked, handing her a new one. "Give me that, I'll throw it out."

They made the switch, and Rachel went back to furiously scheduling. She was a businessperson, someone who always had plans and moves. Her life was organized, and every day was clear cut. Jackson had picked a job in which he reacted to what was happening while Rachel picked one where she controlled what was happening.

"I hope you guys have the best people on this case," Rachel told him as she wrote. "I don't know if you noticed but I don't really have a ton of friends. For some reason." She sneered a little, raising her well-formed upper lip in a curl. "Maybe I'm just too nice."

"I agree. It's always been your biggest flaw."

Jackson stuck his head into Evie's room to check that she was still asleep. Rachel had no ability to whisper, a trait they shared to some extent. Jackson had gotten better at it after spending a few years in the squad car with Marcus. He'd start talking at the top of his lungs, which was his normal way of speaking, and his partner would press a finger into the ear closest to Jack and tell him, "Sotto voce, man. Sotto voce."

"I would never tell Evie this to her face," Rachel said, closing her calendar and leaning against the kitchen counter with a hip popped, "but I'm sorta mad she didn't have one of us staying with her the night that asshole was here."

"Don't tell her. She was worried about you being mad at her. She doesn't need the stress right now." Jackson knew his sister wouldn't dare, but she also had a history of blurting before thinking. Maybe his warning would curb that habit this one time.

"Okay, not mad, exactly. Maybe that's not the word for it." Rachel stared out the window, her eyes glazed for a moment then she snapped back. "It's like this with Evie; sometimes she won't deal with something until it's right in her damn face. I know she gets it from her mom. That woman is a piece of work. But it's frustrating. She's got this tunnel vision that makes her such a great artist who can do these amazing pieces in, what seems like to me at least, no time at all. The problem is when you try to show her what might be outside the tunnel, she acts as if you're overreacting."

Rachel circled the Adonis, pressed one manicured nail deep into its earthy flesh. She retracted her finger and stared at the wet, gray streaks left behind. "She probably couldn't think about anything but this hunk of a man," Rachel joked. "I guarantee she told herself, 'I don't' have time to be stalked; I've got a showing coming up in less than two months.'"

"She did say something about thinking the problem would go away if she didn't pay it any attention," Jack admitted. He wondered if he was betraying Evie by saying this. He certainly felt like he was, but with Rachel's insight, it seemed like a salient piece of information. "Her logic was sound. It was just applied to the wrong scenario."

"Evie in a nutshell; right logic, wrong scenario."

Jackson joined Rachel by the window. They could see Evie from their angle but her face was turned away from them. All they could actually see was a poof of curls. Rachel's face took on a manic darkness, like she'd been caught somewhere between laughing and crying.

Jackson put a hand on his sister's shoulder, an intimate move their new adult relationship made awkward. "Rach, look, you've got a lot going on. Maybe let me deal with being Evie's bodyguard. Ok?"

"You'd probably be better at it than me," Rachel answered listlessly.

Jackson could tell she didn't like the idea of giving up control, but in this situation she was willing to defer to him. Because, and only because, he knew what he was doing.

She sighed. "Let me do it every once in a while, though. You know me. I just...I dunno, I need to."

Jackson agreed and Rachel opened her calendar again. She marked off a few weekend days where she could give Jackson a break.

In the next room, Evie slept soundly for the first time in a very long while.

Her dreams weren't terrible. They weren't particularly pleasant either. But Evie was used to strange dreams. These were somewhere between anxiety dreams and early teenage sex dreams. She kept seeing flashes of body parts, men with pretty smiles and bright eyes. Sometimes the sight of them would cause her muscles to lock up, unable to scream or run away. Other times, she melted, begged for them to bring those parts closer so she could touch them, examine them, learn their lines with her fingers and immortalize them in clay.

One of the men was Jackson, smiling at her with half his mouth, his sharp yet innocent eyes watching her. He and Rachel had different eyes, Evie noticed for the first time in her dream. Rachel's eyes didn't have a speck of innocence in them. They always looked like she was casing the joint, sizing up the competition. Jackson's eyes had a childlike quality to them. The eyes of someone who was excited to be there.

Somewhere in her dream, deep down in the soup of her subconscious, she heard a sentence on repeat.

Get a chance to catch this perv and get a buzz on.

Moving through the landscape laid out for her, she saw a diaphanous Jackson fading into the background, and she touched his arm, bringing him back into solid form.

"What does it mean? You catching the perv and getting a buzz on?"

Jackson smiled with his whole mouth then cast his eyes down and shook his head. "People get mad at me for it."

"What does it mean?"

The dreamscape shifted; Evie felt the ground give way under her feet. There was no sense of fear, no dread of being dropped into the blackness, the void, that was now all around her. It was only when her dream dropped her on the floor that she started awake. She had felt it all over again the way she had when it happened; her body landing on the polished wood of her studio, startling her with how the floor rushed up to meet her.

It was almost twilight. Her room was dark, and the door was closed. Light seeped in from underneath, and she could hear Rachel and Jackson talking back and forth. There was laughing, the sound of a take-out container being opened. Evie considered getting out of bed to join them but waited a bit longer to watch the remainder of the light drain from the sky.

Considering her price range when she moved in, she didn't have too many options, but one of the main reasons she got this apartment was because both the bedroom and living room windows faced the street. She had seen too many places where the windows looked over an alley, nothing but a brick wall right in front of her face and garbage cans strewn around below. No matter how big the space, how nice the bathroom, Evie couldn't even imagine living anywhere without a view.

She didn't need the most glorious, iconic landmark outside her window; she just needed to be able to see the streets and the traffic, listen to people fighting or laughing or making plans. Inspiration wasn't as abundant in alleyways, or at least not at all times. Occasionally she walked past bodies wound together in what she knew was soon to be a beautifully filthy second of passion, tucking themselves behind dumpsters and against the walls that crumbled chalky red bits onto their tugged-up clothes. That she found inspiring; *that,* she thought one time while lingering to watch for a bit, *is true art.*

She envied the ways people could be depraved, could get dirty. It never occurred to her to do any of these things, partially disrobing and groping in alleyways, but when she spotted them, she thought they looked fun. Her mother had taken to calling her prude and uptight around the time Evie entered high school. They'd pass a couple making out on a park bench, the man's hand already resting on the woman's breast. Evie would scrunch up her face in disgust, or at least she claimed, and her mother would cackle and snip, "You muzt want to boring sex life."

There was no doubt her mother had a wild time of it when she was young. Evie had been conceived during a time referred to by her mother as her "Fellini summer." She wasn't even aware of being pregnant until the man in question had left and the days were starting to get short. Evie had been growing patiently in the middle of all the insanity, instinctually repelled by it once she made her arrival.

The window in her bedroom faced west, and Evie watched the burning sun until it was gone. There was still a lot of light since the sun had only dipped behind buildings and trees, the manmade horizon those living in a city create, and the shadows bent in odd directions and angles.

Evie got up and stood in the window for a long time, wondering if anyone could see her. Wondering if anyone was watching right now. This was something she thought about a lot, a game she used to play to see how many people in the city bothered to look up or out or anywhere other than the direction they were headed.

Now, it seemed like a more ominous thought, a question that had an answer she didn't want to face. Instead of the excitement of whether anyone was watching, Evie had the distinct fear, premonition, that *he* was watching.

Chapter Ten

Rachel had written up a very neat and tight schedule for how she and Jackson could keep an eye on Evie, though Evie would resent it being referred to as such, and as per his request, he was on more nights than Rachel was. He hadn't bothered to tell her he'd probably be hanging around on her nights, too. Better to let her think she had it all sorted.

When Evie joined them in the living room after her much needed nap, she was overwhelmed with the discussion, a fact that Rachel had little patience for.

"Evie, you're a dreamer and an artist and that's what I love about you," she said, leafing through take-out menus so she could buy everyone dinner. "But this is a situation which requires a more realistic approach."

"That's not fair, Rach," Evie replied weakly. "I'm not an unrealistic person. This is just...it's a lot to take in."

"I understand that, which is why you don't have to take in anything. The plans are set, the schedule is done. Someone will always be here with you, and between Jack and me, we'll make sure you're safe." In her left hand, she held up a Chinese food menu. In her right, Indian. "Who wants what? It's on me."

Once Rachel was gone to pick up the food, Jackson took the chance to comfort Evie about the arrangement as well as he could. She wouldn't sit next to him on the couch when he asked her to. Instead, she stood stiffly by the window with her arms crossed over her chest and her eyes still glazed from sleep.

"You know Rachel is as freaked out about this as you are," he told her as he joined in the staring. "The difference between you and Rachel is that she's more of a control freak. Making plans and organizing is her coping mechanism."

"Couldn't she just do drugs like a normal person?"

"Knowing Rachel, she'd do something that made her even more of a control freak."

Jackson wanted to put his arm around her shoulder and give her a hug, but he knew better. They were trained to not touch someone who had just had their privacy violated. One time he had rescued a teen girl from an in-progress assault, which he at first thought was a common lewd conduct moment of a couple going at it in the park. When the guy had been arrested and the girl was supposed to get into an ambulance, she ran forward and wrapped herself around Jackson so tightly he was worried she'd snap his spine. Even then, it took a moment for his arms to come down around her. He had never been in her situation, or Evie's for that matter, but it didn't take a genius to see how it could make anyone skittish.

Jackson knew he'd already broken that rule, along with many others, where Evie was concerned. She'd said as much last night. And he had vowed to behave himself.

"Can I ask a favor?" Evie broke away from the window; the eye contact she made with Jackson was startling. The sleep glaze had vanished, and the rest of her expression turned somber. "Rachel's not gonna like it."

"What is it?"

"I don't want her to be here through this. A night or two maybe, but her good intentions shit will drive me up the wall."

"So you want just me? The whole time?" Jackson swallowed though his mouth had gone dry.

"Like a bodyguard. I mean, I can pay you if you want. Not much but something at least. I'll buy your sandwiches when we go for midnight snack runs."

Jackson laughed and shook his head. "Rachel will only hate that for a minute," he promised. "You don't have to pay me anything either. I want to do this for you, Evie. I've felt so helpless lately."

The words hurt coming out of his mouth. They cut his throat as they rose from his vocal cords. Nobody wants to be helpless but coming from a cop, from someone who had prided himself on making communities and people safer, it felt like admitting failure. Worse than failure; absolute and total defeat.

And he'd just said it out loud.

Evie's face was stuck between expressions. Jackson couldn't tell if she was moved by his raw honesty or disgusted by it. He also thought she might be reconsidering him as her bodyguard.

Who would want a cop who can't get himself back onto the force impotently standing by to prove his shortcomings when the time came? Stalking cases were inherently risky, and here he had just told the woman who asked for his protection that he was helpless.

"What happened to your partner wasn't—" Evie started but Jackson didn't let her finish. He threw a hand up to shush her.

"Don't even bother with that," he told her in a cold voice. He could see from her reaction that she wasn't used to him sounding so short, so nasty. "I don't need to hear more platitudes from people who weren't there, alright? That's all I've gotten since it happened."

Evie's face puckered. She shrugged, her jaw set firmly, and turned back to the window.

Jackson immediately regretted speaking to her the way he had but everyone from his captain to his co-workers to his God damned sister had the same speech ready.

After being stalked and terrorized, Evie might have understood how annoying it was to hear the emptiness of the same well-meaning advice on a loop. Bringing it up seemed unwise to Jackson, though the urge to do so was strong. He didn't want her mad at him; he didn't want her to think he was the kind of jerk who cut someone off when they were trying to be caring toward him. On the other hand, he was ready to throttle the next person who told him he wasn't the one who pulled the trigger.

"So, what's the plan for this bodyguard situation?" Evie asked, her tone stiff. She avoided making eye contact with him. Whatever tricks of the light were happening with the buttery glow of city lights and the emerging skeletal forms of autumnal trees was the only thing that had her attention at the moment. "You're going to stay here, right?"

"I suppose so. Rachel kind of made it sound like that was the only option, though she was debating the idea of having you stay out in Queens. With me."

Evie shook her head. The corners of her mouth were slipping further down the sides of her face. "No, I have to be in my studio. I need to work on my Adonis."

"Oh yeah, I forgot about your boyfriend."

Jackson circled the piece, his eyebrows arching as he passed the shapely and specifically toned buttocks. It didn't matter that it was clay; it stabbed a strange knife of jealousy into him.

Evie was facing him now. Her eyes narrowed. "This is a very important piece to me, and it has to be done in less than a month."

"What's the matter? Don't think you can be properly inspired in Queens? I don't live too far from a beach. You artsy fartsy types love the beach."

"Artsy fartsy? Is that a real term you use? Dear God, I thought you were Rachel's older brother. Not her grandfather."

A key jiggled in the lock, and Rachel, with the looped handle of a plastic bag clenched in her teeth, swung open the door and teetered in. She made a grunting noise at Jackson until he took the bag from her mouth.

"Thank you." She rolled her eyes as she crossed to the kitchen. "What a gentleman. Jumps into action after watching me struggle for five minutes."

"Everyone's mad at me tonight," Jackson drawled playfully, but when he caught Evie's gaze, she smiled reluctantly.

There was a brief window of peace as the three of them ate together. Evie, to Jackson's surprise, didn't seem to mind having so many people, so much energy, around her. Her usual need for silence and solitude, especially in her own home, was legendary.

Rachel and Jackson amiably surrendered to her desire not to stay away from her studio, and Evie appeared to relax. Under the shadow of her Adonis, they ate dinner and spent no more time discussing their unfortunate and necessary plans.

"These yours?" Evie dangled a pair of boxer briefs from two fingers, which seemed disgusted to be holding something so intimate. "They were on the floor of my bathroom. My bathroom, Jackson. Not our bathroom."

"I forgot them when I showered this morning. Relax. You're lucky I'm wearing some at all." He crooked a wicked grin her way, but Evie was not amused.

He snatched the boxers and squirreled them away in his bag. Color was coming up in his cheeks.

Evie took some satisfaction in his embarrassment. But she quickly stifled it and made herself give him a stern look. "Jack, I know we've got to at least make this an okay arrangement for a bit, and I'm not trying to be a diva, but there's a reason I live alone. There's a reason I'm in a place with hardly any furniture and nothing on the walls. I need... I need my space to feel like my space so I can get my work done."

Evie bristled at how she was behaving but she couldn't stop herself. Rachel had always jokingly called her a control freak. The way that Rachel jokingly called anyone anything was by snickering lightly as she said it and hoping the addressed party doesn't get offended. Evie argued with her that the term control freak seemed a bit too strong; she was just someone who liked things to be the way she wanted them to be. If Rachel wanted to see a control freak, she should look in the mirror.

"I'll bet it has something to do with being raised by your mother," Rachel would ponder, tilting her head to one sight and sucking in her cheeks the way she did when she was attempting to come across as pensive. "A backlash to her frenetic energy."

Evie wished she had told Rachel to shut up more often, but she rarely did because, annoying or not, Rachel was usually right. Sadly, she was dead on the money about this, though there must be a better term for what she had. Still, Evie held out hope Rachel could be wrong. She didn't want to attribute any of her characteristics to her mother; from Evie's perspective, her mother provided nothing so why should she get any credit?

"I don't even want to give her credit for fucking me up," Evie said whenever Rachel mentioned it.

"Literally nothing about how you process your relationship with your mother is healthy," Rachel answered but she left it at that. Their relationship didn't have to be healthy. As far as Evie was concerned, it didn't have to exist at all.

A few years had passed since Evie had spent a significant amount of time with her mother. She had made a point after college to stop in every few months, duty bound out of a genetic entanglement. Part of her had hoped maybe her mother would start to change by then; that she would be struck by an epiphany in her later years which pressed upon her the importance of stability to children.

Evie once imagined her mother apologizing in her heavy accent that rounded the jagged English words she incessantly spat. There would be tears in her eyes, a trembling cigarette clenched in the fork of her fingers. She'd be shaking too hard to bring it to her mouth, and when she did, the tail of ash that had been steadily growing would rain down into her lap.

In this fantasy, Evie was unemotional, blank even. She'd nod as her mother wept and shook and tried to touch her hand in apology. Her answers to the pain-filled questions being ripped from her mother's throat would be short, polite, but sterile and cold. Once her mother finally got to the apology, the literal words of 'I'm sorry for how I failed you', which Evie was positive her mother would say, Evie would tell her she loved her, she appreciated what little she had done for her, but they no longer needed to pretend they had a working relationship.

Then I'd leave, she always thought when she pictured it. I wouldn't even wait for a response.

It was the coldness that she loved. Her mother was chaotic and moody but cold was never a descriptor that fit. In fact, she ran too far to extremes, and that's what made her impossible to live with. She dove into any fleeting affair or passing fancy as if her life had been leading up to it all along. Then she'd tear it to pieces, leave it behind her, move along to destroy the next passion waiting to bubble up.

To sit expressionless in front of her mother as she poured her heart out, to blink in response to some overly sentimental pablum, was the best revenge she could imagine for a woman who had done that much damage.

Of course, Evie never told Rachel this fantasy. She knew exactly what Rachel would have to say about it, which Evie didn't need to hear. She held no delusion about her scars. Her mother had made her frightened of emotion, frightened to be in touch with pieces of herself. In a way, one that Evie would never admit, she lived in constant fear that she was nothing but a clone of the woman, and the moment she opened the Pandora's box of unrestrained feelings, she'd be just as bad if not worse.

The last time she had seen her mother had been a disaster. Evie had gone to the tiny apartment by the East River Esplanade where her mother's current boyfriend lived. It seemed to Evie that her mother didn't make decisions for herself; she didn't mobilize into any kind of action. There was always a man tugging her along, bringing her into his home then kicking her out again when she acted the way she did. This particular guy, for what it was worth, tried to be nice enough. He was polite and friendly to Evie when she came over without being too invasive. Their apartment was new to him too; he had moved to a bigger place on the East side because he thought it might do Evie's mother some good to be near the Esplanade.

"We take walks along it," he explained to Evie as he pointed out the strip of green that looked as if it spanned the length of the city. From his high-rise window, Evie thought it resembled a runner of carpet down a long hallway. "It's really nice. We went one time around sunset, and it was beautiful. Almost like Paris."

Evie's mother snorted, concurrently lighting a cigarette. "Yes, just like Paris zhis iz." She inhaled and let the tendrils of smoke work their way out of her nose. "The City of Lights iz nozhing compared to zeeing de NYPD fish a body out of zee East River."

It would have been a waste of breath for Evie to remind her mother that she spent a lot of the time they were in Paris complaining about everything. Instead, she started to tell her about the small art gallery that had excitedly selected some of her paintings to display.

"I know it's nothing big yet, but they really loved my work," Evie said. "If nothing else, it was really validating."

"Validating," her mother spat. The words curled off her tongue like poisonous fumes. "Can zis pay zee rent? Validation?"

"No but that's not really the point right now. Besides, the paintings are for sale. I might get validation and money out of this."

Her mother's face went sour. She stared through Evie as if trying to pretend she wasn't there and getting angry at herself for not being able to. The cigarette puffed in short, angry bursts; her eyes went dark despite the glittering reflection of the sun undulating on the surface of the East River.

"You zhink you will be successful, do you?" her mother asked. The words didn't come out as harsh as she probably hoped. Her voice had taken on a higher pitched whine than Evie was used to. "Zee art world will eat you, my sensitive daughter. Et's what et's done to me."

For the first time, Evie saw the age in her mother's face. The thin ridges along her lips grew deeper with each drag of the cigarette that caused them to purse forward like an ancient baby suckling a smoke-filled teat. Circles under her eyes that once only looked startlingly dark when she was tired now claimed permanent residence. She was beautiful still, Evie couldn't deny that, but she finally looked as tired and world weary as she always claimed to be. Her looks had caught up to a lifetime of her gravelly sardonic delivery.

"I'm sorry I came to see you, mother," Evie said, a bit more primly than she had expected to though she liked the effect had on the angry-eyed woman across from her. "If my presence is that annoying to you, perhaps it would be better if we no longer have any contact."

Her mother made a disgusted clucking noise and waved Evie away with one curt flap of her wrist. She was daring Evie to go, calling a bluff she may have known was a genuine threat. The cigarette was brought back to her dried, coarse lips; for the first time, Evie saw the growing stack of ash tremble in her mother's hand.

And she liked it.

Chapter Eleven

Captain Wheeler agreed to meet with Jackson for lunch under one condition; he couldn't ask her any questions about any police activity whatsoever.

"Actually, you can ask if you really wanna waste your breath but I'm tellin' ya right now, Jack: I'm not saying anything."

They sat in Central Park, watching college kids pretend they were being sneaky about drinking in public. A whole picnic of them spread out less than ten feet from the concrete chessboard Jackson and Wheeler used as a table, and the noise they were making steadily rose.

"Should we show a badge real quick?" Jackson jerked his head in the direction of the drinkers. "Remind them public drunkenness is illegal in this city."

"I'm off duty," Wheeler answered with a long sigh. "Come back to me if one of them is about to get behind the wheel of a car."

"That's the upside of living in a place filled with weirdos and stalkers. At least nobody is gonna drive drunk."

Jackson had asked her to meet him for more reasons than just wanting information about the ongoing investigation. He was actually less concerned with that, since he figured she had nothing new to report, and more concerned with Evie's growing resentment every second he spent in her apartment. She snapped at him for chewing too loud, chided him for leaving the bathroom a mess, and got angry that he put on aftershave while she was working.

"The smell is distracting me," she had said, pressing a finger in the gap between her eyebrows. "It's not just right now; I can smell it all day."

"And the musk of a man is that distracting to you? Damn, Evie. When was the last time you got laid?"

Upon repeating this story to Captain Wheeler, Jackson didn't have to bother telling her Evie's reaction. His comment turned out not to be the well-received barb that broke the tension between them as he'd hoped.

"So, what specifically are you asking me here?" Wheeler leaned forward on her elbows, chewing in long, lazy circles. "You want me to tell you how to stop getting on someone's nerves?"

"I guess I didn't realize how easily I could do that."

"Oh, well, you should have asked me earlier. I could have informed you, at length."

Jackson chucked a pickle slice at her, both of them laughing as it hit her cheek and slid limply to the chessboard. Wheeler moved it to a square near him and declared checkmate.

"My bigger concern," Jackson continued, "is that she'll get so annoyed with having me around she'll get rid of me despite still being in danger. I don't know if I want you to tell me what to do or to tell me you're this close to finding the guy or what, but I'm worried about a lot right now, and—" he took a deep breath then let it flow slowly from his nostrils, "I guess I'm freaking out a bit."

"You stopped going to therapy," Wheeler said in that direct, to the bone way Jackson heard her use frequently. She was a more serious person than he gave her credit for, something he was also starting to realize with Evie. He had trouble seeing her as this furrowed-brow artist clambering around on a stepladder to gouge lines next to carved clay eyes, making a perfect male form nothingness.

"I didn't stop going. I just haven't been in a while."

"How long is a while?"

Jackson took another deep breath. He couldn't be sure, but he had a feeling his captain already knew the answer to that question.

"I'm not sure," he lied, weakly. From the face she made, he realized he should have just told her the truth. "I guess it's been about six weeks."

"Two months, Jackie boy, and I think you know that."

"What does my going to therapy have to do with any of what I'm talking about?"

"Maybe you'd know if you were still going to therapy." She took another bite of her sandwich, and chewed in her languid, circular way. "I didn't put you on leave to be a massive bitch. I did it because I saw what that shooting did to you."

"Yeah? And what was that?"

"It showed you how little control you have in this life." She lifted the side of her lip to quickly pick a fleck of lettuce out of her teeth. "Which is something I wish you had known prior to becoming a cop. Men are like that though. Always think they've got the world figured out."

Jackson fell silent. He wanted to be angry but considering the circumstances, he saw what she meant. Evie, lousy with her own batch on control issues, had gone through a turbulent childhood and was now being stalked and terrorized inside her own home. She was several years younger than him, yet Jackson had no doubt she quite keenly knew the limited extent of one's own control. She had probably faced that existential crisis as a kid, watching her dynamic mother spiraling and crashing.

"So what do I do right now?" Jackson asked. "Okay, therapy has to happen again, and issues have to be stared in the face, but for the time being, how do I not make this situation worse?"

"Just think about what it must be like for her. As scared and helpless as you feel, she feels ten times that."

The college kids on the blanket were starting to get rowdy. One of the boys tackled his friend next to him, and they were a rough housing tangle of limbs until the rest of the group broke it up. Captain Wheeler watched all of it with a bemused, if slightly distant, countenance.

"I think maybe part of it is that I still think of her as a kid or something," Jackson said as the picnicking group began to pack up the remains of their meal. "Half the time I don't even wanna take her seriously when she's making a big deal about me being in her way or distracting her from her work."

"Well, she's not a kid," Wheeler replied, sharp and with no room for interpretation. "She's a grown woman with grown woman problems. If you want to do her a favor, don't be another one of them that she has to deal with."

Evie knew Jackson would be back before it got dark, but she felt jumpy anyway. Dark came so quickly in the fall, and on a day as unseasonably warm as this, people had a tendency to forget it was autumn. They'd sit in the park, sunning their faces and legs like they did in the middle of July. Then twilight hit in the late afternoon, and nighttime surrounded them faster than they realized.

She wanted him to come back not only because he made her feel safe but because she wanted to apologize for snapping at him. Part of it had been justified. He did seem flippant when she simply asked him to respect her space, but part of it had just been stress and nerves and anxiety and control issues talking. Evie had dealt with enough of those to know when to admit she was wrong.

Jackson walked in before it was dark out. The sinking sun backlit the artifice horizon of buildings, fading the sky to purple.

Evie sat on the couch waiting for him; she smiled as he opened the door. "Hi."

"You look happy to see me," he said, closing and locking the door behind him. "Happier than I would have thought for sure."

"Yeah, I am. Want something to drink? I ran out to the store earlier and grabbed a six pack. It's an IPA. You know, what all the cool kids are drinking."

Jackson smirked at that and crossed to the fridge. He pulled out two beers, opened them both then handed one to Evie. She accepted it without a thank you, a yielding and unexpected contriteness settled onto her features.

"I didn't realize how late it was," Jackson said, raising the long-necked bottle to his mouth. "It was so warm today."

"I know. It tricks you into thinking it's the summer."

There was no rush for anything that had to be said yet Evie could feel the invisible hand of tension pressing into her, its fingers making imprints in her already frayed nerves. She took a long sip of her beer and noticed Jackson looking at everything in her apartment that wasn't her.

When she finally started to say something, he was staring directly at the glacially morphing lump of clay in the center of the room. He stared at it as if he expected it to shift or move, as if he was seeing the changes Evie carved into it happening right before him.

"That's coming along, huh?" he said, another sip being swallowed down along with the last syllable of the sentence.

"Not really. Or at least, not as well as I would have hoped." Evie cleared her throat, wishing for the tension to dissipate. "Jackson, I wanted to say I'm sorry."

"Sorry? To me?"

"Yes. To you."

Jackson shifted in his seat, extended his legs in an almost successful attempt to seem casual. "What about?"

"I find it hard to believe you don't know what about but mainly that I've been so short with you. I've...this is a situation I've never had to deal with and while it's happening, I still have to go about my day, you know? I have to get this—" she jerked her hand in the direction of her Adonis, "fucking thing done, and I have to take calls from buyers and curators. Now you're here, which is great and I'm insanely grateful for—"

Jackson made the same snort Rachel always did, albeit lighter and gentler considering the situation. "Alright, alright, don't lay it on too thick."

"I mean it, though! I don't want to lie awake in bed every night, and I appreciate you willing to do what it takes to keep me in my home. But I'm not used to someone else being here. Least of all a man."

Jackson wanted to ask what would be the difference of a woman invading her space but he bit his tongue. He was just trying to ease the tension, get a rise out of someone in a spiral. The difference was obvious, and he knew it.

"You don't have to apologize to me, Evie," Jackson told her, dropping his hand on her shoulder then snapping it back briskly. It looked considerably less casual than he had hoped for. "I'm here to help you. Protect and serve, right?"

"Sure, but I still want to apologize. It's not like me to be so tightly wound." A half-truth. Evie could accept that.

She wasn't the type to be snippy and confrontational but there was enough evidence to support a tightly wound personality. It helped lead to success in a difficult industry, and how she had been able to find the perfect, affordable apartment in a competitive city. To discount the tautness of her internal winding did her a disservice. She was tightly wound to a point, but she hated the fact that she had recently started to feel constantly angry.

"Ya know, when my partner got shot, there was nothing anybody could say to me that didn't make me wanna throttle them." Jackson adjusted again, this time sitting more upright. "Even a month after it happened, if someone was like, 'it wasn't your fault, don't blame yourself,' I'd fly off the handle. They're just trying to be nice and supportive, but I wanted to scream in their faces that I knew that already."

"Yeah, nobody tells you how infuriating this can be. Sure, you'll be sad or scared or whatever expected reaction, but no one ever told me that having to deal with some creep would make me assume anything that happened was a personal slight against me."

She had started picking at the corner of the beer label, careful not to rip any of it. Peeling it off cleanly, running her nail back along the translucent brown glass to peel off the last white-capped bits of glue.

Performing the mindless action had calmed her, until she glanced up at Jackson. He seemed to be watching all this with interest, a lot of interest. Evie's finger trembled as she scraped at the final bit of stickiness. She wiped it on the back of the label and folded it all into a tiny square. All the while, Jackson's eyes never left her.

"I didn't leave my drawers behind in the bathroom as a personal slight to you," Jackson said out of nowhere with a lilt in his voice. "I just did it because I'm a slob."

"Well, I figured as much later when I calmed down." She looked at him out of the corner of her eyes and gave him a sideways smile. "You always splash a lot of water everywhere though. Can't tell me not to take that personally."

"That only happens because your shower is so small! Apartments are so tiny in this damn city. Out in Queens, we've got showers bigger than this whole place."

Evie burst out laughing. "Yeah, I heard about that. Houses the size of this building with closets bigger than my studio."

"It's true! You should come check out my place sometime, get a load of what you're missing." Jackson clamped his mouth shut, which made Evie laugh more.

Deciding not to read much into the comment, or her physical reaction to it, Evie focused more on the Zen she hadn't been able to achieve since well before this all started. It would happen when she worked for long hours on a piece she knew would turn out beautiful.

The inexplicable inspiration, the ancient muse of creation as it were, had been absent from her for longer than she cared to admit. The Lafayette Street series had that essence of divine creation, but she lacked it for her Adonis. She couldn't quite get the abs right; she couldn't quite see the shape of the man she was creating.

The two of them shared another beer and ordered some dinner. They had reached a comfortable place for the time being, and the separate anxiety that powered through them each had gone out with the tide.

Yet, despite all that, Evie lay awake in bed that night, swimming through the Zen, sensing the apprehension crouching in wait right behind it.

Chapter Twelve

At around the time of Evie's eleventh birthday, her mother made the announcement that they would be returning to Paris, and soon. She had gotten a ticket for herself to go scout apartments and jobs then she would either return to wrap up the New York based loose ends or simply send for Evie to join her.

For the time she was gone, Evie stayed with Rachel and her family in Westchester. Jackson was about fourteen, and naturally found himself way too cool to spend any time with his pushy little sister and her weird friend. Jackson and Rachel's parents tended to use words like "artistic" and "unique" when Evie would say or do something a tad off. Evie was polite and well-behaved, but she sculpted prostrated forms out of her mashed potatoes and talked openly about watching the prostitutes in her neighborhood solicit in their cars.

"She just says bizarre stuff," Jackson complained when his parents informed him that Evie would be spending most of the summer at their house. "Remember when she was making sleeping bums out of her dinner? She was like, 'this is the guy who always blacks out at the bus stop across the street.'"

"Yeah, that's what happens to kids who grow up in cities," his mom said without missing a beat. She knew what he was getting at. It was startling to see a child so fascinated by the underbelly of the world. "Be thankful we got lucky enough to be able to afford this beautiful house in this lovely neighborhood, and that you don't have to see old drunks outside your bedroom window."

Rachel was obviously over the moon about the prospect of an Evie-filled summer. She loved the weird stuff Evie said; she loved the stories about the excitement just outside her front door. Evie sometimes didn't want to bring up the city, and Rachel would push the issue. She'd ask if the working girls, as she had taken to calling them, had any newcomers, if the bums who shouted at each other and threw bottles were still around.

"Up here it's boring," she said, gesturing broadly to all of Westchester. "I can't wait to live in the city and have every day be as exciting as yours are."

In June when Evie first got there, she thought Rachel was nuts for thinking like that. By August, even as she had fun and enjoyed herself, she missed the noise and the insanity she had grown accustomed to. While boisterous and loud in their own right, Rachel's family couldn't compete with the clamor of a real city.

Evie struggled to draw as easily as she did at home, losing time to the craft as it drew her into a trance. The quiet surrounding Rachel's house was pleasant and refreshing at first but oppressive and grating by the end of the summer. Besides, the woods weren't as peaceful as people believed them to be. Every night Evie heard new noises: hisses and shrieks from nocturnal creatures, groaning creaks from trees whipping in the wind.

Her mother returned from Paris angrier and ruder than when she left. She came to collect Evie and lit a cigarette in the kitchen in front of everyone. Rachel exchanged looks with her mom as if waiting to watch this adult get scolded, but her mom just shook her head and asked Evie's mother how it went.

"Zhat city is a shithole," Evie's mother exhaled, her words formed of smoke and venom. "Eet's good to go back so I remember why eet ees that I left."

"So we're not going to leave New York?" Evie asked, her eyes wide behind her scratched and battered frames. She hadn't gotten new glasses in over a year. "I really want to stay here."

Evie and Rachel had already hatched a probably unlikely plan should Evie's mother decide she had to come to Paris. On a sticky night in July, too hot and humid to sleep, they stayed up 'til dawn whispering what options they had in serious little kid voices.

"My parents would let you stay here," Rachel swore. "I know they would. They think your mother's a loon."

"And it's not like she actually wants me around anyway," Evie agreed.

She stared up at the dim shape of her friend from the trundle bed. Rachel was peering down at her in the dark. All Evie could see was the whites of her eyes moving as she talked.

"Once one of the older kids goes to college, you can have their room. So, like, we'd maybe have to share a room for a year but honestly, that could be fun."

Evie went along with her friend's excitement though the pit in her stomach warned her that she didn't want to leave the city. *Paris might be fun, I guess,* she thought to herself as the world washed to the soft blue gray that heralded dawn. *Would I rather live in the middle of nowhere but be close to the city or live in a different city on a different continent?*

The question never had to be answered, yet Evie never stopped thinking about it. It was the first time in her life she started to understand the complicated nature of inspiration. She had some control over how she created and when she created but felt it increasingly difficult to pinpoint what brought on that flood, that drive to start her work. If the city was what inspired her or the sights and sounds of it, was that a trait she could find elsewhere? Was it inherent to New York as her home or would any city suffice?

Another inquiry without an answer, and one that was nipping at Evie's heels currently. Her Adonis wasn't speaking to her the way she had expected it to. She wasn't finding the trance that came when she hit her stride so fluently.

A call came in last night from the curator of the gallery asking if Evie could come down to meet with a buyer who might want to commission a piece. Evie was secretly relieved that she didn't have to spend the day in her apartment, trying to focus on one male body while not focusing on another. She needed a break from her work at the moment; she needed to give the inspiration a chance to come to her rather than hounding it.

As she was making yet another cup of coffee and getting ready to leave, she heard the shower turn on and Jackson's goofy pop of warbling peaking over the rush of the water. What had annoyed her the day before now soothed her. She went about gathering her things and drinking her coffee, speeding out of her room in such a hurry that she hadn't even heard the shower turn off.

Jackson was exiting the bathroom, a towel bound precariously around his hips. From the surprise on his face, he clearly thought Evie would be gone before he got out. His hand flew to the knot riding up onto his waist as if to hold it in place. Evie screeched to a halt moments before she collided into him, her gaze resting on the water-speckled torso.

"I thought you were still in the shower."

"I thought you were leaving."

Evie nodded vigorously. She pushed her glasses flush to her face and swallowed down the dregs in her coffee cup. "I'm leaving right now. I'm going to have to take a cab. Definitely running late."

Evie flew out the door without saying anything else. Jackson, who had originally suggested he go with her until Evie convinced him she was fine on her own, locked the door behind her, naked and wet and suddenly, entirely on fire.

What are you thinking, Adams?

Jackson knew better than to get involved with Rach's best friend. Wasn't that the first rule of little sisters?

Besides, he reprimanded himself as he toweled off, the last thing he needed was for Evie to see what lurked beneath the surface of his nice guy act.

"I'm not sure what I want exactly," the buyer was saying as he paced around the half-empty gallery, moving in and out of the sunlight vomited recklessly across the floor by the huge windows. Evie normally liked the bright cleanliness of the gallery but today her head hurt and she couldn't seem to concentrate.

The annoying click of the buyer's shoes came to rest uncomfortably close to Evie. "What's your process like? Can I just ask you to make me something beautiful then come pick it up when you're done?"

Evie smiled though anyone could tell it was forced, sickly. "Whatever you'd like works for me. I've got to finish what I'm currently working on but that's for an upcoming show, so it won't be long."

"Do you allow people to see works in progress?" the buyer asked. He started pacing again and moved toward the far wall. "That would be fascinating to me. If you'd allow it."

Evie winced, brought her forced and sickly smile back to life. She knew this man didn't mean anything by it, but she was tired of people asking to be allowed into her space, into her process and her work.

The curator of the gallery, familiar with the expression on an artist's face when they're thinking of how to turn down a request, broke in before the delay got awkwardly long. "It's such a tricky thing to show someone an unfinished piece," he said, leading the buyer away from the blank wall to the piece of Evie's he was there to pick up. "Might I suggest telling the artist what you like about her work. Why you're getting this painting in particular. Information like that can help her come up with an idea for you."

"This piece...well, this piece…"

Evie's painting was propped up against the wall at a slight angle. She watched the buyer step back and forth, studying it with a critical eye. The curator winked at her; Evie swiped a hand across her brow in a relieved response.

The buyer clapped his hands and expelled a teeth-rattling chuckle. "Do you know why I selected this piece? Because it is filled with love."

The painting was of two homeless men on a bench talking animatedly to each other. Pigeons sat near them; in the case of one similarly streetwise looking bird, on them. There was a cheap plastic bottle clutched at the neck by dirty fingers, and an angry curl of dark clouds promising thunderstorms rapidly approaching. The men don't seem to notice anything beyond their conversation, the bottle moving steadily between them.

"I'm glad you see love," Evie said. "I don't think I ever created a work of art from a scene I didn't love."

"Then make me a piece with love," the buyer said, lifting the canvas off the floor. "I trust your instincts."

Dear God, I don't, Evie thought, faintly smiling. She had spent the past few weeks ignoring her instincts because what set off alarm bells in her primordial brain made her skin crawl. Denying it wasn't doing any better, as she had come to find out.

The curator wrapped up the piece as the buyer went out to flag down a cab. He was talking to Evie as he walked in and out of the door, moving between realms and expecting her to catch his drift. There was some mention of inspiration and the mysticism surrounding art then the human desire to put a price tag on what is invaluable. He was loaded into a cab along with his new purchase, and the curator returned inside, shaking his graying head.

"Non-artists might be stranger than us creative types," he said, swinging the glass door shut. He clicked the lock without Evie having to ask him to. They had both lived in the city a long time. At some point, doors get locked through force of habit.

"He seemed nice but a bit much," Evie added. "I'm glad he liked that painting though. When I first finished it, my friend Rachel told me it was a bit too grotesque for anyone to buy. She told me to clean the men up a little, don't make them look so grubby."

"I think that element of it is why it appears to be made with love, as our friend would say. It's a clear-eyed view of reality. Not wanting to erase the ugly bits so other people find it more palatable." He shrugged. "It was the last piece to sell though so make of that what you will."

"There's this old English folk song that has this line; we can all love everything without ever knowing why," Evie told him. "That line really hit me when I first heard it. It was like I understood how inspiration worked. Loving everything without knowing why."

She'd had countless conversations with people outside of the artistic world who assumed being creative just happened, and countless conversations with other artists who decried this viewpoint as dismissal of their hard work. Evie always felt somewhere in the middle. She was consistently hardworking and serious about what she did, but she also liked the unexplained side of her craft, the side that called everything a mystery. Even the overly admiring buyer had given her scattered day a bit of a boost. She was tired of feeling like she was slaving away at a piece instead of feeling the beautiful compulsion of creation.

Walking home, which she had promised Jackson she wouldn't do, she slowed her pace to observe each block the way she used to. She hadn't been able to truly relax in too long. Not just because some stranger was breaking into her home to leave pieces of his fantasies in boxes on her kitchen counter. Her summer had been busy, getting the paintings ready for the big show had occupied so much of her time. She missed her long ambling walks, snapping Polaroids of interactions as quickly as she could before people noticed they were being watched.

Serves me right, I guess, she thought, glib yet half-kidding. All this time I've been the creep, and now someone's watching me.

On her block, she stared at every person who passed or walked behind her, wondering if she saw her stalker, if he made eye contact with her for a split second, could she tell it was him?

She now felt jumpy and suspicious when moments before she had been melting into the cityscape, lost in a sea of people too numerous for her to be noticed. The size of New York was her favorite part. Being one in millions made her feel more secure.

The thought of standing out and getting more and more attention intensified Evie's anxiety. She couldn't help but worry that even if they stopped this guy, and the creep was put away for good, there'd be another one somewhere down the line. What if the rest of her life was an endless torrent of unwanted attention?

She got home and inside quickly. Suddenly, the streets on which she had spent so much of her childhood, and from which she had gleaned so much inspiration pulsed with a sinister energy and the feeling of a thousand eyes focused onto one single target.

Chapter Thirteen

It had been almost a week since the last time Evie's stalker had broken in. Jackson knew full well that a week wasn't long at all. The stalker might be discouraged by the fact that Evie didn't react positively to the gifts, not to mention their bizarre, hair-sniffing encounter. Someone deluded and unbalanced, as most stalkers he had experience with were, might think their attention is desired and their gifts appreciated. Seeing the aftermath of what they had done could rattle the foundation of their warped perspective, causing them to withdraw.

Jackson also knew that sometimes a stalker became even more possessive when there was a backlash, which is why he wouldn't think about moving out anytime soon. Evie, a more concrete person than one would initially assume, was interested in getting a timeline down.

"How many quiet weeks before we think I'm safe?" she asked. She was perched on the stepladder as Jackson did crunches on the floor. "I mean, do we just continue on like this forever unless we catch him or what?"

"One week of no activity is nothing," Jackson panted. He held the crunch as he spoke then lowered himself down to the floor.

"Two weeks? Three weeks? I just want to know where it ends."

Jackson sat up, wrapping his arms around his knees for support. Evie had gotten used to sculpting while he went through his workout, and he saw how much progress she had made on her Adonis in the past week. Its body was starting to look real, muscled and in motion.

"How have you been feeling lately?" he asked. "The times you've had to go out? Do you feel like you're being followed or watched?"

"I can't really tell." Evie shrugged. "I sort of feel like I'm being watched all the time because I'm getting paranoid but then I'm also trying to listen to my instincts more since I didn't take them seriously the first time around."

She stayed perched on the stepladder, and Jackson watched the center of her vision slide across the figure in front of her. There was an issue with it, he could tell by her expression. Something about her creation wasn't sitting right with her.

"Your brow is furrowed," he said, blithely returning to his sit-ups.

"This is what it looks like when someone uses their brain. I imagine a jock like you wouldn't get it."

At the top of his sit-up, Jackson clutched at his chest, his mouth dropping open in mock offense. Evie bit her lip as if buttoning in the laugh pressing against the back of her teeth.

"Yeah, you were never a jock," Jackson said. He extended his legs and folded his upper half across them. "But you definitely used to be a bit...whackier."

"Whackier?!"

"I mean, I just couldn't see you pulling some of the crap you used to when we were kids. Like putting bouillon cubes in the shower head in the upstairs bathroom."

Evie's outburst of hysteria rocked her stance; she keeled over, arms pressed into her stomach. "Oh my God, I remember that!" She calmed herself as if realizing how close she came to falling. "Actually, if you want the truth, that was Rachel's idea."

"Bullshit. Rachel was never that creative."

With a reluctant snicker, Evie went back to work. Her feet were still shaky, and occasionally she let a giggle worm its way past her clenched lips. Jackson wasn't doing sit-ups anymore. Now he was just watching her.

Evie's furrowed brow told him to let her focus, but he had recently found himself drawn into her process, invested in the sculpture that demanded so much of her time. Its presence in the apartment was tacit as if they both inherently understood it to be invasive. They moved around it, worked their daily life and schedule around it. The sculpture was unconcerned with anything having to do with them.

Jackson stood up and crossed to the stepladder. "It's definitely getting there," he said, walking behind her. "If I didn't know any better, I'd think that chest belonged to a real guy."

"A gray guy."

"I would just assume he was in black and white."

Evie laughed again but not the same way she had earlier. That had been special. A moment with the power to yank her out of her trance and shake her body joyously. Jackson had gotten a rush, knowing he had that effect on her.

It reminded him of what it felt like to give someone an orgasm, which had always been one of his favorite activities. Watching whoever he was with writhing and twitching; collapsing to their belly from all fours; bucking as they straddled him and the pleasure won out over their nerves, anxiety, shame. Anything that had to be sliced through to get to the beast in them, the animal that demanded its base appetites be fed. Jackson had always derived pride from being able to get them there.

For the moment, he forced himself not to think of Evie in any other position than the one she was currently in. The moment of levity had piqued his interest, although he'd be lying if he said he was uninterested up to that point, in what Evie might be like in an intimate scenario, but the image of her clutching her sides and doubling over was suitable for now.

"I just..." Evie bit her lip, studying her Adonis. "I don't know what it is that's bothering me about this thing."

"I think it looks great," Jack said, and the noise Evie made in response assured him she considered him a philistine.

"It's not in the aesthetics. Or at least, not in the obvious aesthetics. It's something deeper. Like it reminds me of a statue I've already seen."

"I don't know too many naked dude statues aside from that David one, so I'll have to take your word for it."

Evie stretched to get to the upper part of the Adonis's head where the hairline was beginning to take shape. A sound that was akin to growling bubbled out of her as she focused tightly on the spot she wanted to fix. She wasn't paying close attention to anything else, which Jackson noticed seconds before her tippy-toe posture began to wobble, and she pitched off the stepladder toward the polished wood of the floor.

Jack prided himself on his reflexes almost as much as he prided himself on handing out orgasms. Before Evie even had a chance to feel the sickening moment of her stomach dropping out, he caught her in his outstretched arms. Her eyes were stuck wide open then they blinked rapidly, and Jackson lowered her deftly to her feet.

"Oh, well." She patted him on the shoulder as if trying to thank him, but the motion was uncomfortable and stiff. "I suppose it's good you're here."

"Boy, if I had a nickel for every time I heard that."

"Considering you used to be a cop, I would hope so."

He knew she didn't mean for the statement to wound him the way it did. It had come out of her mouth without her even thinking of how it would land. Jackson exhaled briskly as it hit him, avoiding her eyes as he muttered something about having to take a shower.

Evie lifted a hand toward his back when he passed her to get to the bathroom. They didn't make contact, and the door shut her out.

The hot water in Evie's building was better than Jackson expected. He only lived in a building with that many units for about a year and hated it for a variety of reasons. One of them being that he seemed to run out of hot water exceedingly fast. He was a rookie on the force and coming home to a lukewarm shower after a sixteen-hour shift where he had been up for over a day never did the trick. The heat, the moisture, the white haze of billowing steam enclosed in his tile sanctuary purged his system. After Evie's accidental jab, he needed to be hidden behind a wall of water and fog that was more temporary than normal.

"Used to be a cop," he repeated, pressing both hands flat against the blank walls of the shower stall. Evie's bathroom actually had color, unlike the rest of her apartment. It was a faded aqua that hadn't been updated since the seventies, and it made the walls close in around him. "Used to be a cop."

He was a cop. Or at least, he still wanted to be. He hadn't retired or quit; he was just on leave. But it had been so long, and his progress had stalled. If he was being honest with himself, he realized that his progress had hardly gotten moving in the first place. But saying it stalled and acting like its trajectory had been undeniable was all he could do to keep the tile from crushing the breath out of his lungs.

What was he playing at here? With Evie? Hanging around her as if he actually had a chance in hell to protect her. He never blamed himself for Marcus; he knew there was nothing he could have done. But it rattled the faith he had in being a cop, in being able to do any good.

A hapless criminal with a gun too sensitive and a finger too tense wiped out a life before the body hit the ground. And now he expected himself to stand between a psycho and his mark? He was going to see the signs and move with instincts he no longer believed to be finely tuned? Every second of every day, it seemed more and more unlikely.

Evie waited for him as he exited the bathroom with a concern on her face that stood out despite her attempts to keep her expression neutral. Jackson in his towel paused in the doorway, and a moment of exhilaration exploded quietly in his chest as Evie stammered and swallowed and averted her eyes.

"I have the strangest feeling I've upset you," she said, treading backward toward the stepladder. "What I said..."

"No, hey, I get it. How can I expect you to see me as a cop if I can't even get myself back on the force?"

"That's not what I meant."

"Evie, it's fine."

But she was starting to look worried, and Jackson knew she was picking up on his own concern, on the gnawing insecurity that the peace of mind he was providing was bunk. Neither one of them was comfortable admitting it but both of them saw it written on the other's face.

"I want this to be over," Evie blurted out. She snapped her fingers into her palm, touched her glasses, made any flitting move she had to make in order to not to be standing still. "I hate it. I hate being like this."

"I know."

"I feel so helpless."

"I know."

Evie gave in and sat on the widest step on the ladder. Jackson listened to her breathing, the slow intake of someone calming themselves down. He didn't move toward her, not even when she lifted her head, puffing her cheeks with air then collapsing them.

"Man, becoming a celebrated artist is easy compared to this shit," she said. "I feel like I'm in panic mode all day every day."

Clad in a towel, Jackson sat on the floor by Evie's feet. He self-consciously checked to make sure his bits were covered before he launched into what he wanted to say. Evie was staring at him so intensely that he would have lied and said anything she wanted to hear. Fortunately, what she needed to hear and what she wanted to hear were the same thing.

"Control is one of the most... human things we have to deal with," he started, not completely sure where he was headed with this. "Losing control or having someone take control away from us is frightening. It reminds us that most of life is guesswork. And we don't like that." He snorted, tapped a hand to his chest. "I don't like that."

"Me neither."

Evie's demeanor was bashful, subdued. She'd never been the type to scream for attention in the middle of the room, but Jackson was used to seeing fire in her, a quiet and weird passion for all things beautiful and pockmarked in equal measure.

"Would you believe me if I promised, hand to God, that I won't let anything happen to you?" Jackson put his palm in front of her as if in offering. "If I can control nothing else, I can control this."

Evie relinquished a half smile and slapped her palm onto his in a clumsy handshake. "So, if you can't control this, you can't control anything?"

"I guess so. That must be what I mean."

"I'll take it." She nodded, repetitive yet soothing. "I'll take it."

Jackson gave her hand one last shake. Evie exhaled through rounded lips; Jackson took in the splendor of the Adonis, seeing for the first time the familiarity that had been bothering Evie so much.

A few more days of quiet found Evie uncommonly relaxed. Her work on her Adonis had progressed beautifully in less than two days, and she took a moment to celebrate by bringing home roast beef sandwiches and big bottles of beer from the bodega she and Jackson had gone to in the not-too-distant past.

"I thought you said you didn't drink that much," Jackson quipped when she unloaded the haul into the fridge.

"Oddly enough, I've been getting back into it." She tossed his sandwich to him underhand. It hit Jack square in his sculpted chest. "I thought to myself, 'What the hell? Being stalked is as good an excuse as any.'"

She sat across from him on the small couch, sandwich in her lap and the two beers she brought from the fridge between them. There was no bottle opener within reach, so Evie grabbed a lighter next to her lavender candle and popped the caps off both of them.

"Is there an occasion for the food, the beer?" Jackson winked at her. "The exceptionally good mood?"

"Nothing concrete. My Adonis is shaping up nicely, and it's been—" she held her hands away from her body, palms down as if she was sapping energy from the floor. "Dare I say it?"

"Quiet," Jack finished for her.

"Quiet."

"Well, don't let that lull you into a false sense of security. The last time he made contact probably put the fear of God in 'im but that might not deter him forever."

"What gets in people's heads that they think stalking someone and breaking into their home is behavior that's appreciated?"

Jackson bit into his sandwich without answering. No one, least of all him, really knew what was ticking inside some of those diseased minds. There were psychologists who consulted with the force to explain how people like that thought but even still, it never made any sense to him. It wasn't as simplistic as the power or control that got brought up in cases of sexual assault. As warped as it sounded, that made sense to Jackson; he didn't condone it, but he could see the logic of it. In the cases of stalking, the rationale was beyond what he could grasp.

The one thing he understood was the selection process of it. Someone like Evie was an obvious target in a way he didn't think someone like Rachel ever would be. There was a quality to Evie that begged to be taken care of, to be protected. He felt it as strongly as anyone else might. It wasn't a surprise to him that someone with a twisted, deluded brain would meet her and think to themselves, 'This was a young lady in need of a man; in need of someone to stand guard and keep watch.'

Now, none of this was necessarily true. If nothing else, Evie had proven herself a more formidable mark than anyone would have guessed. She had grown up in the city, no stranger to mean streets and the uncomfortable sensation of danger creeping around the corner. Jackson knew it wasn't about the reality of the person but the stalker's perception of the person. Evie, with her big eyes and slight frame, probably looked to the man who had been following her like a mouse in a world of cats.

"If you're going to be around much longer, I'm going to start putting you to work." Evie shifted her legs under her, eating as she spoke. "You can run errands for me."

Jackson wondered how much of their conversation he'd missed before now. He cleared his throat and said, "Or, hear me out, you can use me."

"Excuse you?!"

"For your art."

Jackson jumped up and posed in front of the emerging Adonis. He moved like a bodybuilder, slow and choreographed. At first, there was no reaction, but he kept at it, stealing a glance at Evie every few seconds. Finally, he heard the high tinkling of her trying to laugh with her mouth full.

"You want to be my model?" she asked, lilting, coy, almost flirty.

"I want to be your muse."

Jackson threw his head back, his arms curled toward his face like cobras dancing out of baskets. A thought ran through his mind that he hoped he was still in the same shape he had been in when active on the force. Unlike some people, he never stopped working out as he reeled from his trauma. He had gone the opposite direction; working out so much it became an obsession. The only time he felt anywhere close to alright, the only time he didn't replay the moment his partner's body pitched back as the telltale crack of gunfire filled in the blanks, was when he was at the gym. Or running. He had taken to running along the beach, sometimes hopping onto the boardwalk to listen to the steady rhythm of his feet slapping the planks covered with hairline fractures.

It didn't take too long for this schedule to wear him down. At least when he was working out, he couldn't spend every waking hour moving. The moving kept the darker thoughts at bay, the ones that asked him why he had the right to be alive.

His therapist, the one he had stopped going to after he mentioned Jackson might be working out compulsively, attempted to explain survivor's guilt. "You don't blame yourself for the incident, and that's good," his therapist said, tenting his fingers as he spoke. "Survivor's guilt is complicated as many people suffer from it without noticing right away. It's not so much the feeling of, 'My God, I could have stopped this,' and more the feeling of, 'My God, why didn't it happen to me instead?' The problems that arise from being a survivor come from the unanswerable questions we all face."

That hadn't sat well with Jackson. Accepting something as unanswerable sounded lazy and helpless to him. He convinced himself the therapist had not a clue of what he spoke, that there was no solace in relinquishing to the ambiguity of life, and that he was going to fix his own problems in his own way. The next session was when the therapist pointed out Jackson's unhealthy drive to work out, and the relationship was thus severed.

He did finally take a break from exercising when he came home one day from a ten-mile run and passed out while doing burpees in his living room. On the fall down, he sliced his hand on the sharp edge of a table, which narrowly missed his head. Upon waking up, he reconsidered his stance, and decided a short break might not be such a bad idea.

But posing in front of the muscular Adonis, Evie's eyes moving methodically across his build, he wondered if he had done enough in the past month or so to get back into fighting shape. He knew logically enough his body wasn't going to fall apart in that short of a time, but the compulsion had already wormed its way into his brain and was telling him he wasn't moving, he wasn't gaining strength. He was faltering and failing and still didn't know why he lived and Marcus died.

"You're going to give me an eating disorder if you keep looking at me like that," Jack said. He dropped his arms to his side. "I mean, I was just playing about being your model. Clearly, whoever ya got for it is one buff dude."

"No, no, it's not that. I just thought of something. That's all." Evie blinked as if extraditing a piece of dust from her eyes. "You look great, and you know it."

"Oh, go on."

Jackson returned to the couch, and the two of them ate quietly. Evie's eyes kept bouncing around from her Adonis to Jackson with only the slightest landing on him before they shifted. Jackson couldn't tell if she was avoiding looking at him because she was uncomfortable or embarrassed for him. Had he taken a moment to think about it, he would have remembered Evie studying her Adonis, murmuring about a familiar sense she couldn't quite place.

A scratching at the door made them both jump but Evie bounded over to it without any explanation. She let in her neighborhood stray, the cat circling the room and its new addition suspiciously.

"What is that?" Jackson asked as the cat approached him, its nose in the air. Its pink little tongue jutted out then disappeared, and Jack realized it was licking its lips.

"This is a cat. You may have seen one before. I know they're rare and all—"

"I know it's a cat but where did it come from?"

"It's just a cat. I told you about her. She comes and goes as she pleases but usually stops by pretty frequently." She tore a piece of roast beef off her sandwich and placed it on the ground. "I'm pretty sure she's a stray. If she belongs to someone, they must have a real relaxed attitude toward their pet wandering because I can't imagine I'm the only apartment she goes to."

"You shouldn't feed her. What if roast beef isn't good for cats?"

"Starvation is probably worse."

Evie watched the cat tear into the small pieces of meat she laid out for it. When it was done, she patted her lap, and the cat jumped up to her.

"Does it have fleas?" Jackson asked, his face registering the disgust he was attempting to keep out of his voice.

"Fleas? I don't think so. You're acting like you've never encountered an animal before. You and Rachel grew up in the woods with those screaming raccoons. I'd think a cat is pretty tame from your experience."

"We didn't let those raccoons in the house. Big difference." Jackson tilted down a slight bit as if he wanted to examine the cat but didn't dare get too close. "Plus, this isn't some beautiful, glossy coated house cat. This is kind of the ugliest thing I've ever seen."

Evie's mouth dropped open. She pressed her hands to the cat's ears. "Don't say that in front of her. Cagney's had a rough life on the streets. You wouldn't look as good as you do if you had to live like this kitty."

Jackson smirked. "I look pretty good, huh?"

There was no answer Evie could give. She tried to fight down the smile that wrapped her lips involuntarily upwards. Giving Jackson the satisfaction of the last word was bad enough; she couldn't let him know just how many times she found herself staring at him, thinking about him, wondering what the parts of him that she hadn't seen looked like. She was curious about the inside of his thighs, the curve of muscles that built out his ass into the pert shape she saw under the towel when he emerged from the steam room of the shower.

"Did you hear that Cagney?" Evie asked, stroking down the cat's head with the pad of her index finger. "A boy is fishing for compliments."

"Did you hear that Cagney? Evie's becoming a crazy cat lady despite not even owning a cat."

"I should be a crazy cat lady," Evie agreed, sipping her beer. "I don't want to have people around me all that much. They mess with my process and their, I guess energy, is overwhelming. A cat would actually be a nice addition to this apartment."

"Not a single cat, Evie. If you want to be a crazy cat lady then you're going to need an army of cats."

"Legions of cats!" Evie exclaimed with such enthusiasm Cagney sprung out of her lap and meowed disapproval over her shoulder at both of them. "Maybe not. Maybe cats are too sensitive."

"Yeah, but they might keep you safe. It's not like they could be like an attack dog or anything like that but if a guy was obsessed with you then found out you lived with a million cats, he might be like, 'Never mind. That chick is crazy.'"

Evie laughed again, surprised at how much levity she had inside of her. It felt good to relax; it felt good to not be worrying about every little thing like she had been doing since well before the stalker.

The only problem she could see was the pulsing attraction she had been fighting down.

Later that night, studying her Adonis for one last time before going to bed, she confirmed what she had noticed earlier.

Yes, he looked familiar. Yes, there was a sense that she had seen his form before. It was just that now, after seeing Jackson posing like a Grecian statue in front of it, she knew exactly why.

Chapter Fourteen

"I feel like it's been years since we hung out," Rachel said when she called to invite Evie to lunch. Or dinner. Or anything Evie thought she had time to fit into her schedule. "How's it going with Jackson? Ready to throttle him yet?"

Evie gave some roundabout answer to hopefully not show her hand. Rachel wouldn't be angry or freak out over her adult friend and her brother getting cozy but rather, she'd be annoyingly excited about it. Perhaps even excited in the way she used to get as a child where she'd babble and explode and tell everyone who would listen exactly what was going on.

During college, Rachel and Evie shared an apartment together in Brooklyn. They had very different schedules, not surprising since they were going to different schools with different majors, so they had a set date every Sunday night to make, or more often take out, dinner, and catch up. It was during one of these dinners that Evie began to tighten up in regard to what she would tell Rachel.

Rachel had always been her biggest cheerleader, her biggest supporter, her biggest protector. If Evie mentioned someone being rude to her, Rachel was ready to break a bottle and have a showdown. When Evie mentioned a classmate she thought was cute, Rachel would be flipping through the directory and scanning for his contact information. She was, for all intents and purposes, the sister Evie never had, and as much as Evie appreciated her care and concern, there was more of it than she was used to.

Evie never doubted that much of Rachel's approach came from the fact that Evie's mother was scattered and emotionally absent, and that Rachel's parents were fast to tell horror stories about the realities of growing up in the city. They would never say anything around Evie, that would be beyond rude in their minds, but when Rachel asked questions about the things Evie had to worry about like being alone with a stranger on a subway platform, her parents held nothing back. And Rachel never held back when relaying those 'talks' back to Evie.

"People in that city are out of their minds," Rachel's mom told her. She was grilling in the backyard the summer that Evie stayed with them. Evie was still safely away by the pool so she let Rachel ask anything she wanted. "This crazy guy pushed a woman onto the tracks a few years ago. Right as a train was coming. I can't even imagine trying to raise a family there."

Rachel's parents were Puerto Rican and wanted their kids to have as many siblings as they both did, a common thing in their old neighbor even with the confines of an apartment. They also wanted something different for their kids, which included a house surrounded by nature and plenty of space for them to explore. They had said that exploring in a city isn't as much fun, despite the fact that they also told giggle-inducing stories from their own childhood that sounded like a better time to Rachel than wandering through the woods.

So Rachel grew up hearing that New York City was dangerous and disgusting but also magical and exciting. She both worried about Evie and was impressed by her ability to navigate in a world like that. When they moved into their shared apartment right before freshman year, Evie told her that the best piece of advice she ever learned about living in New York was to simply be alert.

"My mom's boyfriend, the one who lived on the Upper East side, remember him? He told me that. He told me that tourists always freaked out and came with pepper spray like they expected to get mugged right out of JFK. He said people made themselves look like marks."

At the time, Evie had thought his advice pedestrian and redundant considering that she had spent most of her childhood there. Later, she thought it sound and reasonable. On her way to Rachel's for their "old-school college night," she knew the advice was well-meaning but painfully naive.

The only type of crime it took into consideration was of opportunistic variety; people snatching wallets, beating someone up for their shoes. There was a dollar value attached to actions like these, an obvious motive and impulsive action. He didn't understand how some crimes were perpetrated by people who didn't think what they were doing was wrong. No amount of keeping herself alert would have protected Evie from a man who suddenly decided they had not only a history together but a future.

Rachel's apartment was the opposite of Evie's in every possible way. While Evie's was austere and functional, Rachel's was lush with the intention of parties and gatherings built into every corner. Beyond that, Rachel lived with another person, which Evie had sworn never to do again once she graduated college. She didn't hate living with Rachel but living with another person meant another schedule and another life had to be worked into the fabric of her day, and it became hard for her to focus, to lose herself in her work the way she liked.

For Rachel, living alone was not an option. She had wanted a bigger apartment anyway. Even with her formidable salary getting anything more than a studio would have been a pinch, and the silence of coming home to an empty apartment would have driven her nuts. Her life never featured much solitude, and Evie knew she wasn't missing it.

Evie let herself in and took her shoes off by the door. Rachel had given her the key back when she first got the place. It was intended to be the spare that Rachel could grab should she ever need it, but it made its way onto Evie's personal keyring, and nobody seemed to mind. Rachel's one condition, a residue from childhood, was that Evie take off her shoes anytime she came in.

"If we're out of town and you wanna bring a boy over or something? Cool!" she told her. "But he has to take his shoes off too."

Next to the door was the neatly lined up pumps of the two professional women who lived there. Evie's thick soled boots, shapeless and cumbersome, got tossed next to them. She constantly wore shoes around the house; it didn't even occur to her to take them off when she came home.

"Hello, hello!" Rachel called from the kitchen. Neither one saw the other yet, but the noises made were so familiar that they stood in for visual confirmation. "Evie, I'm actually cooking something for you tonight!"

All the kids in Rachel's family had been taught how to cook from a very young age. Partially to share in their heritage but mainly because it was a frugal way to live, and their parents never wanted their kids to be careless with money. Still, Evie rarely saw any of them cook. The ones who had settled in the city spoke openly about surviving on take-out, visibly breaking their mother's heart.

Evie had never learned to cook and didn't care all that much about it. Food was a necessity; she enjoyed it for what it was. She was impressed when she saw someone making a difficult dish or inventing a new one, but if it came down to it, she could have survived on canned soup and crackers for the rest of her life. Seeing Rachel in the kitchen, not the first time but certainly not a common sighting, Evie noticed a glow in her friend's eyes.

"Cooking, eh?" Evie said, leaning against the alcove of the kitchen door. "And here I thought you were just going to pick up take-out on your way home."

"Oh my God, no." Rachel haphazardly tossed her wooden spoon into the pot she was stirring, turning to Evie with her hands up and ready to assist in her story. "That's so funny because I was thinking that too but then a few days ago, I was like, ya know what? I know how to cook. I've got this beautiful kitchen. Why not? So I called my mom to ask for her recipe for mofongo, and I spent the next ten minutes telling her to stop crying."

"Yeah. She spent all that time teaching you guys how to cook and none of you do."

"Like you're such a gourmet. What kind of French person doesn't like food?"

Rachel went back to stirring, and Evie climbed up onto one of the high-seated stools by the breakfast bar. She leaned her chin into her palm, watching her friend bustling happily through the heavy-scented air. For the first time, she felt guilty noticing the differences between Rachel and the brother who had been dominating her thoughts lately.

Pushing the sight of his bare chest out of her mind yet again, Evie said, "Funnily enough, I'm really hungry. Your brother's got me into a bad habit of eating roast beef sandwiches."

"Oh, and beer?" Rachel paused at a drawer by the fridge, moving her eyes slightly toward Evie. "Bodega sandwiches and beer?"

"Yeah. How'd you know?"

"That used to be his 'big brother to the rescue' kit whenever I broke up with someone or didn't get a job I interviewed for. Comfort food, I guess." Rachel snorted. "He was always such a mom. He wants to be big and tough. Mr. I'm-The-Protector. In reality, he's all maternal and shit."

Evie heard a timid scoffing noise and was startled to find out that she had made it. She wasn't sure why that was her reaction, but Rachel turned to her with an amused expression on her face and waited for an explanation.

"I must have found that funny," Evie said after a long pause.

"It almost sounded like you don't agree." Rachel touched a finger to the edge of her spoon then put it in her mouth. "You don't find Jack to be maternal?"

"Sort of. I get what you're saying but—" Flashes of him posing in front of the statue, of the shape she could see hanging flaccid against the terry cloth of the towel. Evie blinked rapidly. "What do I know about maternal, right? For me to think he was acting maternal, he'd have to be chain-smoking cigarettes and whining on about the unfairness of life."

"God damn, your mother."

Rachel opened the fridge and pulled out a bottle of wine. In the humid atmosphere of the kitchen, the bottle began to sweat rapidly. The drops that gathered along it were large; Evie could see her reflection in them. Her face was pulled into the long teardrop shape, and her forehead and nose protruded like a cartoon character. She wished there was a way to capture the image so she could paint it later. A self-portrait, perhaps. A feat she had never taken on. She didn't consider herself the most impressive subject, especially not when she lived in a city that breathed and moved with millions of other options.

"About Jackson…" Evie started.

Rachel grabbed the cold wine bottle, her fingers knocking through Evie's reflection.

"Is he driving you nuts? Does he still leave his underwear on the bathroom floor all the time?" She uncorked the bottle and searched around for two glasses. "I mean, I know he does. I've seen them on the floor at his place."

"Yeah, but there's something else too." Evie creased her brow, knowing the look was going to give her away no matter what she decided to tell Rachel. "I'm not sure even... I guess what I mean is... he and I have gotten... close the past week or so."

Rachel stopped pouring and narrowed her eyes. "How close?"

"No. Just regular close. I've actually been enjoying having him around. Sometimes. Other times he gets in my way and I want to kill him."

"And you would tell me if you two were—" Rachel raised her eyebrows in quick succession. "...doin' it, right?"

"Doin' it?" Evie mocked. "What are you? Twelve?"

"Yes, I am. I'm a twelve-year-old, and I'm about to drink all of this wine." She pushed Evie's glass toward her as she took a sip. "Evie, baby, you can do whatever you want. You know I love you and Jackson with all my heart but let me tell you one thing about Jackson, ok? He's super fucked up."

"You mean from his partner dying?"

"From a lot of stuff. Not like he's violent or anything but he's always had control issues, and they've only gotten worse as he got older. Between the two of you, I just don't know how well it would work out."

Evie shrugged and sipped her wine as well. She didn't have the heart to explain to Rachel that she wasn't considering a long-term relationship where she and Jackson got married and had a bunch of kids. As it was, she didn't consider that an option with anyone. What she was considering with Jackson was a catharsis, a release. A moment where the two of them could forget they were frightened and hurting and disappear into that powerful void sex somehow managed to provide.

The Adonis was getting there. Evie hesitated in saying it was almost done. With other projects, the moment she thought that was the moment she realized she had to fix a piece of it, and that was going to take weeks longer than she expected.

When Jack asked her how it was coming, small talk honestly since he could see the progress for himself, she just replied with, "He's getting there."

"He. Not it, but he."

"Of course. He's my Adonis. If I called him it, that wouldn't be very nice of me." She drew her hand back from the clay then pulled the stepladder over to reach a higher point. "I want this sculpture to look so good women fall in love with him. To achieve that, I must first acknowledge his humanity."

"You're so weird," Jackson said.

The moment he said it, Evie bent to shape a portion of the chest, letting the loose neck of her t-shirt dangled low. Just past its ribbed cotton mouth was a slice of bra-clad breast, plump in its miniature cup.

Evie was paying close attention to her top, and her body, and the way Jackson was staring at her. When she crouched down a little further, she heard the awkward silence of someone watching her, a feeling she was getting good at recognizing. Her eyes flashed up to Jackson's, and he immediately looked away.

"Are you alright?" Evie asked as Jack took a stumbling step away from her. She fought the urge to bait him further, knowing full well what she was doing. "Don't hurt yourself."

"Yeah, I'm gonna go run some errands. Maybe pop into the station, see if Wheeler's got any new info for us. I'll be back in a few hours. Definitely before it gets dark."

He managed to get out of the apartment without doing any more damage, making any more of a fool out of himself. The rest of the day was spent idly on his part. Even with errands and meeting up with the captain, he had plenty of time to kill. Evie needed her space to work, and he needed to not be there leering at her like a masturbator on the subway.

They had dinner together when he got home, though Evie ate next to nothing and kept climbing up the stepladder to work. Jackson kept his eyes consciously forward whenever she was on the move, avoiding the stare with all the willpower he could muster.

Evie, for what it's worth, wasn't put off by what had happened. Jackson couldn't be sure if that was the actual case or if she was just acting like it didn't bother her. He decided that a line of follow-up questions would be impertinent, so he took her reaction at face value.

Nights were getting harder though.

Usually, he was a believer of 'nothing sacred' when it came to fantasies, but there was too much attached to this for him to feel alright about it. On the cramped little couch, the one where he couldn't even stretch all the way out, he did everything he could not to picture Evie bending over, Evie's shirt hanging low, Evie's big green eyes filled with knowing accusations meeting his. He forced himself to sleep despite the whirlwind of frustration spinning ceaselessly inside of him.

"Jackson," came the voice, soft and enticing and so close to him. "Are you comfortable out here, Jackson?"

Evie crouched next to the couch dressed in the black lingerie that had been left behind by her stalker. Jackson would have thought it an odd choice and would have remembered that it was taken by the cops as evidence, if he had any blood left in his brain at all. Streetlights washed the inside of the apartment yellow in a color both sleazy and sexy at the same time.

"This couch is too small," Jackson told her though he didn't feel his mouth moving and appeared to have no control over his words. He was merely along for the ride at this point. "I miss sleeping in a real bed."

"I've got a real bed," Evie said, toying with the thin straps of her lingerie. "Maybe you'd like to share it."

The straps dropped down along her shoulders, the black lace front folding open toward him. Jackson saw the swell of her breasts like he had before. An erection was seemingly in bloom, but it felt very far away to him. Warily, he reached forward and pulled the straps further down until she was exposed, vulnerable, and completely in command of him.

"What're you doing to me, Evie?" he asked, his voice sounding almost as distant as his hard-on felt. "I'm supposed to protect you."

"So protect me." She moved his hand to cup one of her breasts. "Stay so close to me that you're inside of me."

"I can't do that."

Her nipple was rock hard; it pressed into his palm like an insistent little finger. She stood up and let her panties slide to the floor. Naked, bathed in the surreal never-ending glow of a city at night, she climbed onto him, pressed her body to his.

"I know what you want from me, Jackson," she said, curving her spine backward so her chest hovered right in his face. "More than you understand."

Again, he had no say in his actions. His mouth opened and gently closed around her eager nipples. He moved between them, sucking and biting and watching the reflective surface of Evie's back wriggling as he did. When he bit down hard, she squealed and bucked against him.

"You don't even know what I want," he said, his tongue flicking against the tip of the nipple he had just bitten. "You're guessing that you could give it to me."

"I know everything you know."

Evie rolled off of him and started toward her bedroom. Her hips swayed in a way Jackson had never seen before from her; fluid and smooth, her feet floating across the floor, moving through swaths of light then shadow.

At the door to her room, she hesitated and turned back. "Are you coming?"

Jackson rose from the too small couch, each step toward her like a peal of thunder in the midnight silence. She waited until he was almost to her then she crossed the threshold and curled herself on her bed.

"Tell me what you want," Jackson said as he knelt at her tucked up knees. "Tell me what you want, and I'll give it to you."

He brought her knees to center; Evie sighed contentedly, shifting onto her back. Jackson split her legs apart and stared at the V between them. The dim light of the apartment was plenty for him to see the parted lips, the coarse and beautifully curled tufts of hair. He wanted her body to envelope him, to take him into her warmth and use him for its own purpose.

Unlike most of the men he knew, he never saw sex with a woman as her surrendering her autonomy to him, his body penetrating hers. To him, it always seemed to be the opposite. He was being devoured by whoever he was with, and her body was built to swallow him whole.

As he parted Evie's legs and lowered his face to the cleft between her thighs, he had a heady flash of disbelief. There was a moment of uncertainty that this was happening, but he ignored it and pressed his mouth against her. Evie arched her back and moaned, Jackson's tongue lapping against her. She tasted of vanilla cream.

He stroked himself just enough to keep from exploding, which considering the moment and the build-up and the excitement seemed like a strong possibility.

"You want to know what I want?" Evie breathed, her fingers gripping into Jack's hair. "I want you inside of me."

Jackson didn't have to be asked twice. He worked his way up her body, kissing her stomach, suckling her small, pointed breasts. When he reached her throat, he let his tongue trace the length of it before their mouths connected.

She wrapped her legs around him; he fit smoothly inside of her.

Fortunately for Jackson, he was able to stay and see his favorite part, the moment of climax where Evie dug her nails into his back and shook so violently under him that he was convinced she was having a seizure.

Unfortunately for Jackson, the garbage truck that usually came around 6 a.m. was running early, and its clattering ruckus outside yanked him from his dream before he got to finish himself.

It was dark save for the streetlights, and his feet sticking off the end of the tiny couch were cold. There was no naked Evie whispering in his ear, no licking and touching and savoring each other's bodies. He was alone on the couch in the darkness, the sound of the garbage truck outside the window and his painfully throbbing erection clutched in his right hand.

Chapter Fifteen

In many regards, Jackson was a late bloomer when it came to sex. He was certainly good looking for girlfriends and hook-ups, but his mom had scared him as much as she had scared Rachel when discussing how easy it was to get pregnant. Lots of his friends in high school had laughed at the idea of him being worried about pregnancy. They reminded him that it had nothing to do with him, and he could just walk away, a fact he truly never considered.

"Because you're not a piece of shit like those guys," Rachel told him when he brought it up to her. "If you got someone pregnant, you'd step up and do whatever you had to do."

Aside from the fear of being thrust into parenthood, which was never really a goal in his life, Jack also felt unsure about what he wanted from sex. Early encounters were pleasurable, but he got bored so fast. Not with his partners but with what they were doing together. Within a few years of being sexually active, he wondered if this was really all there was to it.

"This is what people get so worked up about?" he asked Wheeler one time. She wasn't his superior yet, but she had been on the force longer than he had, and he knew she was open to discuss pretty much anything. "I feel like I must be missing something if I'm already bored with sex."

Her face went from empathetic to knowing so effortlessly Jack was positive she practiced doing it. She mentioned that there were places they could go if Jackson wanted to see a more intense side of sex.

"Look, kid, we live in New York, ya know?" she said with a cough. "If there's anything we do right, it's sex."

"I'm not paying for it," Jackson replied, misreading what she meant.

"Paying for it's illegal," she shot back. She leaned in, motioning for Jackson to follow suit. "There's clubs around the city for this kind of thing. Totally above board. Just weirdos who want to be weird with other weirdos."

In all honesty, Jackson hated the idea of it but agreed to go anyway. The few times he'd gone to kink clubs with friends of his it seemed to him like people were more concerned with strutting in their creaking pleather outfits and discussing how wild they were. He didn't want to have to exist in that world and hoped it wouldn't be the only way he could enjoy sex.

Where Wheeler took him was different though. For starters, people actually appeared to be having sex with each other, though not in the common room around the bar area. There were rooms for people to disappear into, and any number of toys and fantasies to indulge. Still not sure what he wanted, Jackson asked if they could wait a minute and take in the sights before they made moves.

There was a woman dressed entirely in black with sharp, lean stiletto heels by the bar that Jackson could not look away from. Men approached her throughout the night, and she would inspect them as if they were horses. Only a few were brought into another room with her; Jackson was dying to know why.

"She's here a lot," Wheeler said when she saw where Jackson was looking. "I'm pretty sure she works as a professional dominatrix. Maybe this is where she gets her clients."

"That's a gray area legally, right?"

"Truth be told, a lot of stuff is in the gray area legally."

Jackson swallowed down the last of his drink and crossed the room. The woman watched him the whole time, grinning like the Cheshire cat when he made the trip.

"New to this game, I see," she said, leaning against the bar. "You don't seem to know the protocol."

"Should I crawl to you on my hands and knees? Lick your shoes?"

"These shoes are too expensive to get your slobber on them," she told him, pulling him into her by his waistband. "But I can tell you're curious and inexperienced. Two of my favorite qualities in a man."

She brought him into a private room and ordered him to strip. Jackson, who spent most of his life in control, the concept of not having to think for a while was thrilling. When he was naked, she had him kneel on the bed, and she whipped him until he had to shout at her to stop.

"I like it," he said between gasps. "It's just a lot."

"How about one more for good luck?" she asked, running the crop between her fingers. "Just to make sure you like it."

Jackson shut his eyes tight and nodded. The final lash landed softly against his butt; he let out a groan of disappointment.

Later, as he left with Wheeler, she asked him if he found what he was looking for. He hesitated to say yes, still concerned with the idea of coming across as some sort of sex fiend, but he told her he was interested in coming back again. The thought of being naked and whipped had turned him on more than anything else since he started having sex.

Control is a funny thing, and its prevalence in humans is as important to survival as it is detrimental. Jackson knew he had issues with the concept of control. It was part of the reason he became a cop. There were more problems in the world than he knew what to do with but if he was doing something, if he was taking real actions toward fixing them then he didn't feel so helpless.

In his personal life, he exhibited control as well. Whereas other cops complained about not having the energy to work out or being unable to turn down a free pastry offered from a bakery on their beat, Jackson had no problem with that at all. His home was tidy, he always got an oil change when he needed it, and there was never a birthday or important date that snuck up on him. Sometimes people would ask what his secret was to being organized and on top of things, but he never wanted to admit to them that he needed to be whipped a few times a week to keep himself collected.

Wheeler knew, but that was fine by him. She wasn't the type to talk about other people's business. Besides, she understood it more than anyone. Often times they took trips to the club together so he could be whipped, and she could have a big butch lesbian rough her up and call her dirty names.

"If only I was straight," she said once when they were stumbling out into the brisk city night, their faces red and tacky with sweat, "we'd be an NYPD power couple."

"Yeah but then we'd have to find someone to overpower us both," Jackson joked. "To think, I might have gone my whole life without knowing this."

As he got more involved with his own tastes, he developed the other side of his sexuality. He saw the appeal in being dominant too, in having someone begging for pleasure. There were a few doms at the club who he had heard were selfish and uninterested in anyone else's enjoyment. Jackson couldn't even fathom that; his favorite moment had always been watching the zenith as the woman's body gave into itself. Being so concerned with his own simplistic and boring orgasm missed the forest for the trees, in his opinion.

Which was why he felt so unsure about any part of the situation involving Evie. Not only was he supposed to be protecting her, but he was having trouble picturing her as a powerful force in the bedroom who would whip him when he needed it and submit when she needed it.

He wanted to imagine her in skin-tight leather grasping a cat-o-nine-tails, but it never seemed right. After his dream, he tried to picture her as a pouty submissive salivating for the pleasure he had promised her, but that didn't seem right either. For all the reasons it was a bad idea, and there were plenty of them, Jackson considered it best that he let the fantasy go. If Evie wanted him, he figured, she'd tell him. Or not. And in that case, it wasn't meant to be.

Jackson, maintaining the position of que sera sera, avoided thinking about Evie in any way other than the most chaste. He wasn't blind to the fact that her eyes drank him in plenty, and that she didn't complain about watching him work out, or 'accidentally' let her blouse fall open in front of him, but for the time being, self-control was the right course of action until circumstances dictated differently.

Accidents were not infrequent in Evie's life. She wasn't a klutz, but she was known to carry more weight than she could handle or try to get too much done at once. With her Adonis becoming more manly by the day, she was certain she saw the finish line, and it made her more determined to reach it post haste.

What he needed was accessories, a thought which made Evie laugh. But it was true; his form was done and all that remained was his sword and shield. The shield was the easy part. It would be attached to his arm that ran along the lower section of his abdomen. The sword she wanted to be swung over his head, raised in a frozen moment of battle.

She shaped each accessory of their own before, not wanting to futz around with them on the sculpture until she was positive they were ready. The shield was done as Jackson was heading into the shower, and she planned to be adjusting the sword before he came out. Evie had a bad habit of rushing once she was close to done. It was common among artists and other creatives, their imaginative eyes always focused on the next project they were waiting to conquer.

The stepladder Evie had wasn't as tall as she thought. She had been able to get to the head of the Adonis without too much trouble, though she did have to stand on her tippy toes a lot, but the extent of the sword was out of her reach. The clay she used was wetter than she anticipated, and it wasn't staying upright the way she hoped it would. Its tip pointed to the floor, pathetic and limp.

"God, Evie," she muttered to herself as she manipulated it. "You want it big and sticking straight out. How God damned Freudian of you."

Nothing was working; there was a buzzing behind her eyes and a shortness to her breathing. The sword kept slipping, lowering its point down as if aiming to stab directly into her Adonis. She grumbled without opening her mouth and wrenched the piece back into position.

On the floor next to the leg of the stepladder was a mop bucket of water anchored on top of a tarp. All around the Adonis there were tarps decorated with the inevitable splatters of clay. While Evie was busy yanking the uncooperative sword into place, she didn't notice the slipping leg inching toward the bucket. One final tug from Evie, and everything turned into a wet, crashing blur.

She fell backward off the ladder, seeing a spray of stars as her head connected with the floor. The bucket vomited its contents across the tarp, which did little to keep it in one place. Evie in her daze pulled the edge of the tarps toward her and it billowed upward with a minute tidal wave of water and silt.

Jackson threw open the bathroom door. He was in the process of getting dressed but hadn't gotten past the point of putting on his boxers when he went into protector mode. Seeing Evie twisting under a wet piece of plastic, he threw himself on top of her and surveyed the apartment for intruders and sickos.

"What happened?!" he asked. He shouted it louder than he probably meant to, but he was swollen with adrenaline. "Is there anyone else here?"

"I fell, you idiot!" Evie shoved him hard off of her then sat up and ripped the plastic from her face. "I was leaning too far on the stepladder, and I fell, alright?"

She plucked gray pearls of leftover clay from her curls. Her glasses were crooked, and her hands were shaking as she adjusted them. Then she saw that Jackson was coated in a layer of clay also and reached over to brush a hand down his chest.

"I'm sorry, Evie. I didn't think. I just—"

"You never think! Jesus, the sculpture. Did I ruin it?"

Evie scrambled to her feet. Her shirt stuck to her where the water had soaked it. She rubbed her head, muttering to herself as she circled the sculpture. A big piece of it was lying on the floor in a shapeless mass but when she crouched down, she saw it was the sword. For an awful moment, she had thought she knocked his head off, and was quite close to crying.

"It's okay," she said with a shaky sigh. "He's okay."

Jackson got up, and Evie did a double take. "Why are you naked?" She clutched her hand to her chest, the one that had just been on his bare chest without the slightest thought.

"I was in the shower when you screamed. You're lucky I had my boxers on already or that would have been a very awkward situation."

Evie squeaked, a high and unconscious noise. She took a step closer to Jackson, pushing her hand into the clay on his stomach to leave her prints behind.

"With this clay on you," she traced down a line of his abs, "you could be him."

"Him?"

"My Adonis."

He pressed a hand against the small of her back, drawing her into him. Wet clay and all. "Say it to me this time," he told her.

"Say what?" Evie asked, her lips curling and her eyes sultry. She felt a sudden hunger like she'd never known before.

"You know what. Say it to me."

"My Adonis," she repeated, her fingers grazing down the long muscle that reached from his hip to his pelvis. "My Adonis."

She shoved him toward the couch and straddled his lap, kissing him fiercely on the mouth. Her hips rocked as his hands made contact with her, groping under the soaked t-shirt to wrap around her bare breasts. Jackson pulled back as if surprised at how much force he used but Evie matched it, her teeth closing down on his lip in a quick, hard bite.

"I wanna drive you wild," he whispered to her, his mouth finding her nipples. "I want to make you beg for my cock."

"Well, you'll have to go harder than that," she purred. Then she shrieked as he applied more pressure.

His teeth dug into her skin then pulled back. Each flash of pain caused Evie to wriggle helplessly in his lap.

"That's what you want, huh?" Jackson slid his hand up the leg of her shorts; his fingers pressed into the cotton covered curves. "You want it rough. You want it dirty."

"And I'm sure you just want plain old missionary," Evie teased. "Just want me to lie back and think of England."

Jackson cocked his head to the side. "What are you talking about?"

"You've never heard that? It's an old saying. It's what they used to tell women to do during sex so they could get through it and procreate but not enjoy it."

"You're so weird," Jackson told her but then he kissed her neck as his fingers worked past the cover of her panties, and before long, Evie's body twitched and pulsed like a bolt of electricity ran through her.

"The bed's probably better," Evie whispered as she ground herself onto Jackson's hand. "More space."

She climbed off of him, slipping a little on the water they had yet to clean up. Jackson walked so hotly on her heels that his erection threatened to stab her if she stopped short. Thankfully, there was no stopping for either of them, and they tumbled into bed together, the last shred of clothing being tossed off in a hurry.

Jackson was big, bigger than anyone else Evie had been with. The idea of fitting the whole thing inside of her made her stomach and knees go weak. She wanted it, God how she wanted it, but she wondered where it would all go, where it would all fit.

When she had put her fingers or toys inside herself, there didn't seem to be a lot of space. She decided she'd give it a shot with her mouth first but as she moved toward it, Jackson flipped her on her back and spread her legs apart.

"Do you know what I want to do to you?" he asked, running his hands down the insides of her thighs.

"I can take a guess." She didn't want to guess, though. She wanted him to fill her up, make her cry out in ecstasy, and she wanted it right now.

"I want to make you come so many times you beg me to stop. I want you to be so drenched with pleasure that you literally can't take anymore."

Evie smirked. "I'd like to see you try." She scooted down toward him, making her intentions clear.

Jackson's face vanished into her pubic hair. His tongue worked from top to bottom, tracing the outer lips and slipping inside of her. Occasionally, he glanced up and they made eye contact between her legs.

Evie's hand touched the side of his face then moved around to the back of his head. She pressed her hand there, forcing his tongue deeper into her. Jackson must have liked her taking charge because he let out a moan that vibrated against her clit. Evie pulsed her hips into his face as she held it there, and Jackson obliged her nonverbal request with enthusiasm.

"Fuck, I'm gonna come." Evie's whole body tightened. "Keep going like that, I'm gonna come."

Jack did as he was told.

She pressed her fingers harder into his scalp as her body shook, racked with a thundering release. She jerked upward like she was being tugged on invisible strings. For the briefest moment Evie wondered if her soul was leaving her body.

When she settled, she felt him slide alongside her, his hand gently working his shaft. She could barely open her eyes, but she wanted to see. She had this animalistic urge to watch him pleasure himself.

"Did I do good?" he whispered, bringing his face close to her ear. She could smell herself on him; earthy and tangy. Her mouth watered.

"You did very good," Evie answered, breathlessly. "Very, very good."

Jackson kissed her neck, his erection protruding between them.

Evie pulled him on top of her and positioned him so he could enter her. There was no motion at all for a long pause. Evie's breath caught in her throat with anticipation. Of what, she wasn't sure. She braced for the pain of his size, but his oral skills had her expecting pleasure.

Then Jack thrust himself forward, filling her in one fell swoop.

The shock of it sent another wave of sensation through her. Pleasure and pain mixed in a wild crescendo. Evie felt herself losing control, surrendering to his body, and for some reason, she fought it. Some pent-up thing inside her broke free in that moment.

"You know what you want, don't you?" He moved deeper into her with each word. "You don't hesitate to get it."

"What I want is not that hard to get," Evie told him, inhaling tightly as he hit a spot so deep inside of her she felt the pressure in her stomach. "Most guys are down to fuck."

"You pretend you're not a freak, but I see you." He bit down on her nipples hard. "I see everything about you."

Evie's body was still tender from her first orgasm, but she wanted more. She rolled Jackson onto his back and slid herself down on him with ease. The aroma of her own juices wafted up and she felt her control returning. She'd made him pleasure her. He did her bidding, not the other way around.

Her hands closed around his throat. She didn't apply pressure; she just held them there and watched his face. "You can't even pretend you're not a freak," she said as she moved on top of him. "You're hopeless."

Jackson's face went slack, relaxed. "I know what I am, Evie. I've never pretended to be anything else."

Evie let go with one of her hands and rubbed herself as she rocked on him. Before they started this, Jackson had been worried about losing control, hurting her. But now, with her using him like a plaything, he wanted nothing more than to push both of them to their limits.

When she was going to come again, her body hunched over, and she rattled from the very core of her. Jackson had never seen anything like it. He had seen some explosive orgasms but never with so much intention behind them. Such power.

To him, it seemed like Evie was on a mission to come. The same intensity she brought to her work and her art came roaring out of her. She grinded on him, pushing the head of his cock so far inside her he could feel the end of her.

Jackson forced himself to hold on, to fight through the pleasure long enough for her to use him up. This moment had always been easy for him with the others. Never once had he spilled too soon. But now, watching the shadows of lust and anger and need play across Evie's face, it was all he could do to not flip her over and pound his load into her.

As it turned out, he didn't have to wait much longer. She came the second time, grunting like an animal and bucking so hard he should have worried she'd snap his cock clean off. When she was done, she flopped down, her body unable to support itself any longer. Jackson felt the muscles in her twitching against him, clenching and unclenching around his erection.

"I hope you're alright with not coming," Evie said as she managed to ease off of him and down onto the bed, "because I don't think I've got much more in me."

"Oh, is that right?" Jackson pulled her against him, his finger pressing into her wetness. "You're such a selfish lover."

"Obviously."

He raised up, hovering over her, and slid inside of her one last time. He didn't bother starting off slow. She had used him and now it was his turn to use her. He relished the memory of her riding him, all while taking in the shape of her now beneath him. Her eyes closed, mouth slack, she looked sated as never before. He wanted that feeling for himself, needed it. That sweet release.

He thrust deeper, urgent. Sweat poured down his brow. His arms shook from the strain of holding himself up, and from the force of what he knew was to come. His whole body tensed and a low growl began in his chest.

"Fuck," he said when he didn't think he could take another second.

Then, right before he let go of an orgasm more powerful than anything he'd ever experienced, he saw another climax possessing Evie.

Her eyes rolled back into her head and she spasmed like a cattle prod had been pressed against her. Jackson stopped thrusting and pushed, hard, into her. He didn't dare breathe for fear of tipping over the edge himself, a danger that still threatened with every ripple of her body.

He'd been so caught up in his own climb, this one had snuck up on him. From the expression on her face, she hadn't expected it either.

When she relaxed and let out a contented moan, Jackson found the last bit of his control failing. He pulled out and released into his hand as well as he could. Evie was a rag doll next to him, her chest lifting and lowering steadily as she returned to earth.

When Jackson got back from cleaning himself up, he was surprised to see her sitting upright with the covers pulled to her chin.

"Well," Evie said, unsure of where to go from there. "That certainly happened."

"Are you alright with this?" Jackson asked. "All of a sudden I'm thinking I breached some really important ethical boundary."

"No, God no. If we're being honest, I made the first move. I guess you diving on top of me could be considered a move though."

"Hey, now. That's part of my job description."

He sat next to her on the bed, tucking his feet under the folded quilt at the edge of it. Evie stared past him out the window. There was a slight smile on her face but then she cleared her throat, and her eyes focused on Jack.

"You can understand why I feel a little weird about this," she said. She wriggled under the covers, relaxing into the mattress. "I didn't expect anything like this when you said you were going to be staying here with me."

"I would hope not," Jackson teased, holding a palm to his cheek as if gasping in horror. "Taking advantage of your poor little bodyguard like that."

"Oh, c'mon. You either get to be my Adonis or my bodyguard. You can't have it both ways."

Jackson curled up next to her, their bodies just touching. He looked as if he wanted to tell her something, a deep dark secret that only came to light in the warm afterglow of lovemaking.

But what they'd just done had nothing to do with love, so Evie made a show of yawning and settling into her spot on the bed. Besides, she had enough of her own secrets to mull over tonight. Like how she lost control so completely at the hands of her best friend's brother.

Sure, she'd gotten rough before, way more than what had happened tonight. But it had always been by design, preplanned and agreed upon. Hell, she'd even signed a contract with that one guy from Club Nightpulse, though how binding it was she didn't know. He'd signed it Blayd.

Evie rolled her eyes at the absurdity, but her cheeks burned when the memory brought with it a flash of how that nobody had been packing the biggest dick she'd ever seen... until Jackson. Her insides quivered with remnants of his power.

"I'm glad this happened," Jackson said, bringing Evie out of her memory haze. His eyes drooped as if the onslaught of post-coital sleep threatened to pull him under. "I've been thinking about this for a while now."

"You have?" If she hadn't been so drowsy herself, Evie would have sat straight up. She'd been semi-plotting her conquest for days, but now it seemed her prey hadn't been so meek.

Jackson nodded, his eyes closing. "I had this dream about you a few nights ago. That's not where it started though. I had already wanted you by then."

"You did?"

Jackson exhaled a response, but he was fading fast. Under his breath, he mumbled something that sounded like, "Don't tell Rachel about my... behavior."

Evie started to reply with, "Only if you keep your mouth shut, too," but it was too late. Jackson's head lolled to the side and his breathing slowed.

She tried to succumb to sleep the way he had. She was loose and relaxed from her multiple orgasms, yet something kept her tense. Jackson's hands tugged at her as he slept, and she heard his voice on a loop telling her he had been thinking about it for a while. The last thing she wanted was someone to commit to.

She gazed down at Jackson's dozing face and sighed as she snuggled next to him and closed her eyes. Whatever awkward conversation they needed to have could wait 'til tomorrow.

Chapter Sixteen

Anxiety dreams plagued Evie that entire night. There wasn't one narrative she remembered clearly, more like a cloudy jumble of cords wrapping around her, flesh enveloping her. She woke up with a sweat-soaked gasp somewhere in the colorless breath before dawn, Jackson's arms bound tightly to her waist. Peeling them off without waking him up didn't seem to be possible so she wriggled free, unconcerned if it jarred him out of sleep.

Standing over the bed and watching him readjust, since her movements hadn't bothered him at all, Evie wondered if this night had been a bigger deal with him than it was to her. She enjoyed herself, more than she'd anticipated, but there wasn't much else she wanted from him.

She could only hope he felt the same, though his coma betrayed that hope. She knew he'd not been sleeping lately, so she convinced herself it was just the physical release that sated him. Nothing more.

That thought carried her to the kitchen and through making a modest breakfast for the two of them. Still, her mind had been awakened and wouldn't stop turning last night over like a worry stone. By the time she finished cooking and headed to start working on her sculpture, she'd all but driven herself mad over it.

Independence was a trait Evie prided herself on; her need for solitude was non-negotiable. More than one potential boyfriend was put off by this, a fact Evie accepted and cared little for addressing. A guy she had been seeing briefly after college told her in no uncertain terms that she was cold and hard to love.

"It's like you're never excited to see me," he said when she asked him not to show up unexpectedly at her apartment. She had answered the door with her elbows since both her hands were caked in cracking gray clay.

With a bruised pride look he added, "I'm here to surprise you, and you're angry with me."

Evie gave a half-hearted attempt to explain she wasn't angry, but he didn't want to listen, and she wasn't that thrilled with the relationship anyway. He hadn't been good in bed and that was all she needed him for. She knew she'd find a replacement when she felt the need.

To her, work was the priority. Her passion. Her life force. Men were available and easily accessible; work was a drive that required as much energy as she could afford. Without that, without devoting everything she had to it, she was positive she wouldn't succeed.

Rachel had introduced her to a flighty artistic guy she had met at some faux-louche, bougie lounge, claiming how well the two of them would hit it off. Evie reluctantly agreed to the meeting, but left after one drink as Rachel chased behind her asking what was wrong.

"Nothing's wrong. I just don't want to have anything to do with that guy."

"But why not?" Rachel asked, out of breath from keeping pace with Evie while wearing heels. "You're an artist. He's a writer and, like, musician or something. You guys would be a perfect match."

Evie stopped walking. They were a few blocks from the bar so there was no chance of an uncomfortable encounter with the guy unless he'd tagged along behind Rachel.

"I don't want to date an artist," Evie said, pushing her hair back from her face and holding it in the clamp of her fingers. "I want someone who doesn't have an artistic bone in their body."

"I'm well aware of the only bone you give a shit about," Rachel had said, hands on her hips.

And she was right.

Artists always thought they were the brilliant one in the room, Evie knew that. She had plenty of problems with normal men demanding her time and attention. An artist would want his girlfriend to be a support system, which she didn't want to be. She pictured him wanting her to prepare meals and clean up after him. If preferring to be alone and focused on her work made her cold-hearted and hard to love, then fine. Evie had no response to that beyond complete acceptance.

She didn't know what kind of person Jackson would be within a relationship, and the longer she stood in the living room staring at her Adonis while his soft sleep noises billowed in, the more she knew she didn't want to find out. The risk of becoming a couple only to have her hate him in a few months was too real and big to be worth it. She resolved to have a long, frank discussion with Jackson once he was roused from what sounded like a deep, necessary sleep.

Through her somewhat limited dating life, Evie had formed the perception that being alone was her only option. Even the men who told her they didn't want an official girlfriend and were happy without putting labels on things, had a set of expectations she had no intention of meeting. There had been a few casual arrangements, that Rachel so helpfully referred to as fuck buddies, but those fizzled after a while for various reasons. One left town, another came over for one last round before telling her on his way out that he was seeing someone seriously.

"No hard feelings though, right?" He stood shrugging and shuffling in her doorway as if he was waiting for her to tell him off. "I mean, we both knew what this was."

When Evie said she was fine and he could leave now, he kept one foot on the threshold, watching her face for an undefined moment he had been anticipating. It took her longer than she cared for to explain to him that she wasn't mad and didn't care and could he please, for the love of God, leave so she could lock the door and get back to work? There was no response from him after that aside from sulking away, but Evie saw the look on his face as he stepped out, and she knew what it said. You're cold; you're hard to love.

Funnily enough, this was one of the only traits, good or bad, about herself that Evie didn't blame on her mother. The fact that her mother wasn't partial to showing love and spent most of her life being self-absorbed should have raised some flags, but she was too attached to her freedom to deign to give her mother credit. Besides, Evie had assumed she was the way she was because she was like her mother, not because of her mother.

Nature versus Nurture.

The difference between them came down to Evie's ability to be alone. She enjoyed silence and doing whatever she wanted whenever she wanted. Evie's mother always attached herself to someone; sometimes she drained them of their happiness so thoroughly that they left her, and she was back to square one. Having heard, or at least inferred from sideways comments and glances, that she wasn't exactly a bubbling font of warmth, Evie figured it was better for everyone if she didn't pursue a relationship too vigorously. And she included herself in the count of 'everyone.' From where Evie stood, it wasn't worth it to be loved.

She started some detail work on her Adonis as the sky turned the pale sherbet color of sunrise. It took so long for the light to flood the whole city, the horizon of buildings both impeding and assisting the deluge. Instead of the sun coming up and spreading all at once, it bounced and refracted off thousands of windows, surfaces, chrome and metal behemoths hulking along the streets and cast long shadows at their feet. The constant play of luminescence and shade was what Evie loved about places like New York, cities allowed to grow as tall and wild as the imaginations of the humans within them.

A dry cough resonated through the mostly bare rooms, and Evie knew it was only a matter of time before Jackson awoke. He was probably stirring in the middle ground of consciousness at that very moment, his body and mind preparing to face full reality. She avoided thinking about how he might meet the day with a new sense of peace or contentment only to have it smashed by her inability to commit.

Evie ran her hand down the shaped clay of the Adonis and sighed. "I can commit to you," she told it as she heard Jackson climb out of bed. "That's about all I can handle right now."

Jackson had left after their conversation, stating he had to go meet with his captain. When he was gone, Evie called Rachel. "Got a minute?" she asked, putting the phone on speaker to not get clay all over it. She'd been warned by her carrier that they didn't care how much insurance she bought; she wasn't getting another one.

"Gotta make it quick," Rachel told her, chewing into the phone as she spoke. It was still early for her, so probably cereal or some other easy grab. Rachel didn't consider it rude that Evie would be calling at an unusual hour as long as Evie didn't consider it rude that Rachel would not stop whatever she was doing to pick up the phone. "Jack called me a minute ago, and he's on his way over. He says he's got something to talk about. Since you haven't been abducted, I'm guessing it's got nothing to do with you."

Evie stumbled through a reason to get off the phone then hung up without saying goodbye.

The conversation with Jack had gone fine. Not great but not awful. Better than Evie had thought it would, but he was obviously less fine than he let on.

When he'd come into the living room, Evie immediately said, not bothering to step down off her ladder, "I'm worried that we might be on different wavelengths here. In general, I tend not to have serious relationships."

"So you want this to be a casual thing? I can get behind that."

"See, I'm worried that casual can't happen as long as we're living under the same roof." For the first time since Jackson came into the living room, Evie made eye contact with him. "How can we be casual while we're living together? Whatever the circumstance."

Evie was thankful she had the excuse; it made perfect, sound sense. She could tell Jackson agreed with it even if he didn't want to readily admit it. In his mind, he probably thought that 'casual' and 'sharing a living space for the time being' was a wonderful fit. But still, that was the part that seemed to knock the wind out of him. There was the awful sense of both people now performing when as recently as last night, they were completely uninhibited.

He had left soon after.

Evie let out an audible sigh once she was alone again, relieved the moment was over yet sad it had to happen at all. As she went back to work, she found it impossible to focus on the task at hand. Her mind kept slipping in shots of Jackson supine under her, his chiseled torso bending into itself as he stretched forward to kiss her. She didn't want to encourage a relationship, but she'd be lying if she said she didn't have fun, that she wasn't quite attracted to him.

If only it could be enough.

Chapter Seventeen

Jackson, on the other hand, was speed walking his way to Rachel's apartment. He hardly looked up as he moved between groups of men gathered on street corners and other New Yorkers rushing to their next destination. The tempo of the city had thrown him off the entire time he was staying with Evie; it made him feel like time moved too quickly. Either that or he was standing completely still.

At Rachel's, he took a deep breath before knocking on her door. She called out that she had unlocked it already, and he entered to see his sister sprawled out on the couch, a bowl of cereal balanced on her chest and cartoons parading around the TV screen.

"You're not really watching Saturday morning cartoons, are you?" he asked, knocking her legs off the couch so he could sit. "How old are you again?"

"It's my weekend, I can do with it what I like."

Rachel shoved the remainder of the dry cereal into her mouth then wiped her lips and reached for the remote to turn the cartoons off. Jackson stayed her hand, reclining into the couch with a defeated slump.

"I'm ok with cartoons for a bit," he said, his eyes moving along with the action on the screen. "When was the last time I got up and watched something on a Saturday morning?"

"For me it was last week." Rachel spun so she could face Jack. "What's up? You said you needed to talk about something."

"Doesn't matter," he answered blankly. "I'd rather just watch cartoons."

Nothing needed to be said, and no comment was offered. Rachel had gotten used to the labyrinthine way Jack would discuss what he was dealing with, and he knew she would wait him out. As the colorful characters battered each other across the screen, Jackson heaved deeply then covered his face with both his hands.

"I did something stupid, Rachel," he announced through the digits folded over his face. "I did something so, so stupid."

A dryness curdled the spit in Rachel's mouth, one wrenching thought surfacing in her mind. She had never suspected Jackson as the one stalking Evie since he'd never shown an interest in her before, and he was pretty aware of how breaking into a woman's apartment wouldn't be received well, but now she stared back at him as his fingers slid down his face and pulled it into a stretched mask of itself. If there was one thing life as a woman had taught her, especially in a city like New York, everyone was capable of being awful.

"Jackson, you would tell me if you were the one doing all this shit to Evie. Wouldn't you?"

Jackson snorted. He snapped his hands away from his face, his head whipping toward Rachel so fast that his neck made a popping sound. "You think I'm stalking Evie?"

"No! I don't actually think that. I just thought maybe you were about to confess to that, and then there's gonna be this drama I gotta spend my Saturday dealing with when I really just wanted to watch cartoons and maybe take a bubble bath."

"A bubble bath?" He gave her a look, twitching the base of himself so he shimmied into an upright position. "You're regressing."

"Excuse me?"

"Watching cartoons, eating cereal, taking a bubble bath. You're gonna be a baby again if you don't catch this in time."

Rachel kept her face steady but released a tired, annoyed groan from the back of her throat. "What stupid thing did you do, Jackson?" she asked. "Get to it so I can kick you out and not feel guilty."

Jackson's expression took on a halting, sickly pallor. For a fleeting moment Rachel was positive he was about to vomit on her rug. Another mess of drama she didn't want to spend her day off dealing with.

"I slept with Evie," Jackson said, his voice quiet.

"You what?!"

"Last night."

"And she let you?!"

"Of course she let me. Jesus, what is it with you? You think I'm a stalker, you think I'm a rapist. I'm a good-looking guy, Rach. I don't need to attack women to get sex."

"Oh please, you know as well as I do that sex crimes are about power. Not sex."

"Touché." Jackson pressed the bridge of his nose with two fingers. "Look, Evie and I slept together, and now it's weird. She was sort of cold and stand-offish this morning, and I don't want her to think I'll turn into another crazy man she has to worry about. On top of that, I think I really like her so it's not gonna be easy. Pluuuus—" he dropped his hands to his lap, looking very drained and tired. "I'm kicking myself for letting it happen because it feels like some ethical breach even if it technically isn't."

"Yeah, she's not a prisoner. She can consent."

"But part of me is wondering if it's right to be in a protector position for someone and making moves on them."

Rachel touched a finger to her lips. "You made the first move?"

"I guess so. Actually, not really. I mean, she definitely had her hands on me before I went anywhere near her but she caught me, ya know, staring."

"At her tits, huh?"

"Rachel, please."

Rachel stretched her legs long across the couch, kicking at Jackson the way she used to when they were kids. She laughed sharply then folded her arms and rested her head on them.

"I can't picture you and Evie together," she said after studying Jackson's worn-down expression. "She's so...cerebral."

"I feel like I'm being insulted here."

"No, it's not that you're some bumbling idiot. You're just a more physical, social...honestly, more normal person than she is. You know how much I love Evie but she's a weirdo. She always has been."

"You think I should just let it go then?"

Rachel shrugged. "I don't know what you should do except say if she doesn't want to hook up again then that's that. Evie's pretty good about saying exactly what she means."

Jackson stood up, his sight fixated on the TV screen. After a moment, he lulled his head down into his chest then straightened up and slapped his hands in one bright burst of noise. Rachel watched all this with bemused interest, familiar as she was with her brother's odd rituals. This one she attributed to his stint in high school of being in plays. It was a coarse moment of focus, forcing out the creeping intrusion of unwanted thoughts with little more than an energetic superstition.

"That's that then," Jackson said with such conviction that Rachel almost believed him.

"That's that."

"Thanks for your help, Rach. I'll let you get back to your cartoons."

Jackson started toward the door, Rachel not bothering to get up to let him out. When he was about to leave, Rachel hopped onto her knees and leaned forward over the back of the couch. She didn't say anything at first, but Jackson had seen her out of the corner of his eye, and he froze, hand on the doorknob.

"I was thinking," she started but her voice petered out as if she ran out of air after only three words. "No, nothing. Never mind."

"Are you serious? Now you have to tell me."

"I was thinking that you and Evie might make more sense than I realize but there's one thing with Evie I think you should know."

"Yeah, what's that?"

"Evie's not really a relationship person," Rachel said, settling back down into the couch. "I'm not saying it can't happen, but it tends not to."

"So what does she want?"

Rachel shrugged, her focus back on cartoons. "I'm really not sure, Jack. You'll have to ask her."

Asking her was out of the question. Jackson wouldn't dare bring anything up to Evie about sex or coupling or relationships or whatever else he could think of that was even remotely related to what they did the night before. He went for a long walk before starting toward Evie's apartment, the flickering images of his brain twisting into recognizable forms as he drifted through the cooling autumn streets.

The sheer amount of Evie in his thoughts wasn't that unusual but he was having trouble staying away from the dirtier side of his imagination. Before long, his blood was churning hot, and he was picturing her slinking toward him in nothing but silk panties, her arms stretched over her head as she walked, levitating her small breasts higher over her opening rib cage.

"You really think you can control yourself from fucking me?" the Evie in his mind asked, her fingers teasing the elastic band of her panties as if promising to drop them. "Nothing but a thin sheet of drywall separating us."

"I'd punch through it in a heartbeat," he told her as his hands crested up over her stomach to close around her pointed tits, her hardened nipples.

"I know you would. I can see it in your eyes how badly you want me."

Jackson managed to pull himself out of his own fantasies by hitting on a note of truth. Evie was going to be able to see how badly he wanted her, no matter how well behaved he was. It was only a matter of letting his guard down once, and then that soft adoring look he'd only given to a few women up to that point would take over. Evie would see the glaze in his eyes, the dumb smile on his face. No matter how much he swore he was fine with the arrangement, she would know how he really felt.

"Christ, this is gonna get bad," he muttered to himself as he rounded the last corner toward Evie's place. He knew he would have to spend less time with her, that the joking around and sharing sandwiches would have to be nixed right alongside sleeping together.

Mentally preparing himself to go inside, Jackson stood on the sidewalk as the early sunset hit darkness even earlier, and the sun fell behind a building. It was still the afternoon, but nighttime seemed to sneak up on him faster every fall. To him it felt like one day it would be eighty degrees with the sun hanging in its slow decline until past nine o'clock then the next it was crisp and windy and completely black by five.

I can't leave her alone once it's dark, he thought, willing himself to put the key in the door. For God sakes, it's my job to make sure someone's there when it's nighttime.

He tried to be as normal as possible when he came through the front door. Evie was perched on the stepladder again as if she had been up there all day. She gave him a quick smile as he came in.

"You went to see Rachel, huh?"

Jackson froze, halfway in the door. "Did that blabbermouth really tell you that or are you just an amazing guesser?"

"I called a little after you left this morning. I was going to see if she was around so we could hang out and talk. Imagine my surprise when she told me you were on your way over."

"Well, then you probably know I told her everything." He paused and reconsidered that as he closed the door. "No, not everything. The broad strokes."

"Yeah. She doesn't need to know everything."

Evie lowered her hand, the tool she was using nestled firmly between her thumb and her forefinger. She turned away from her Adonis and leaned forward on her knees to address Jackson.

When she didn't say anything, he smirked and settled on the arm of the small couch facing her. "What?"

"Nothing. I was just going to ask you what Rachel's reaction to us was?"

"Us?"

"You know what I mean."

Jackson rubbed the heel of his palm against his forehead, exasperated and gruff. "Well, the first thing she thought was that I'm your stalker."

"She didn't." Evie's big green eyes grew wider. Her mouth gaped, then the corners of her lips curled upward.

"And then after that, I dunno, she seemed ok with it. She was surprised more than anything else."

His eyes flashed up to Evie's, then out the window to the still blue sky. It was much brighter up there than on the sidewalk, the sun only partially hidden at that height. Jackson flicked the overhead light on; he saw Evie blink rapidly as she adjusted to it.

"Sure. Surprised makes sense." Evie shrugged. "I mean, both of us were surprised, right?"

"Then she said we weren't a good fit. She said you're a smart weirdo, and I'm a normal meat head. Or something like that."

Evie furrowed her brow, straightened up, and returned to scraping and shaping the intricacies of her Adonis's chest. "I don't think we're that different. It's not the most obvious pair of people but it's also not like we're getting married and having kids. When it comes to being with someone like this, it's more about attraction anyway."

"Maybe she thinks one of us is a hideous beast that should never be seen by human eyes."

"Oh man, she definitely used to call me that when I wouldn't let her straighten my hair."

Jackson relaxed, a breath escaping his body. He had been wracked with anxiety the whole day. There were so many big and little things to worry about, and he didn't want to spend any more energy on them. Worrying all day about what Evie would think when he was around, how uncomfortable it might get between them had been exhausting.

A tsunami of tension broke over him then receded; he pressed his lips together tightly, convinced he was going to cry. Not cry like he was hurt or in pain but cry the way a child does when they're overwhelmed and can't sort out what they're feeling at the moment.

When he'd regained control of his voice, Jack said, "I'm glad we can be like this." He motioned between the two of them. "I was prepared for you to ask me to leave. Since it's been quiet, too. I was worried you were gonna think it was too much of a headache to have me around when there hasn't been much activity lately."

"Honestly, even if I felt weird, I'd want you to stay."

Evie paused her work to study the cuts and lines in the torso. It was impossible for her to deny that it was Jackson. She had to see the likeness.

When she pushed her hand against him, when the muscles under his skin surfaced against her palm, Jackson knew she understood the inspiration that was pouring out of her every minute of the day. Even when she wasn't working on her Adonis, she seemed to be thinking about him, about how beautiful she was going to make him.

Jackson knew last night, standing before her in all his naked, sexual glory, she couldn't still think she was crafting from an imaginary man in her head, but rather the one who had been in her space and getting in her way for the past two weeks.

Jackson peeled his eyes off of Evie who, likewise, was staring at her sculpture, probably realizing the same things. "I want you to be safe," he told her, acting like he was moving toward the bathroom when he was just awkwardly shifting his weight. "If you didn't want me around, I'd hire someone to stay here with you and cover the costs. I mean it."

Evie turned her face to him. Her eyes were hidden behind the reflection of the lenses, but the soft smile and slow nod said all he needed to hear. She looked as if she was about to speak. In a long, stretched out moment, Jackson watched her mouth start to move, her cheekbones start to pull upwards.

Later, in recalling this split second to the police, Jack would swear he didn't hear the shattering glass at all. The only thing he clearly remembered was that lingering expression on Evie's face and the sickening thunk of the brick flying through the window and connecting with her temple.

Then Evie pitched forward off the stepladder, and he grabbed her before she hit the floor, her eyes rolling backward into her head and a trickle of blood oozing down her jawline.

Chapter Eighteen

"Where is she?" Rachel asked as she burst into the hospital waiting room. Jack was sitting with his hands pressed together as if in the trance of a silent prayer. At the sound of Rachel's voice, he snapped to attention. "Jackson, where is she?"

"She's alright. She's still unconscious but that's because the doctors gave her something. Thank God the brick didn't do any real damage."

"Brick? Jesus Christ. You're telling me—"

Jackson put a hand against Rachel's arm in the hopes of grounding her frantic, manic energy. "Whoever this dude is, he's a real piece of shit."

Rachel was shaking so hard that Jackson's hand rattled on her arm. He applied more pressure as if to steady her, noticing the tremors seemed to move outward from him. Retracting his grip, Jackson stumbled back into a hard plastic waiting room chair and held his quaking hands out in front of him. "God, I'm a mess."

"Are you ok?" Rachel sat down next to him. Her shoulder pushed into his in a comforting way, a way that reminded him of the closeness they shared. "Did you...see what happened?"

She wasn't asking for an account of the incident. Jackson heard in her voice the reluctance to pry; the force of her question came from what was implied within it.

Jackson nodded. "Yeah. Right in front of me."

"Jesus."

"I know." Jackson sunk into the plastic mold of the chair, a faded orange cushion holding him like a curled palm. "I haven't even gotten the last one out of my head."

"You never really get them out," Rachel said. She sounded certain of that fact, and Jackson didn't have it in him to ask why. He was well aware of how much trauma befell women just for existing.

"When I was waiting for the ambulance to arrive, waiting there with Evie, holding her hand and talking to her, I told her she couldn't die right now because I'd never be able to come back from that." Jackson started their shared sibling snort then choked it midway through. "I hope she doesn't remember that. What a selfish thing to say."

"Will you give yourself a break? You weren't being selfish. If it was me, I would have said that I'll kill her if she dies in my arms and scars me for life."

"Yeah, but you're super selfish."

Rachel pinched the soft underpart of her brother's bicep. Jackson gave a small cry of surprise then laughed as he rubbed his injury and stared at Rachel in disbelief.

"There wasn't much there to pinch," Rachel noted. "I guess you've kept on your exercise regimen while at Evie's."

"Did you really just do that? How old are you?"

"Look, it snapped you out of it for a second, right? I can't really put up with you acting like you did anything wrong. You had a split-second thought about not wanting to deal with another helping of trauma. That doesn't make you selfish or shitty or anything else but the solid dude you are."

A scrubbed-up doctor strode toward the waiting area. Because the hallways were so long and wide, Rachel and Jackson watched her walking for what seemed like twenty minutes. From her steady gait, they both felt the slow dread of impending bad news. She didn't appear to be paying attention to anyone else other than them, her face somber with the gravity of her message.

"Are you family members of Genevieve Hansen?" the doctor asked. Her approach caused Rachel and Jackson to rise from their seats, fingers clutching each other.

"We are," Rachel answered without hesitation.

Jackson almost said no.

Rachel gave him a squeeze that said, in that sibling way, *Fucking boy scout.* Then, to the doctor without missing a beat, she said, "Is she alright? What's going on? Does she need blood or an organ or something?"

The doctor lifted her hands, turning them like a magician proving they were on the level. "She's fine. She just woke up, and we wanted to come get you. We didn't expect her to come out of the anesthetic so easily. She is slightly concussed, so we'd like to keep her overnight either way."

"One of us needs to stay with her," Jackson said. "Not just the way most family members say that. This is a matter of safety."

"Yes, I understand. We spoke with the police once we assessed her situation. They told us it was an assault."

"That's not even the half of it," Rachel muttered, but Jackson had no desire to stand around rehashing the past few weeks. The doctor was fine with them being there, and that was what mattered. He pulled Rachel away from the waiting area and started down the hallway.

"Excuse me? Mister, uh, Hansen?"

Rachel could barely contain her startled snort laugh.

The name stopped Jackson cold in his tracks. The doctor was standing in the same spot with one finger raised in the air.

"Yes?" Jackson asked, the name "Mr. Hansen" playing on a loop in his brain. Rachel was intermittently shaking next to him, and he knew she was trying not to laugh again. "Is there something else we need to know?"

"Genevieve's room number, I should think."

Jackson thanked her then continued yanking Rachel along after they got the information. "I guess that was to be expected," he said as they hurried up the stairs. "You need a better poker face, though."

"Oh please. You look way more insane than I do. Hopefully, she knows you're a cop so she's not on the phone with the police right now."

When they got to the door of Evie's room, Jackson went pale. He didn't want to see her in that bed. Knowing she was relatively unharmed didn't make it any easier. There was a different quality to people in a hospital. Whether it was the terrible lighting or the stark whiteness or just the mere context of the building, Jackson couldn't tell. What he did know was he had seen too many people he loved lying on the sterile beds, and if he never saw another one for the rest of his life, it would be too soon.

Rachel rested her hand on the knob, watching him with measured concern. "Ready?"

It didn't matter if he was or he wasn't. They had to go in; they had to see Evie. One of them, more likely both if Rachel got her way, had to sit there all night under those lights that drained the life out of everyone's face, and watch Evie in bed, both of them trying not to sleep.

The room turned out to be not as bad as Jackson had pictured. The lights were only on along the far end, so the death glare he had winced at upon its anticipated arrival wasn't present. Evie looked small and vulnerable in the hospital bed but no more than Jackson's other loved ones. Her eyes were open, dark circles under them, crescent moons the color of a fresh bruise. The side of her head where the brick struck was bandaged, and Jackson noticed a bare spot near her hairline that was shaven.

"Thank God you're alright," he said.

He wanted to touch the bandages, see the damage done. He wanted Evie to tell him she felt fine, and that it was hardly more than a scratch.

But for the first time since this all started, Evie had nothing to say.

Jackson had expected in desperation that when they opened the door to her room, she and Rachel would start chatting away like they always do, and Evie would ask if anything had happened to her Adonis. He had enjoyed the brief fantasy, but the sinking realization came that this was worse than the previous incidents, as frightening as they were.

Evie's ability to roll her eyes and shake off danger wasn't going to work this time. This time was a different beast.

"I'm tired of getting terrifying phone calls from my brother about you, young lady," Rachel joked as she sat next to the bed. She wasn't steady as she spoke, wavering with nascent tears gathering in her throat.

Evie barely smiled at her. When she managed it, both Jackson and Rachel could tell that it was a smile for their benefit, not hers. They could plainly see that Evie wasn't up to smiling.

"They told me," Evie started slowly as if fascinated by the way her mouth formed each word, "that it was a brick."

"Yeah," Jackson said. "It was."

"Someone threw it through the window."

"Yeah."

Evie stared up at the ceiling, blinking, and touched her face as if wiping away tears, but there was nothing there.

"We're gonna stay with you all night, babe," Rachel promised. "The doctor said we could. You don't have to worry about anything."

"Sure," Evie answered. Her tone sounded eerily placid, making Jackson's skin crawl. "Sure."

Jackson swallowed. "Captain Wheeler is spear-heading this now. She's got two plain clothes cops casing your neighborhood and keeping an eye on your building. If that creep comes around, they'll get 'im."

"So, it was just a brick?" Evie asked. She didn't move her focus from the ceiling; her sight slid slightly to the right as if she was reading. Jackson realized she was counting the holes in the textured institutional tiles. "That doesn't seem like this guy's M.O."

"What do you mean?" Rachel asked. "He's a stalker. He's a psycho. Hurling a brick through a window sounds par for the course to me."

"I guess," Evie acquiesced.

Jackson had planned to keep the final piece of the story to himself. Attached to the brick, was a crude note.

Jackson had told the cops on scene, though he refused to hand the actual evidence over to anyone except Wheeler. One of the officers gave him an attitude about it, which only strengthened Jackson's resolve. He had too little faith in humans and their impulsive nature to give up an object of such importance to a person he didn't know.

"There was a note," Jackson admitted softly. He thought that if he said it quietly, she might not really hear, and he wouldn't have to tell her. "He attached it to the brick before he threw it."

"And the note was for me?"

"Without a doubt."

"What did it say?"

Rachel and Evie were both riveted to Jackson as he swallowed again and exhaled a trembling breath. "It said," he inhaled again, exhaled again, "I'll kill you for this, you cheating bitch."

Chapter Nineteen

So he knows a man is staying with me, Evie thought as she sat up that night in her hospital bed watching the reruns of M*A*S*H that played at two in the morning. *He knows a man is staying with me, and he possibly knows that we slept together.*

Rachel and Jackson were sleeping in shifts though, like Evie, nobody was getting much rest. There had been a half hour or so where Rachel nodded off, but she woke up like an alarm, her eyes popped open and her hands outstretched, fending away invisible threats.

"I hate being in the hospital," Evie said. She was watching the TV and refusing to look anywhere else. "I mean, normally I do. This time is so weird. It's like I feel safer here than I would at home." She broke away from the TV to make eye contact with Jackson. "Even with you there."

"I know what you mean," he agreed. "I feel safer with you here than at home, too. I wish there was a way for them to let you stay here."

Evie rested the tips of her fingers against the bandages on her head. She wasn't sure how many stitches it took, only that it was a lot. The doctors had tried to explain it to her when she was in and out of consciousness in the emergency room. Evie had been able to absorb that they needed to shave part of her head. She was pretty sure she nodded her consent, but blackness swarmed over her right after, and she melted into the void.

She would never freely discuss it with Rachel or Jackson but there had been a few glimpses of oblivion as she plummeted further away from consciousness. Being ripped out of the floating blackness where her body was vapor and her mind ceased its incessant pulsing, to hear snippets of tense voices calling to each other about stitches was cold water thrown in her face. Hearing someone mention they were going to give her something for the pain, something that promised to return her to the ether from which she was pulled, had been a moment of peace. When she followed whatever they gave her back into the nothingness, she left herself as the shell in the emergency room and accepted the inert afterlife.

Later, when morning came, they explained in more depth the ramifications of head trauma, and all the strange things it can do to a mind. "We're always trying to hold our equilibrium," the doctor said as if she had seen the light in Evie's eyes burn out and was giving an argument for staying alive. "The extremes to which our brains will go to keep us functioning is really remarkable."

My brain opened the void up to me, Evie thought, thanking the doctor for what she did as Evie and Jackson prepared to leave the hospital. *My brain wasn't frightened of going dark.*

Jackson had insisted on getting his car so he could drive Evie home, even if they weren't sure where they were headed. Instinctively, Jackson headed toward the Grand Central Parkway to his place. Rachel's apartment was an option to, but Evie told them both that that was out of the question.

"This whole situation is getting way out of control," Evie said, causing Rachel and Jackson to exchange looks. 'Situation' must have sounded too tame and trivial for what Evie was facing. "I don't want anyone else to get hurt."

"You getting hurt is fine though," Rachel said dryly. "Ok, I see."

"My place is out of the city," Jackson reminded them both.

"If I stay in Queens…" Evie shook her head then cringed and touched the bandage. "I need to be able to work on my Adonis."

"Get the fuck outta here with that shit," Jackson practically snarled. "Your Adonis can live without you fawning all over it, alright?"

"Fawning?" Evie asked sharply.

"That's how you look at it," Jackson told her. "Like a schoolgirl watching The Beatles."

"Regardless," Rachel cut in, "you need to go somewhere this guy doesn't know about. If it's not Jackson's, fine, but then you come up with a place."

Evie and Rachel both must have thought they'd been friends for too long if this was their way of discussing the aftermath of a frightening assault. Rachel and her solution-oriented thinking versus Evie's tendency to minimize problems. As long as they were problems unrelated to her work. Those she dove into headfirst.

But Evie was actually grateful for Rachel's approach, as brutish as it was. Now was not the time for tears and handholding. Now there were accommodations that had to be made, and silly sentimentality from an avoidant artist was only bogging down the works. Very little debate happened once Rachel demanded Evie provide her an answer. Evie shrugged, mumbled something about how she was going to need rides into the city, and the three of them headed to the parking lot.

"Drop me off at Evie's, and I'll get her things together," Rachel said as they sat at a red light. "I can head out that way later today. I'm sure Evie will be happy to see me by then." She wiggled her finger against Evie's cheek until Evie slapped it away. "Or maybe she'll still be mad."

Evie sighed. "I'm not mad at you."

"Well, that's good."

"I'm mad at this... fucked up situation."

"We all are," Jackson told her, giving her a flash of a grin as he changed lanes. His straining neck and the short burst of movement like a facial tic turned the grin into a grimace. The sight of it turned Evie's stomach with nerves.

Jackson dropped off Rachel and continued on in the direction of Queens. Before they got onto any bridge, a thought on where to stay came to Evie's mind. Her mother was in Paris for the next few weeks so her apartment would be empty. The only reason Evie knew about this was from a brief message her mother had left for her explaining that if there was an emergency, Evie should use the spare key to get in.

"But don't let zee scum I waz dating in at all," her mother had said, clipping each word as she spoke. "He iz not allowed."

Evie hadn't met her mother's latest mark. She figured it was a toss-up whether he was scum or a nice guy, toward whom her mother had turned angry and hateful. Considering her own experience with the woman, she presumed the latter.

"You think your mom's place is safer than mine?" Jackson asked as he barely avoided running a red light. They needed to go the other way, and he was trying to do that quickly and without making an illegal U-turn.

"Honestly, I have no idea. I just...I don't want to leave the city."

"Rockaway Beach is hardly 'leaving the city.' Don't act like this is Green Acres or something."

Evie wasn't really sure what he meant but she got the gist of it. Logically she knew she wasn't being ripped away from her urban playground to make do in the middle of nowhere. It was becoming more and more of a control issue though, a fact she didn't dare admit to Jack. She thought it ridiculous that she should have this reaction to people doing their best to keep her safe, to protect her. In the end, she at least wanted to be allowed a decision or two, but to say that plainly was out of the question.

If Jackson knew her frivolous rationale, they'd be heading to Queens before Evie could blink. Evie had seen the control issues that manifested in him the same way they manifested in her.

Before they made it to the east side where Evie's mother's empty apartment sat, Evie asked if they could make a stop at the grocery store. Jackson found one with a small, cramped parking lot so they wouldn't have to carry anything very far. Once parked, he drummed his hands on the steering wheel and surveyed the area as if he was anxious about something.

"What's the matter?" Evie asked. The side of her head where the stitches were was starting to hurt again, and she wanted to get groceries and be inside where she could just lie down and not have to think or worry. "You're not going to stay in the car, are you?"

"Of course not. I just don't love the idea of you being so exposed in public. This guy is watching you, Evie. Enough to know that you slept with the man who's staying in your apartment."

"We don't know he knows that much," Evie argued. "For someone like that, he just needs to see a man anywhere near me. Any man in my vicinity is going to make me a cheating bitch to him."

"I would just rather get you to the safe house, and have Rachel pick up the food and provisions."

"Rachel's already bringing my underwear and tampons and taking Cagney to her place. Let's not make her do anything else."

Evie got out, slamming the car door. Jackson followed soon after her, sighing every step of the way. He couldn't stop staring at the shaved and stitched area on the side of Evie's head, knowing how lucky she was and not wanting to tempt fate any further than they had.

They reached Evie's mother's place in the early afternoon. Rachel had been notified of the change of location and was on her way with Evie's things. Jack figured this was shaping up to be an alright decision but then they got inside.

The apartment was in shambles; books and paintbrushes strewn across the floor, empty wine glasses with dark sticky drops drying onto them. A stale odor crescendoed over them as they walked in. It reminded Jackson of the time he had to assist the fire department with a health check on a shut-in. The windows were sealed closed, and the man had papered them over with anything he had handy. Food containers sitting empty by the trash cans reeked of grease and salt.

"Are you sure your mother didn't get robbed?" Jackson asked as he helped Evie carry the groceries into the kitchen. "It sorta looks like someone tore this place apart."

"Yeah, that person would be my mother."

Evie put the food away then began furiously straightening up. Jackson wanted to stop her, force her to rest, but he also wanted to be able to sit down somewhere in this place. She gave him orders, softening her voice slightly. They were going to have to deal with each other for the foreseeable future and he figured she didn't want him to think she was turning into a monster who barked commands and needed to be in control.

Jackson, for what it was worth, felt quite grateful for the direction. Obviously, this was what Evie had to have; he recognized the grasping of control in a futile situation.

"I guess you knew there wasn't gonna be any food because your mom was away," Jackson said as they tended to the pile of dishes left in the sink. Evie's mother wasn't one to cook or lovingly present food so they were both surprised at how many plates were there. When they reached the bottom of the pile, it was evident the stack had been growing for weeks.

"There's never food here," Evie told him. "If my mother wants to eat, she'll go out and get something. But if I'm being honest, she doesn't really eat that much." She held up a wine glass, tacky with the residual nectar. "She prefers to drink her calories, if you know what I mean."

Jackson remembered his mom saying that to Rachel one time when she asked why Evie's mother was so slender while the women in their family were buxom and curvy. When she was told that Evie's mother didn't eat enough, Rachel nodded and followed with, "Yeah, that's why she always looks tired too."

Lately, Evie had been taking on a similar pallor, the look of someone running their system on empty and powered solely on nervous energy. Now that the apartment was closer to habitable than it had been before, Jackson pulled Evie out of the kitchen and pushed her toward the couch.

"Sit down. I'm gonna make you something to eat."

Evie resisted, cleaning things as he moved her forward. "I'm not hungry. I still feel sort of off from whatever they gave me at the hospital."

"Sit down. I'm gonna make you something to eat," he repeated.

Evie was his charge and it was high time he started acting like it. No more tragedies on his watch.

Evie let herself be forced onto the overstuffed couch in the living room. "Hmm," she said.

"What?" Jackson asked as he moved toward the kitchen.

"I'm surprised to see a piece of furniture so comfortable in this place. That woman was not known for enjoying the cozy, fun side of anything. And this," she said, pointing to the TV set right across from the couch. "My whole life, TVs were considered verboten. If I dared to bring up the option of getting one, she would sneer and call me 'hopelessly American.'"

A moment passed in silence as Jackson began scrounging for something edible.

"Maybe that crazy bitch *has* changed," Evie said from across the room.

"What?"

She motioned to the TV set. "I just can't believe after all these years of lecturing me that a TV would rot my brain, here she is with one right in her face. And she was one to talk, that wino drank her meals and smoked a pack a day, but that was apparently fine."

"You two seem like you have a real healthy relationship."

A knock at the door made them both jump. Jackson rested a finger against his lips as if Evie needed to be told to stay quiet. She made a face and rolled her eyes, causing Jackson to laugh at his own dramatics.

"You guys, it's Rachel. I know you're in there."

Jackson snorted, and opened the front door. "Yeah, I guess we should have figured it was you, huh?"

"I mean, I'm not a cop but tell me, Jackson, do stalkers often knock?" She shoved a bag of groceries at him. "Here. I brought food."

"Oh, we did that too," Evie said, and Rachel locked the door then joined her on the couch. "I knew there'd be nothing here."

"Well, I'm assuming she left a storehouse of wine."
"Maybe. I think she probably drank it all before she left."

Jackson listened to them talk as he cooked. He found an open bottle of white wine in the fridge and poured himself a glass, sipping it thoughtfully. It had been a while since he'd drank wine; he was taken aback by how much he enjoyed it. He found it more soothing than the beers he and Evie shared those other nights. The glass was empty before any part of the meal was done so he poured another one, and sighed heavily.

When the voices stopped, Jack looked up to see Rachel standing in the alcove of the kitchen. "Oh, so there is wine here."

Jackson held up the near empty bottle. "There was," he corrected.

"That woman always has something stored around."

Rachel began opening cabinets and looking through the musty, forgotten shelves of the pantry. She emerged with a triumphant 'aha' and a green glass bottle without a label held by its graceful throat.

"You're gonna drink that?" Jackson asked. "It's a million years old. There's not even a label."

"It's not like booze goes bad," Rachel shot back as she prowled around for a corkscrew. "If it smells like it's gonna kill me, I'll run down to the bodega and grab something better."

The cork popped out easily though it started to crumble to pieces when Rachel tried to remove it. She shrugged, and Jackson knew she was thinking. Now they had no choice but to finish the bottle. Rachel poured two huge glasses for her and Evie and left him with the remainder to drink while he finished cooking.

Once Rachel was out of the kitchen, the discussion started up again as if there hadn't even been a pause. Jackson envied the ease that seemed inherent to female relationships. As a kid, he rejected the notion that men and boys were the less complicated gender, more laid-back with clearer emotions.

The men he saw were always angry and offended by the smallest perceived slight while the women were fast to forgive and move on. When he and Rachel got to the age where they hung out with each other among friends, he found himself gravitating toward her cluster of teen girls. They were the ones who wanted to go see bands and see if they could get away with sneaking into a bar. His friends wanted to break bottles in parking lots and challenge other boys to drag races.

Becoming a cop didn't shift that perspective at all. Jackson dealt with too many crazy men deluding themselves into thinking their actions were appropriate; to think that they were the gender with the handle of their emotions. To say nothing of the guys on the force. Again, he found himself seeking out the companionship of women, considering them less tasking to spend time with. He had been concerned when Wheeler told him she was partnering him up with another male officer and begged her to reconsider.

"Don't worry," she had told him in that flat intonation that Jackson could never read. "You'll like this guy."

She had been right, and his devastation in the wake of Marcus's death was the lasting proof of that. There were so few men that Jackson held as loved ones. The closest people to him in his life were his sister and mom. *And now Evie,* he thought as he plated up two dinners for her and Rachel. *I know we might not sleep together again but…*

He wasn't sure where they stood, so he had no way to finish that sentence. Instead, he let it trail off in his mind, and carried the dinner out to the sound of Rachel's excited, celebratory shouts.

But he couldn't stop the hope that welled up in his chest at the sight of her.

Masochist.

Chapter Twenty

They were alone again soon after dinner and the house had settled into a nervous quiet.

Rachel had left with the reminder to call should they need anything, but what they actually needed was for her to stick around. She'd been their buffer all night, and now she was gone.

Evie had wanted to clutch at her friend's arm on her way out the door and beg her to stay, beg her to hold tight in order to save Evie from her own bad decisions. She felt the swirling confusion, anxiety, desire she knew were about to converge into a laser-focused drive to sleep with Jackson again.

Sex just made her feel better; it always had. Starting from a young age, sex intrigued Evie. She'd been fast to approach boys about it. Her first time was wildly disappointing; he finished in an instant and wouldn't consider any other position aside from lying on top of her.

When Evie matured a bit and got the nerve to take control, the world opened up to her.

She and Jackson sat on opposite ends of the couch, staring at the TV and digesting dinner. Evie fought the urge to extend her leg toward him, run her toes up along the line of his thigh. He seemed like he was absorbed in the show so, for a while, she thought it would be rude to interrupt him. Even for sex.

After a half hour or so, she couldn't contain herself any longer.

Jackson blinked at the sight of her slinking off the couch and settling on her knees in front of him. Her hands rested on the top of his legs, inching toward their goal. He didn't stop her until they had reached it.

"Evie, what are you doing?"

"I'm sucking your cock. I thought that was obvious."

"Weren't you the one who just said we shouldn't do this again and that we should be friends? I could have sworn it was you."

"It's like you've never heard of someone changing their minds."

Evie pushed herself between his legs, her hands freeing his erection from his pants. She smirked at him, and left her thoughts unsaid. A hard-on like that had been waiting for her warm, supple lips, the coarse surface of her tongue, the stretching muscles in the back of her throat.

Jackson surrendered with a sigh, his hands falling placidly to his sides.

"You're driving me crazy," he said, quietly, as if it wasn't meant for Evie to hear. "The entire time we've been sitting here all I could think about was fucking you."

"I can tell," she chuckled, letting her lips and hot breath brush past his tip.

"I wanted to toss you over the arm of the couch and..." His voice cut off as she ran her fingernails around the pulsing head of his cock.

"Then you should have."

"Don't tease me, Evie."

Evie licked up the length of Jackson's shaft then sat back on her haunches. She tugged her shirt over her head, exposing her small, but full tits to him. Jackson touched one delicately then grabbed the meat of it with his entire hand.

"How bad do you want to fuck me?" Evie asked with a grin. "Enough to take it, even if I didn't want you to."

Jackson sat back, his expression drawn downward. "I would never ever, Evie. Never."

"Jesus, I know that." Evie threw her hands up and groaned. "I wasn't saying... I was trying to be sexy. Like, you're this big strong man, and here's little old me just dying to suck your dick."

Evie got off her knees and flopped down on the couch next to him. Her shirt was still off, and he couldn't avoid watching the pointed tips of her nipples bounce as she settled.

"You know me," he told her, tearing his eyes away from her chest. "I can't help but be a boy scout."

Evie rolled her eyes but as Jackson's hand crept down the front of her, and she noticed he was still completely hard, she arched her back and pouted. "You're thinking about fucking me again. I can see it on your face."

Jackson rested his hand on the waistband of Evie's pants. "What happened to 'I don't think we should sleep together again?'" He lifted the band slightly off her hips, a flash of pubic hair displayed then covered. "Or is that just a rule when you say it is?"

"Don't think too hard about it, Jackson. Now's not the time for that."

Evie straddled his lap and kissed him firmly on the mouth. When she lowered herself, she could feel the hard head of him straining, desperate against the thin cotton of her sweatpants. Her body ran hot, flushed as Jackson kissed down her neck until he reached her breasts.

"So that's the game, huh?" Jackson rolled one of her nipples between his fingers, pressing tighter with each word. "You snap your fingers and I give you what you want?"

"You get what you want too," she whispered. Then she yelped as Jackson twisted her nipple. Her hand flew to her chest. "That hurt."

"That's what my cock feels like having to sit next to you after you tell me we're not fucking anymore."

Evie bit her lip, smiling as she pressed herself strategically against Jackson's cock. "But it's all worth it when you get to fuck me."

Jackson gave a rough war cry and flipped Evie onto her back on the couch. He yanked her sweatpants off with one hard tug and pinned her down by pressing himself into the v of her legs. Evie tossed her head back, pulling him closer. She moved to place a hand on his chest.

Jackson snatched her by both wrists, his free hand holding her face forward. "Don't act like you don't love it."

He sneered at her in a way that made the blood in her body pump harder. His fingers pressed against the vulnerable spot on her wrist; the spot that gave away how fast her heart was beating. She wasn't sure what aroused her more about his new attitude, this callous rudeness.

The fact that she felt like a bit of a liar and a drama queen for relinquishing her decree so quickly after making it played a small part. It excited Evie that Jackson wasn't letting her pretend she was doing him a favor.

"I like it well enough," she said, wriggling slightly as she linked her legs behind his back. "Take it or leave it, in my book."

Evie tilted her hips as her legs pulled him toward her. She had lost control of the situation where her main goal had been to get him inside of her, and now Jackson was easing his hips back, the tip of him circling the folds and waves of Evie's cunt but never making the plunge in.

"Take it or leave it," he repeated. He kissed the open base of Evie's throat, and released her hands. "So right now, you could just leave it?"

"C'mon, Jackson. You're being an asshole."

Jackson shrugged and sat up, snorting at what looked like genuine anger on Evie's face. He reclined with his hands behind his head. Evie, naked and thrust suddenly into the cold from the balmy undulations of impending coitus, raised herself onto her elbows and glowered at him.

"I'll fuck ya, Evie," Jackson told her with the same shrug, "but you gotta tell me ya want it. Don't be coy. You gotta tell me exactly what you want from me."

Evie got onto her hands and knees, resting against Jackson while staring down at his lap. "I thought I did."

"Say it."

"I want your cock. I want you to fuck me as hard as you can."

Somewhere deep inside Jackson's mind, a tiny voice shouted that he shouldn't take her up on it, that she was a person in distress and screaming her pain through this release. He had, for a second, considered that the voice was right. Then Evie rubbed against him, warm and naked and begging for it, and he told the tiny voice to shut the hell up.

She wasn't a kid, someone deferring to him as an authority figure. If her demands were to be believed, she was the one in charge. A spark Jackson almost recognized, the way a person in a dream recognizes a face they've never seen, powered through him. He pulled Evie onto his lap as he thrust his hips upward, impaling her right where she leaked wetness onto him.

"You're sick, baby girl," he whispered through the curls that covered her ears as her hair got increasingly more mussed. "This is what you want, huh?"

"I don't want to think, Jack. Make me not think about it."

Desperation spoke to Jackson. Losing himself in obsessive workouts was the only way he had been able to make sense of the world after Marcus was killed. There didn't have to be explanations, understandings of meaninglessness and random chance, when he was sweating in pain; the moment was exactly what it was. Much less to consider than a cruel twist of fate, happenstance outside of human control.

He flipped Evie onto her stomach and slammed his cock into her before she could even position herself on all fours.

"I see you," he panted through thrusts. The feeling of Evie pushing backward, throwing her hips into him, nearly made him come right then. "I know what you want."

The dirty talk had ceased; by now, Jackson was speaking of silence neither of them could find, and that claustrophobic feeling of being trapped inside one's own head. They both needed the same thing, to be seen. To be heard. And if one of them could find that, Jackson would let it be her.

Evie's hand flew to the fork of her crotch, rubbing her clit as she rocked to Jackson's rhythm.

Before the other night with Evie, Jackson hadn't had a proper orgasm since well before what happened with Marcus. At one of the seedier clubs he frequented, a patron had spotted him as a cop and kept waving at him with a riding crop calling, "here, piggy piggy," for the rest of the night.

The sex he had found with polite women he took on dates, the ones who dropped to their knees and slobbered all over him exactly as he liked, were uninspired, if he was being honest.

He hated the idea that he was more turned on by Evie because she had initially pushed away from him when he was growing attached. Being drawn to her because of her frighteningly human way of diving into sex rather than deal reality was the healthier option in his mind.

Plus, Evie wanted something different.

She pressed down as he thrust forward; she rubbed her holes against him and pouted over her shoulder. Jackson was no stranger to this behavior. He wound his hand through Evie's curly hair and yanked her head to the side.

"Yes," Evie breathed as he pressed his mouth to her neck. "Please."

The world disappeared as the rhythmic pounding of Jackson's cock inside her became the only thing she cared about. The only thing she knew.

"You want to act like it's not your decision." Jackson's tongue traced the inner curve of Evie's ear. "Like you're just going along with it."

For the first time, Evie handed over control of her body.

"Oh God, yes."

They moved in sync, Evie's fingers flying over her clit as she rocked. She let him lead her in this primitive dance. Jackson would decide when and if she came, and she was too far gone to care.

Jackson's hand twisted around more of her hair, pulling her head closer.

Evie let out another moan, wordless, thoughtless.

"Don't you dare," Jackson ordered as Evie felt the first tremor of an orgasm begin to tear through her.

"I..." She couldn't form more words. The sensation was building, too fast and hard.

"Not yet!" Jackson slapped Evie's hand away from her clit and she let out a whimper.

He grabbed her by the hips and flipped her over again, effortlessly. His stare was intense as he drove into her.

In one motion, Jackson pulled her closer and thrust deeper, filling her completely.

She didn't need her fingers. She was gonna cum now, no matter what.

Her back arched. She ground against him, pushing and pushing until there was no room left between them. Nowhere else to go.

"Not yet," Jackson said, and slowed his pace.

"Please," Evie whispered, then again with more force. "Please!"

"You may." The words barely escaped his lips before his thumb pressed against her swollen clit. He arched his hips, angling his cock up toward his thumb, toward that spot, and Evie could do nothing but let him.

It was too much to bear. Every muscle tensed then exploded as she climaxed uncontrollably. Every inch of her twitched with a spontaneous firing of nerves. She lost herself on him. Completely.

A rush of blood hit Jackson heavy in the head. He knew he wasn't far behind.

Raising Evie's pliant body up higher on the arm of the couch, he pulled out of her and positioned his cock above her rounded tits.

She looked spent. Sated. Content.

And he'd done that to her.

That smile on her drowsy lips was because of him.

His hand worked his shaft furiously but he didn't need all that. He was so close to coming that a few strokes brought forth the eruption.

He spewed over Evie's chest and splattered up her curved neck.

She looked faintly surprised as the warm cascade landed on her still-sensitive post-orgasm flesh.

Her fingers lazily played with a spot of it by the open of her throat.

"Oh, fuck," Jackson muttered, his face slack as his body regained its equilibrium. "I... should have... asked."

"Don't worry about it," Evie told him as he collapsed on top of her. She was having her own trouble speaking, and her voice sounded distant, floaty as if she had stood up too fast despite being on her back.

The semen that stuck their bodies together like glue slowly dried as both Evie and Jackson disappeared into a deep sleep, roused less than an hour later by the screaming fight of the tenants next door and the shouts from across the way for both of them to knock it off.

"Jesus, fuck. Am I scared."

They'd been laying in her mother's bed for hours, talking and... not talking. But Evie hadn't expected those words to come plainly out of her mouth.

"I won't let anything happen to you."

A sound ejected from the back of her throat against her will. "I know you'll do whatever you can do to keep me safe."

"What the hell does that mean? I'm serious. I won't let anything happen to you."

Evie rolled onto her back; her sight went soft-focus at the ceiling. She did this when she needed to think, or stop herself from thinking. She vaguely remembered counting holes in the hospital ceiling after the attack, which only made the fear stronger.

Jackson ran a fingernail lightly down then back up her arm, and she returned her gaze to him. He was a much better sight anyway.

"I don't doubt your commitment, Jack," she said, finally.

"Alright, alright. Don't say anything else, ok? I can hear every word in that sentence, and I hate them all."

Evie knew the words because she was ready for her own version of them. There were going to be legions of people hearing about her story if she started to take off in the art world, and legions of women who wanted to look her in the eyes and commiserate, share an ancient pain of their kind. There was only so much gossip she could deal with.

She hated herself for thinking of it in such cynical terms but in that angry vacuum in that desperate night, there was no human with whom she wanted to emotionally share; no person worthy of seeing the void gradually absconding with her identity.

Except for Jackson. Jackson lived through the pablum the non-grieving say to those in grief; stared it down like trauma in its own right. Like Evie, he wanted to be alone in his process, though he also watched himself receding into the ether like a drug addict fatally hooked on his own spiral.

They slept fitfully, alternating their shifts of waking and moving. For Evie, the hours after midnight were the worst, and she kept getting up to go to the bathroom, get a drink of water, and lie back down in a useless loop. After the third time, she brought her glass of water to the window in the bedroom and pulled a chair close to the sill. She forgot she was naked, and didn't understand why she felt so cold until she noticed and pulled a knit blanket around her shoulders. When she had gotten there, the blanket was in a pile on the middle of the floor. Evie had folded it into a perfect square and arranged it just so over the curve of a beaten armchair her mother had been using as a hamper.

It satisfied Evie to clean her mother's apartment; it satisfied her in a sordid, depraved little way. She would leave it even more spotless than she found it, and the cabinets would be filled with staples her mother never bothered to buy. It would be after all this, and she and Jackson wouldn't be locked together in desperation, and she wouldn't be terrified of once again waking up to a man lurking in her apartment, and her mother's show or whatever the hell she was doing in Paris would have been a failure and—

Evie took a sip of water. As a child, she had discovered a way to pull herself out of the avalanche of negative thoughts that came from nowhere and pulsed forward with a most assertive destination in mind. She came to this knowledge by watching her mother rant about the pointlessness of it all, driving deeper into a sadness and a rage for which she had discovered no catharsis. It struck Evie as odd that someone who fancied herself an artist couldn't harness these emotions into her work, and that was when Evie landed upon the difference between a dilettante and a true creator. Naturally, since she was about ten at the time, she didn't quite think of it in those terms, but she began to see the world as people who talked about how special and talented they were and people who actually had something to show for it. Her mother, suffice it to say, was teetering toward the former.

But there was skill there; Evie couldn't deny that much. She hated to give credit at all to either of her parents, the one who raised her or the one who simply jizzed inside of a warm body and shrugged at the idea of creating new life. But from the little her mother did create; Evie was inclined to think her talent was indeed inherited.

Her mother's artwork embodied no love. That had always been the problem. At least, not the way people seemed to find love and adoration in every corner of Evie's. People were moved and saddened by what Evie's mother created. They spoke to her at length about how powerful her installations were, never buying a piece for fear of having to face that chokehold of emotion every time they casually glanced at it.

Evie's mother did portraits the way Evie did snapshots of daily life; everything in motion. In Evie's, they were the motions of the city, the motions of a life powered from a million different outlets all running at a different frequency. In her mother's, they were the unblinking faces of people in the shadow of decay, the scraps of humanity clinging like barely noticeable fat on bones.

Evie could paint a depressing scene and find the one moment where everyone was laughing, light coming through the trees, and the day was decided, by and large, to be a fine one. Evie's mother would feel the sad subtext of how every person there was dying, and that laughter was limited, time was finite.

"Et's because I am French, see," her mother would say as she displayed the portraits of skin dissolving away from skulls, not entirely but just enough to make everyone squint and look a second time. "Zee French understand zhat life iz without a point."

"Then why make someone else go through it?" young, angry Evie would ask, demanding an answer that no parent in any generation or country could ever whip up an answer to. "If it's so awful and terrible, why have me and make me do this whole fucking thing?"

Evie's mother's mouth twitched, the closest she got to a smile. She found nothing wrong with a child cursing, especially when it was in a heated moment. "Because otherwise I would have to be miserable all on my own," she replied, and that seemed as good a response as any.

The east river esplanade was almost empty at that time of night. Evie watched what looked like canoodling lovers on a bench then leaned closer to the window in fascination as she saw the woman in the couple stand up and bend over, her panties like handcuffs around her knees. The man was licking from her pussy to her ass, splitting her cheeks apart so he could feast on the most intimate part of her. A flair went off inside of Evie, and she crept back into bed.

"Jackson," she whispered, closing her fist around his limpness. "Jackson, wake up."

"What's the matter? What's going on?"

"Nothing's the matter. I just wanted you to be up."

Evie's mouth closed around Jackson's cock, pulling on the loose, flaccid skin until she felt it engorge and grow, pushing her teeth apart and closing off her air. She reared up, inhaling sharply as she did.

"You got your wish."

Evie straddled Jackson's lap, rubbing the tip of him around the puckered hole of her ass. She considered it, sitting lower and letting his size stretch her open slightly before she thought she better not, and slid him into the safe warmth of her cunt. *There'll be plenty of time for all that,* she told herself as she rode Jackson hard. Her fingers enclosed around his throat as his hands squeezed her breasts like he was juicing them.

Plenty of time for that.

She came hard again, the pain from Jackson's strong grip sending her zenith spiraling upward and out of the crown of her head. Her mind told her that her body was levitating for a moment before it faltered back to earth, landing in a sweaty pile on Jackson's still erect penis. He rolled her over and mounted her, telling her to breathe through her tiny whimpers of not feeling like she was there, and feeling like she was walking somewhere in space.

Chapter Twenty-One

Of all people, they were woken up that next bleary morning by Captain Wheeler banging on the door. She had gotten the address from Rachel when she called her after having trouble reaching Jackson.

"Falling off the face of the earth like that," she said as she forced her way into the apartment and slammed the door behind her. "After your little girlfriend gets hit in the head with a brick."

"She's not my girlfriend," Jackson argued. He sounded like a grade school kid being called out about a crush. "I didn't realize you were even paying attention to me."

"Oh, what is that? A shot at us not doing our job or something? Look, Jackson, you show up at my office one day telling me—"

The sight of Evie, pale and sleep-deprived with her curvy legs sticking bare out from underneath a t-shirt, brought the captain's tirade to a pause. She cleared her throat and plastered a practiced cop expression on her face. It was a neutral, steady line of emotion; aware that an event was occurring but not willing to throw everyone into a panic.

"We were just trying to find somewhere safe," Jackson said, taking the advantage Evie had given him simply by existing and invading his life at the right time. "It's not like I was on official police business."

Captain Wheeler pulled her mouth to one side then fluttered her lips as if it wasn't worth her time to argue. The silence between their angry snaps at each other went on too long, and the heaviness of the air reminded Evie of a play where someone had forgotten their lines. Everyone looked uncomfortable, nobody willing to be the one to step up in hope that someone else was going to. It was a pleasant moment for Evie in a way she couldn't exactly articulate. Considering the highs and lows of her life recently, a commonplace awkward pause brought her to normalcy, and that was a place she hadn't been in a while.

Evie cleared her throat, her eyes brightening. "Can we get you some coffee, officer? Sabrina, right?"

"Uh, yeah. Sure. That sounds good right about now."

Evie disappeared to the kitchen, leaving Jackson and Sabrina to discuss whatever they had to discuss. She bristled at the thought that she had found a reason to excuse herself like a complacent housewife tending to the needs of the men as they talked business. There was a small piece of her that wished she stayed in that cramped entrance way and waited patiently as Jackson and his captain muddled through the uncomfortable ambiance and told her everything that was being disclosed.

She couldn't help but notice the steady stream of low held chattering voices weaving its way into the kitchen. *Plenty to talk about now that I'm gone,* she thought as she started the water for the French press. An ex-boyfriend of her mother's had once gotten her an American style coffee maker telling her how much easier it would be when she could make a whole pot at once with the push of a button. She unceremoniously dropped it out the window when they inevitably broke up. It landed with a satisfying crunch next to where he stood shell-shocked on the sidewalk.

"Never trust zee man who wants to make zees things easy," she told a then-teenage Evie as she slammed the window shut and dusted off her hands in a theatrical flourish. "Zhat ez how a lazy person thinks."

Less than a week before the coffee maker incident, Evie had released a storm of anger at her mother, and somewhere in the barrage of insults, she told her that her little stunts were tiresome and far less shocking than she wanted everyone to find them. Her mother absorbed each stab and word with a countenance that turned chillier, dark, more dead behind the eyes. Evie would wonder forever if her mother did all that just to show her up, just to seize a moment of utter astonishment from her daughter and clutch the memory of it when she needed to be reminded of what she was capable.

Evie let the kettle whistle for a torturous amount of time. She could hear it like a siren blaring somewhere in the recesses of her mind but more a noise coming through a dream, and she couldn't quite think of what to do next. When she finally turned the stove off, Jackson leaned his head into the kitchen to make sure she was alright.

"I thought maybe you blacked out or something. Do you need help with anything?"

Evie didn't turn in his direction. "No, I got it. I was just a million miles away when it started going off."

The boiling water curled under the grounds as she poured it into the French press, lifting and roiling them in their own tiny circular paths. She loved watching the tide of coffee rising, the individual grains twisting alone then with each other in a big earth-colored cloud. Breaking the head with a spoon and watching the rich brown foam of the crema had always been her favorite part.

One of the few warm childhood memories she had of her mother was watching her poke a dark wooden chopstick through the puffed up collection of grounds and water then stir rapidly as the curdling waves of caramelized sugar rose to the top. It was the memory she thought of when her mother let go of the American style coffee maker with a shrug and a flick of her wrist. Evie couldn't deny that the long, time consuming way of making the drink was, at the very least, more interesting.

As the second hand rounded the face of the analogue clock above her mother's sink, Evie pressed the plunger down into the still steaming liquid. The clock was fast by an hour, and Evie knew her mother's latest boyfriend must have been gone prior to daylight saving time ending. Her mother could never be bothered to deal with petty details like that.

Out in the living room, Jackson and Sabrina were talking in overly bright, animated tones that sounded disingenuous to Evie. She decided to take that as a sign that they were done with whatever they had needed to discuss. She brought out the coffee she had prepared for Sabrina and herself. It wasn't until she settled on the small, and from what she could tell broken, club chair across from the couch that she realized she didn't bring any coffee for Jackson.

"Oh, there's still some in the French press," she said with a laugh by way of apology. "Sorry. I don't make a great hostess or housewife."

"It's fine. We need to let you know a few things, ok?" Sabrina, not Jackson, said to her in an official tone.

Evie nodded, sipped her coffee, tried to steady her breathing. No sentence that started that way ever went anywhere good.

"We got a description of a guy," Sabrina said. She cupped her hands the entire way around the mug and held it firmly in the middle of her lap as she held Evie's attempted casual gaze. "A few people noticed him lurking around outside your building. I guess he asked one of your neighbors if he knew you, and if you were going to be around later. That neighbor flagged down a cop on that beat and told him what happened. That's when some more people started letting us know this guy had been around a lot lately."

"Well, that's sort of good news, isn't it?" Evie's voice cracked. "I mean, it's at least a step forward rather than us reacting to shit." She cleared her throat. "Stuff."

"Nah, you meant fucking shit." Sabrina laughed. It disarmed Evie however momentarily. "It's better than no news but it's not great. Your neighbor was really helpful but there's only so much we can get from a witness trying to remember a face." She unfolded from her pocket a police sketch of an average looking man that Evie would have walked right past on the street. "Know this guy from anywhere?"

"Never seen him in my life."

Evie kept her hands clenched and hovering above her lap even as Sabrina pushed the drawing closer to her. She waited for Evie to take it, a long and unmoving pause. Again, Evie felt the ambiance of artifice as if one of the three of them was waiting for a cue to bring the scene to a close. This difference this time was that it was Evie for whom they were all waiting.

Sabrina lifted her weight off the couch to stretch the drawing closer. "Are you sure? You can take a good look at it. Give yourself a minute to think."

"I'm sure."

"Evie," Jackson slid forward on the couch, "it's ok to be freaked out but if you want this to be over, then you need to work with us."

Evie coughed out a dry laugh. "Listen to you. You sound like a cop."

"Please, Evie," Sabrina said, gently shaking the picture toward her. "Just take a second and really look at this."

The way the two of them were positioned together on the couch they looked like worried parents extending a hand to their troubled child. In Evie's own memories, she had never encountered a sight like that, though she was one time lectured alongside Rachel when the two of them were caught trespassing on the elementary school playground at two in the morning. Her parents' faces had seemed so stern, so hurt by the tacit betrayal of sneaking out and breaking rules but Evie had to fight back giggles at how seriously everyone appeared to be taking it. She wished for that sentiment to flood her again. Instead of being trivial, it was becoming increasingly more intense.

Evie took the drawing in her hand despite the fact that she trembled when she touched it. Sabrina and Jack exchanged concerned glances surreptitiously. Both of them were in the mode now; neither of them wanted to frighten the victim.

"I... I mean, I still don't think I've seen him before." Her laser-focused pupils jerked along the lines and contours of a face she struggled to recognize. "It's also hard to tell. Sometimes I think he might look like someone I know but it's not a match as much as it's a resemblance."

"Plus, at some point everyone starts to look the same." Sabrina took the picture from Evie and studied it, her eyes squinting. "Imagine how we feel putting out an APB; Caucasian male, 5'9, brown hair, driving a Honda sedan. Around here, that's like every third guy."

Sabrina got to her feet. "We're obtaining CCTV footage from the place across the street. Hopefully we'll be able to get an actual photo of this creep."

"And they're putting a watch on this place," Jackson said. "Now that they know we're here."

Evie stayed seated as Jack walked Sabrina to the door. She listened to them saying normal good-byes then their voices dropped, and she knew they were talking shop again. Her legs were so tensed that she was starting to get cramps in her upper thighs. By the time Jackson closed the door behind Sabrina, Evie felt her whole body shaking.

"I wish I hadn't seen that," she whispered. "I wish I didn't have a face to put to all of this."

Jackson hesitated on the threshold between the living room and the door. Rushing to comfort her would have been counter-intuitive, which he seemed to recognize. It made sense even through Evie's growing anxiety. The trembling, the spiking adrenaline wrenching rage upward from wherever it had; it needed to pass on its own.

"People never imagine that the person who hurt them is so plain looking," he said, taking one slow step toward her.

"I don't know what I expected him to look like but not just like an old guy." She pressed the heels of her hands into her head, wincing as she almost pressed into the stitches on her temple. "There's nothing to show everyone what a creep he is. There's nothing even remotely remarkable about him. He's just a boring guy who for some reason decided that I'm the woman he loves."

"I get it. When I was brought in to ID the little shit who... after what happened to Marcus, he looked nothing like what I'd expected. Watching him flee the scene, I remembered him as sweaty and desperate, with specks of spittle gathering at the corners of his lips. Like rabies. I honestly thought he was rabid. A rabid fucking animal.

"Then, at the line-up, I kept staring at the face I knew was the right one, wondering why this terrified looking kid was there instead of the snarling monster I had witnessed. I pointed at him, demanding they bring in the person who did it, the person who looked just like him but deadly and vicious. It had taken me a solid five minutes to calm down and make the identification."

Evie placed an arm around his shoulder.

"They're not monsters," Jackson said. "That's the hardest part for us to accept."

"You're right. I was expecting a picture of the devil."

Evie's gaze went glassy as she stared toward the window overlooking the East River Esplanade. The curtains were parted, and she could see the spot where the lovers had licked and sucked and enjoyed each other's bodies in the early morning hours that gave so much darkness as validation for their acts.

"It's gonna be ok, Evie," Jackson was saying, though he sounded like he was drifting away from her. "I'm not gonna let anything happen to you."

"I know that, Jackson," she replied absently, unable to move her gaze from the spot.

She had let herself be lulled in a moment of levity and escape when Jackson plunged inside of her the night before. Reaching out for him, she felt as if she was falling through the floor, through the body of the building. She waited for the moment of impact, her splatter against the crooked, cracked surface of the city sidewalk but Jackson caught her before she hit the ground, her eyes fluttering backward into her head, her mouth dangling open.

"Can you hear me?" Jackson brushed a curl out of Evie's face. It sprung into place the second he released it. "Evie? Evie?"

Evie blinked, and shivered, staring up at Jackson as if he was an apparition in a dream. "I was dreaming…"

"You alright? You stood up too fast, I guess. Or the whole situation, I get it. Either way, you passed out."

"Passed out?" She reached up instinctively to the stitches at her temple.

"Fainted. Whatever." He held a palm against her jaw, careful not to make contact with her stitches. "You feel ok? You want water or something?"

Evie shook her head, and let Jackson help her up to a seated position. Her head pounded and her eyes didn't want to open. He had carried her to the couch after catching her, and even in the small one bedroom apartment, Evie was disoriented. She placed a hand on Jackson's forearm, pressing into the skin like she was checking that he was real.

"I was dreaming about this park we used to go to when we lived in Paris," Evie told him, her tone ethereal, speaking from another world. "This park near our apartment where my mother liked to paint. And pick up men, I imagine but maybe not. I was too young to notice anyway." She laughed and patted Jackson affectionately on the cheek. "When I woke up out of that dream, you were leaning over me, and it was all very confusing."

"You're ok now, though?"

"I'm fine. I'm hungry, and I'm fine." She lifted herself to her feet, inching up the way elderly people did. "Let's take a walk. See if we can't find a place around here that does sandwiches."

"Actually, Evie, we're gonna do things a bit differently."

Jackson ushered her back down to the couch then went to the window and pulled the drapes shut. The deadbolt was locked already but he touched it to check it, a compulsive behavior Evie saw in her own life. He went into the bedroom and returned momentarily.

"What did you do in there?" Evie asked.

"Closed the blinds. We've gotta rachet this up a notch."

"Rachet this up a notch?"

Jackson sat next to her on the couch. He took her hand in his. Both of them were shaking to some degree. "There's gonna be a squad car outside your place and this one. Anybody coming in will be seen but this guy doesn't seem to be discouraged by anything we've done so far. The fact that he's been asking people about you is a huge concern. It's an escalation. He's not hiding out after the brick incident. Not like we thought he might be. He's bolder now."

Evie drummed her fingers against her legs and blinked before speaking. "Alright, fine. So we can't go get sandwiches?"

"Let's order some delivery. What do ya say? Anything you want."

Evie nodded as Jackson went to go rummage through the kitchen drawers for take-out menus. She was pretty sure he wouldn't find much but she let him go anyway to have a moment to collect her thoughts. What she assumed would be a flurry of manic concerns was relatively quiet except the annoying repeated line of 'this is real.' She nodded again as if in agreement with herself.

"Man, your mother doesn't do delivery or anything, huh?" Jackson appeared with a menu for a Chinese food place and a pizza parlor. "I was hoping she'd have one for a spot that did sandwiches."

"I don't care what it is as long as it's food." Her stomach agreed and Evie wondered absently how long they'd gone without food. Then, she remembered all the extra exertions of the past couple days and smiled through the pain.

"Chinese then. If it's all the same to you." Jackson was on a mission and didn't notice.

Better that way, Evie thought. She was in no condition to mess around. *Right?*

Jackson placed an order, Evie's toes skimming the top of his pants the entire time. He shot her a look out of the corner of his eye. As he hung up, he wrapped his free hand around the foot closest to him.

"What do you think you're doing?" he asked hoarsely. He yanked her toward him by her foot, her legs splitting around him. "Distracting me when I'm on the phone."

"We've got nothing but time to kill now, Jackson," she told him, rubbing her crotch against him.

"So we might as well fuck, is what you're saying."

"If that's what you're hearing, that's what I'm saying."

Jackson rolled up the edge of Evie's long t-shirt, exposing her panties. Slowly, he inched it over her stomach and ribs until her breasts were unveiled, and he could extend his eager tongue to each prominent nipple.

"You know, I felt what you did last night." His tongue trailed between the hills of her chest, traipsing through the valley like a happy traveler. "I felt where you were trying to fit my dick."

"Where?" Evie asked with an innocent lilt. As if she didn't know what he was talking about; as if she hadn't been dreaming of his thickness spreading her puckered hole till it was smoothed.

"You want me to fuck you up the ass," Jackson said, his fingers tracing the outside of her cunt lips, clad in the white cotton of her unassuming panties. "At first I thought, no, she must not realize what she's doing. But then you did it again, and I knew it wasn't a mistake. I knew what you were hoping for."

"I haven't found anyone who's good at it," she told him with an impish half grin. "All the other guys just ram it in. It's like they don't care about whether I like it or not."

"So that's why you like me, huh? Because you know I need you to like it. I need you to like everything I'm doing."

Evie raised her hips so his fingers were positioned outside the opening. The tips of them pushed into the resisting fabric, threatening to burst through and dive inside of her. She whimpered.

Jackson stood up and yanked Evie's panties off. He held her knees to her chest, smiling as both her holes split open and up at him. "This is where you want it" He ran a finger around Evie's ass. "You're not supposed to want it in there."

"I know that, but I can't help it."

Jackson gently eased his finger in, and Evie moaned as he penetrated her up to his last knuckle. Her hands rubbed her clit, stroking it in a steady rhythm. She writhed against the couch cushion, breathing heavily, as Jackson moved his finger faster and deeper in and out of her.

"I've never seen a woman go so crazy over having anything up her ass."

When he pulled all the way out, Evie gasped and pouted at him. She tried to pull him back toward her.

"You looked like you were about to come," he said, a dash of authority resonating. "Do you come from your ass a lot?"

"Probably about half the time."

"My God, you're a secret anal fetishist."

Jackson bent down and licked her from hole to hole.

When she was ready, and nicely wet, he slid his cock into her ass. She had expected him to be big, much larger than anything she'd had in there. And until that moment, she hadn't expected to like it as much as she did.

Jackson moaned along with her, as if relishing her clenched teeth shriek of pain-spiked pleasure. She hiked up her hips and began thrusting before he was fully in.

Jackson laid his weight on top of her, shaking his head.

"Come on, please," she whimpered, begging like a greedy child. "Please put it in."

"You can't even wait for it. You start pulsing the second a cock gets anywhere near you."

"Not just a cock. Your cock."

Evie watched her words send a shiver through Jackson's body; she knew he couldn't have held off any longer once she said that.

With a low, guttural groan, Jackson drove himself into Evie's ass, his teeth biting into her neck as he filled her to bursting and she enveloped him in warmth.

"I'm crazy about you, Evie," he said in gasps as he pounded into her. "I'm seriously so crazy about you."

"God, if you keep fucking me like this!" She spasmed, her throat running dry.

Her body pulsed under his, and her fingers kept stroking her clit as she shook. Pressing her legs around Jackson's ass, she locked her ankles so he was in her as deeply as possible.

Evie came more wildly than she had the night before. Each stroke pushed her farther over the edge until the muscles inside of her clenched around his cock.

"That's my favorite part," he told her, touching her face. "Watching you come like that."

"It's my favorite part too," she exhaled, her eyes closing and a fine layer of sweat breaking out over her skin. "Me coming."

"We have so much in common, then."

Jackson moved slowly, as if suddenly worried that Evie's body was too heightened, too sensitive for any more activity. She took a deep breath and wrapped her arms around his neck, hugging him down to her.

"Come for me, Jack," she whispered. "Come inside of me."

Before she could ask again, Jackson exploded inside her ass as if she had willed him into an orgasm.

Commanded.

They lay linked and entwined with each other, the sweat that coated both of them slowly drying, until the doorbell rudely buzzed, and they were reminded that they had ordered food back there in reality. In the space between their bodies and orgasms, both of them were far away from anything as stifling and scary as reality.

Evie watched in satisfaction as Jackson pulled a blanket around his waist, answering the door to a surprised delivery driver and grabbing the food as if this was just any other day.

Their power dynamic had shifted in this torrid affair. She wasn't ready to call it love, but now lust wouldn't do either.

He owned her body, and she now owned his.

Nothing would ever change that.

Chapter Twenty-Two

Jackson could tell Evie was cabin fever, fast. Had her Adonis been there, her crawling the walls wouldn't have started or at least not so ferociously. But without him, she paced the small apartment, fidgeting with her hands and driving them both crazy.

"I hate having the curtains drawn, not being able to go outside."

"You know it's for your own good." Normally, he wouldn't give in to her theatrics, but he was bored, too.

"Are you gonna make me beg to walk around the park like a dog?"

"The walls are closing in around me," she told him as he pulled her away from the window. "I hate being inside doing nothing."

"Here, watch some TV with me."

"I can't watch anymore TV." Evie stalked across the living room, spinning on her heels when she reached the other wall. "What do I do for fun indoors? What can I do to not be thinking about the same shit over and over?"

"Does your mother have any books? Maybe you could read something." He knew what the answer would be, but he liked watching her mind work. The way she screwed up her nose when she was lost in thought.

Evie stalled mid-pace. She cocked her head to the side and shot a sardonic laugh out of her nose. "I don't even read, really. God damn it. I never thought about it, but I guess I don't do anything for fun. All I do is work on my projects."

"I guess that's why you're the one on your way to being a famous artist, and I'm just some schlub hanging out with you."

"What do you do for fun? Like, indoor fun?"

He raised his eyebrows at her and let his grin do the talking.

"Clothed fun."

Jackson shrugged. He couldn't really think of much either. His first answer was 'watch TV,' followed closely by 'workout.' Neither of those seemed to appeal much to Evie.

"I think we have similar problems," he told her. "I can't really think of anything, either."

"Man, I hope they catch this guy soon," Evie muttered, dropping to the couch.

"I'm sure they will."

"Oh, save it. You have no idea if they will or won't." She surveyed the small living room made dark by the drawn curtains. "This could be what it's like for the rest of my life."

Jackson was out of his way to comfort her. All his attempts felt impotent, feeble. No matter how well he understood how she felt, he knew there was a difference between what he went through and what she still faced.

For Jackson, acceptance had been the name of the game. He had to come to terms with his trauma and find a way to move past it. For Evie, that stage couldn't even start yet.

They found an old movie on TV that seemed to occupy Evie's busy mind for a few hours. She looked tired even though they hadn't done much at all that day, but the constant anxiety plus being closed in like they were drained the life from her. By the early evening, she was nodding off against Jackson and jerking back to consciousness with a violent thrash.

"You seem tired," he said as she settled into him to repeat the process again. "You can just go to sleep, ya know."

"Then I'll be up at four and it'll be the longest day of my life."

"Well, maybe you can fall asleep even earlier tomorrow."

Evie sat upright, rubbing her eyes with balled fists the way kids did when they were jarred out of a nap. She didn't seem to be completely awake.

"I feel like if I go to sleep, that's when it'll happen." She was staring off into space as she spoke. "That's when it happened the other times. He came in when I was sleeping."

"But I wasn't with you those times. I can sit up all night keeping watch."

Evie turned her head to him, and Jackson could see the faintest upturn of a smile on her lips. A full, grateful overjoyed grin was not in the cards, but he was happy to see that much. Just a tiny sliver of evidence that Evie didn't feel so scared and alone in the world as she did before he arrived.

"I... you know something, that actually makes me more relaxed," she said. "I know you would fight your absolute hardest to keep me safe. If that guy is strong enough and scary enough to defeat you then it's like he is an actual monster. You can take any human."

"I hope so," Jackson responded, smiling back at her. He watched her lean in, and he closed his eyes as their lips connected. "It means the world to me that you trust me."

Evie rested her head on his shoulder. "You don't know how weird it is to me that I trust someone who isn't your sister. I think she might be the only person in my entire life who I trust without hesitation."

"And now me."

"And now you."

Jackson put his hand on Evie's knee and shook it affectionately. He fought the erection starting to swell in his pants. If Evie had brought it up, he would have been ready, but this moment felt more tender to him, perhaps even more intimate than sex.

"The idea of losing another person," he started, his chest rising and falling with heavy breaths, "is unthinkable to me. I don't know if I could forgive myself a second time."

"You didn't have to forgive yourself for your partner getting killed. There was nothing you could have done."

"It's a different type of forgiveness. You have to forgive yourself for being the one who stayed alive."

Evie wrapped her arms around them, and they sat in this position while the credits of the old movie began to scroll up the screen.

"Ok," she said as the production company logos, crackly in their static, glowed silver and blue on the TV. "I'm going to bed."

As anxious as Evie had been the past few weeks, to say nothing of the horrendous forty-eight hours she had just gone through, Jackson was thrilled to see her finding solace in sleep. He had noticed that at her apartment she slept fitfully, routinely getting up for a glass of water, then crossing to the bathroom and not always using it. He assumed she was used to this behavior, that her body had grown accustomed to sleep being interrupted by menial tasks. The other lingering thought was that she could no longer sleep peacefully through the night; her mind believed it to be too long of a time to be unaware. Not ready to fight back.

The private joke Jackson had made with himself in regard to Evie's odd sleep pattern was that she knew he would wake up when he heard her tromping around, and he'd see her from his uncomfortable question mark shape on her awful couch.

He liked the idea that she was sashaying around in the wee hours of the morning for his benefit, to get him more interested in her than he already was. Saying such a thing out loud to anyone, especially Evie, was unthinkable, of course. No woman in the process of being stalked would be flattered by her protector hoping her sleepless nights were for him.

That night in her mother's apartment with Jackson keeping watch on the couch for most of it, Evie slept more peacefully than she had in a while it seemed. Jackson heard a thunder rumble of snoring through the wall and was shocked to discover its origin. He figured it was a neighbor or the cloggy sound of old pipes coiled through the building like nests of snakes. The sound of Evie so far gone in sleep was a sheer delight to him.

He went to the room to lie next to her, careful not to wake her. Listening to the steady rise and fall of her contented breathing turned him on, got him hot. Not in the traditional way where he fantasized about sliding under the covers next to her and kissing her neck until she woke up. Like learning to forgive himself for being alive. He was aroused by how much vulnerability Evie would gift him with; how safe she felt with him standing guard.

"He'd have to be an actual monster," he whispered to her in the early dark. It was barely 10 pm; Jackson knew he had a long night to go. "He's not a monster. He's just some regular ol' guy. And I won't let him near you."

The crashing noise that alerted Jackson to trouble in the bedroom only barely pulled Evie out of her sleep. She was dreaming of the park again, and of her mother sitting naked on a bench and cooing like a pigeon at passersby. Her head was swimmy and clouded when the sound of a full-grown man tumbling through the window finally roused her the rest of the way.

She blinked into the dark, certain she saw a shifting shadow but also not positive she had yet woken up. Her mouth dropped open; she could have sworn she was calling out for Jackson but there was nothing but a faint heaving, the sound of a stranger's labored breath.

The bedroom door swung open; the lights flicked on. Jackson stood with his gun steadied and aimed, his finger under the trigger but ready to move. In the corner was a man looking very much out of his depths.

It had already started to get cold in New York that time of year, but he only wore a thin t-shirt and torn jeans. His arms were ropey and veiny, his eyes more sad than wild, raving lunatic.

Not a monster at all.

Evie looked to Jackson. Was this the feeling he'd been talking about? Seeing the monster for the broken man he was? If so, his face didn't show it. And neither did his steady finger on the trigger.

As ineffectual as this man seemed, he had managed to do his damage, to find the object of his desire despite her attempts to hide from him. Evie's skin bristled at how close they truly were to each other, how close he'd come to succeeding.

Jackson spoke, a loud, intruding noise in the silent fear Evie had been nestled in. "So, you're the one causing all this trouble?" He kept the business end of the gun trained on the intruder. "Hands up. In the air. On your knees. Do what I say."

Evie pulled herself up against the headboard of the bed. She was still in the middle of them, close enough for the man to lunge and hurt her if he wanted to. Jackson wasn't moving from his stance, and all Evie wanted was for him to be in front of her. She wanted to be out of the way of the stalker, out of the line of fire, and currently, they both posed a threat.

"I'm doing it, man. I'm doing it." The intruder's voice was nothing like Evie had imagined. Weak and cracking, he sounded more like a puberty-ravaged child than a grown man, a full-blooded monster.

The man lowered himself down to his knees. His movements were awkward and shaky. Evie noticed the dark circles under his eyes, the skin so ravaged and paper thin she was astonished it managed to contain his blood.

Had her throat been working, she would have said something to Jackson about how strange it was that a man so skinny and frail looking had been able to hurl a brick through her window, two stories up, and hit her with enough force to warrant a night in the hospital. Since all she could think about was keeping herself and Jackson alive, none of these thoughts made it out of her mouth into the tense air that surrounded the three of them.

"Don't you fucking move from that spot, do you hear me? You move from that spot and I'll light you up."

The man sneered. "Fuck the police, man. Fuck the NYPD."

There was the monster she'd been waiting for.

"Keep running your mouth. I'm about to put your ass in a God damned cage."

Jackson reached to Evie, motioning for her to get out of the bed and stand behind him. Evie did so in a flash. A sudden chill passed through her as she realized she was in nothing but a t-shirt, and she tried not to notice that the man seemed to be enjoying the sight of her legs.

He's watching me.

"Eyes to the ceiling, pervert," Jackson ordered.

"You fucking pig," came the snarled reply but he did as he was told.

Evie wanted Jackson to continue bossing him around, humiliate and insult him. Instead, Jackson merely got behind him and handcuffed his wrists together.

"You have the right to remain silent. Anything you say or do may be held against you in a court of law."

The man snickered balefully and did the next part for Jack. "You have the right to an attorney. If you cannot afford an attorney, one will be provided for you."

"Don't be a smart ass, pal."

"That's not one of my rights, and I'm not your pal." He nearly spit the words through his thin, dirty lips.

Jackson yanked the man to his feet by the cuffs. The man groaned and grimaced as the metal cut into him.

"Evie," Jackson started, "go into the living room and stay there, alright? I'm going to bring this guy out to the officers in the squad car. Don't let anyone but me in. I don't care if they're wearing a uniform and waving a gun around, ordering you to open the door. Keep it locked."

"Yeah, you don't have to open the door to pigs," the man said, daring to let his eyes rest on her near-naked form before adjusting them back up to the ceiling.

Evie left the bedroom and tucked herself into a corner of the living room where the man wouldn't be able to see her when Jackson dragged him out the front door. She wasn't feeling any safer, no matter the fact that Jackson was marching the man down to the street and into the custody of the authorities.

He had gotten too close to her; he had found her in hiding and clambered up a fire escape to get to her. The heavy breaths of hyperventilation came on; Evie bent in half, unsuccessfully slowing her inhalations. Part of her allowed itself to be momentarily relieved but it didn't stem the tide of her panicked swallows of air. She trembled all over; suddenly she felt very cold. It was as if she had been holding the pieces of herself so tightly and precariously since this started and now her strength had failed her. Her fingers were slipping, and everything she had managed crashed at her feet. Without any warning, Evie burst into tears.

I've got to keep it together, she thought, wiping angrily at her cheeks. I can't be blubbering like this when Jackson's here.

Crying had never been a particularly powerful catharsis for her. In fact, she considered it cheap in regard to any sort of cleansing. She liked a catharsis to come from stamina and endurance, from the elation and exhaustion one feels when they push past their breaking point and find a new limit they didn't know they had. Crying was too simplistic; a baby could do it. A child not even knowing how or why could do it. Evie always needed things to be more challenging, even down to allowing herself to experience relief.

With a shudder, she thought of how her mother used to mock people who ate for comfort and sat with glazed eyes in front of TV sets. Evie's mother told her everyone had become too lazy and dumb to stare their issues in the face. Worse still, they didn't even have the stomach to find comfort in the dangerous tonic of drugs and alcohol.

"Pick zee Happy Meal and poof!" She would toss her hands in the air dramatically, fluttering them down to her sides as she spoke. "Zhey are happy."

"If it actually works then what's the difference?" Evie would argue, but she knew the difference. The same way she saw crying as too easy; the same way she had to drive her body to the brink before she could let herself relax. There were some things in life that demanded more from their user; things that couldn't be done as part-time habits.

People were talking loudly in the hallway, and Evie made out snippets of it. Someone was asking about the crashing noises; others were convinced the squad car currently on their block had been sitting there all night. Someone else told that person they were just being paranoid. The round robin of New York City apartment gossip started over again. Evie listened to the doors opening and closing, friends and people who had lived closed to each other for years discussing the life of someone they didn't know.

"Was it the French woman's apartment?" a voice asked. "I thought she had gone back to Paris for a while."

"Maybe she brought a house sitter in and the house sitter had a man over and the man got too rough and she had to call the cops," suggested another voice, rich with condemnation.

"Maybe it's her kid staying there. I'm pretty sure I've heard her mention that she has a daughter."

"Really? I didn't know she had a kid. I don't think I've ever seen anyone but men come in and out of here."

"She might not visit much. That woman's not exactly the easiest person to be around, if ya know what I mean."

"Doesn't matter. Family is family. Her daughter should make more of an effort."

There were a few more sentiments expressed and questions left unanswered. When it seemed like the scene was ending, the lingering coffee clutch in the hallway dispersed, leaving Evie frighteningly desperate for more noise. She didn't love hearing absolute strangers speculating on whether or not she was a good daughter but found comfort in hearing it, in knowing that there were people right outside the door should she scream bloody murder.

She wasn't sure how long Jack stayed downstairs with the handcuffed man. It seemed like it was taking him forever, but Evie didn't have the best sense of time at the moment. She was still tired even though her anxious heart was pounding loudly in her ears. All she wanted was to go back to sleep but she didn't dare close her eyes until Jackson was back with her, and she knew she wasn't alone. She turned on the TV and switched briskly through the channels. There wasn't anything in particular she was looking for but she landed on an old black and white movie, and released a shaky, reluctantly relieved breath.

She picked up the phone to let Rachel know the ordeal was over.

"It's all over now," she told herself, practicing, but her self didn't believe her.

Chapter Twenty-Three

Around the time Evie hit puberty but still a little before she got her first period, she was accosted by a man. She'd just crossed through the park on her way to anywhere that wasn't in range of her mother's infinite foul moods. It wasn't the middle of the night; she wasn't off in an isolated place where it was easier for men with eyes like predators to lurk and spot their game. A pool of sunlight had splayed itself across the manicured path, and Evie had just stepped into it when she noticed him staring at her. In the bright glare of the sun, Evie thought to herself that she had nothing to be scared of.

He never made it close enough to grab her but his intent was clear. In one hand, he gripped what looked to Evie, even at her tender age, to be an unimpressive cock, beating it furiously as he limped toward her.

"Come here," he had said, attempting a comforting smile though Evie had already learned how hard it was for the seediest creatures of that city to genuinely smile. "Come here. I just want to talk. I won't hurt you."

Evie didn't exactly freeze in place, though she didn't make a break for it like she always assumed she would in that situation, either. Instead, she swiveled her head from side to side, positive there had to be someone else in the vicinity; a grownup who could at the very least shoo the man away. Maybe kick him in the balls a little. It was such a nice sunny day, and she was right in the heart of the park. How could it be possible that no one else was around?

"Come here," the man repeated, his hand working faster. "Don't make me chase you. Because I will."

Evie took one calculated step backward. The man was haggard; he looked to her young eyes as quite old. He clearly wasn't in good health, and one of his feet dragged behind him when he walked. She thought she could probably run faster than he could, especially if he didn't let go of his cock.

At first her plan was to turn on her pubescent heels and sprint in the opposite direction, then she reconsidered and decided to run directly at him, take him by surprise. There was no way, she had thought, that this creep would see that coming.

Before she could put her plan into action, a jogger materialized from around a bend, coming toward the torrid scene at a decent clip. When he saw the man looming over a child, sneering his sad excuse for a smile, he bolted right toward them, shouting wordless exclamations. The masturbator took off but not before pressing a hand to Evie's fast-budding chest as he stumbled past her.

"Ya alright, kid?" the jogger asked in a heavy New York accent. "Where ya live? Ya want me to call your ma to come pick you up or something?"

Evie watched the receding spot that had been her assailant as it morphed into the surroundings of the park. She nodded without saying anything, suddenly realizing that as she grew, she became more of a target. Children were told to be careful and wary of strangers; children who lived in a city even more so. Evie had never skipped through the streets of New York thinking she was completely safe from harm. This was the first time she had been specifically spotted, the first time it had something to do with what formed on her body and her basic internal biology.

The jogger walked alongside her until Evie remembered she hadn't been heading for home, that in actuality she had been heading anywhere else. She laughed a nervous, lilting little kid laugh and smiled weakly at the jogger.

"I forgot that I was going to the movies," she lied. There was a tremor in her voice, and she was worried he'd be mad at her.

"Well, maybe ya feel like heading home now. It's alright if ya feel freaked out or whateva."

She liked how his accent sounded. For some reason, his coarse handling of words put Evie at ease. She agreed with him, and asked if he wouldn't mind walking her home.

At her mother's apartment, the jogger explained what happened in the hushed voice of an adult discussing the adult world. Evie's mother's face was tight, loosening only when the jogger mentioned that he got there before the man could do his worst. He hadn't seen the fingers close around her breast, though Evie entertained the possibility that he had but thought that didn't do any damage... considering.

Her mother thanked the man in her stiff, dry way before closing the door in the middle of him telling Evie that he hoped she was alright. Naturally, her mother was as suspicious of the jogger as she was of the leering predator who lumbered through the park, cock in hand.

"I don't trust someone being zhat helpful," she said, deadbolting the door. The perfect punctuation to almost anything she would proclaim.

"He was totally nice, ma," Evie replied, copying the jogger's over-the-top New York accent. She was delighted and startled that her mother laughed at that.

"Et's not normal for a man to care zhat much."

She crossed the room and tugged Evie toward her as she sat on the couch. The motion was more maternal than Evie was used to; somewhere inside of her, she wondered if she was in trouble.

"I didn't do anything with that man in the park," Evie swore, her big eyes getting wider. "Honest to God."

Her mother's face softened. She clasped Evie's hands in hers. "Oh, my girl. I know that."

In the depths of Evie's memories, this was the only one she could dredge up where her mother loved her. She didn't do it in the warm motherly way of petting Evie's hair and dropping hollow promises of protecting her until the end of time.

The more Evie thought about it, the more she resented the idea of being comforted like that, and it spoke to the respect her mother must have had for her that she didn't treat her like a child. Plenty of times growing up, Evie would have sold her soul for a mother more caring, more normal. Right then and there, she was thrilled she lived with an adult who felt an obligation to level with her.

"Zhat man in zee park was a sick freeeek," she told her, dragging the word out with a world-weary rattle in her throat, born from a lifetime in a female body. "You? You did nozhing wrong. Zee rest of your life you will hear people say zings, lettle zings, that might make you zhink et es your fault. Zhey are wrong. Zhey are why zee world is a sad place."

Evie gaped in wonder at this peeled back, raw layer of the woman she had so recently been escaping. They would never be close, never the smiling portrait of mother and spitting-image daughter that Evie had seen among Rachel and her family. But for that long, stilted pause where they sat as equals, and her mother impressed upon her adamantly that she was never to blame for the action of men, Evie felt a love for her that she hadn't experienced before.

"He had his thing out of his pants," Evie said, her little chest heaving with the onslaught of confessional tears. "He grabbed my breast when that jogger chased him off."

Her mother still didn't hug her or hold her close. She nodded as Evie divulged each upsetting detail then touched her daughter's face, and said, "Zank God zat man was zhere."

The implication in the statement brought the temperature of the room down. Evie didn't want to think about what was impossible. Once the notion of what could have happened was introduced, it took up space in Evie's brain forever. No amount of Zen contemplation, obsessive control issues, or any other type of mental sage could banish the thought. What could have happened that bright sunny day would trail behind her, a rabid snarling puppy demanding to be taken wherever she was going.

There was never a heart-to-heart where Evie's mother poured out her own traumas and experiences, comparing her scars solidified by time to her daughter's, fresh and new and only about to get worse. This conversation where she told Evie nothing was her fault and her salvation had been a lucky turn of events was it, but it was satisfactory.

Evie had already been reluctant to become a woman, and this had not helped the matter. She felt like she was perfectly complete being a little girl. She didn't have the desire to fill out sweaters like Rachel did and daydream about dating the barrel-chested and stubble-faced creatures that were only ever fleetingly in her domain.

"It's going to be fun," Rachel had promised her over and over again as they graduated from training bras to the real thing. "Let's dress all sexy and hit the town."

Rachel adored being beautiful, curvy, leggy. Her hair was a mane from the time she was a child so in her teen years, it was quite the glory to behold. She was always on the prowl for the perfect shoes, the best outfit to highlight each and every asset she possessed, and there were many.

When Evie would arrive in Westchester for a long weekend, Rachel would take her shopping. Evie was rarely interested in getting more than t-shirts and jeans. Her most adventurous purchase was a pair of leather ankle boots with a thick heel. She didn't have much in the way of an hourglass figure, and while she admired Rachel's, as an artistically inclined person is apt to notice anything aesthetically appealing, she never coveted it the way others did. Being busty and sexy and alluring was pretty low on her overall list of goals.

She'd seen for herself how dangerous that could be.

Somewhere in her, that fear she felt when her mother tugged her toward the couch had never dissolved, even when she knew she wasn't in trouble. It was the fear held by women through centuries that for as long as they were alive, danger was close by.

Trouble wouldn't have to come from a disciplinarian, an authority figure with the neutered power of scolding and punishing, but from a person who saw her as an object, a trinket to be collected. She had dressed like a tomboy her whole life, kept herself plain to avoid extra attention. It hadn't worked. Nothing had worked. Her mother's world-weary rattle replayed in Evie's mind as she sat in the empty apartment and waited for Jackson to return. "Zhey are why," she heard on loop in her head, "zee world is a sad place."

Street level that night was a very different beast than the closed-in room of quiet desperation where Evie currently resided. Jackson, discreetly jubilant, led the man who had broken in down the square spiral of stairs that terminated in the dark wood paneled lobby. The whole building reminded him of those classic New York movies from the seventies where even the slums had a cool look to them. One entire wall of the lobby was mirrored, and Jackson caught a glimpse of the pair they were. In the yellowed surface, reflective now due only to its most basic functional nature, Jackson saw pride on his face. Pride was so long lost to him that he stared too long as if he didn't recognize the person looking back.

By contrast, the man he was marching out into the crisp autumnal night wore a dead-eyed expression of complete regret.

Jackson didn't realize how much he had been sweating until the wind hit him in the face. Swinging the heavy wood and glass door brought a gust in like he had opened a portal into the vacuum of space. The man in his charge shivered, his own body covered in a sickly sheen of moisture. To Jackson, it appeared he was starting to go through withdrawals.

"Damn, pig," the man complained as they headed toward the squad car about ten feet away. "Can't you give me a jacket or something? I'm freezing."

"It'll be nice and toasty in the cruiser. Maybe even more so downtown."

Jackson rapped on the hood of the cop car. It startled the officer inside, and Jackson was distressed to see that he hadn't been paying attention. In fact, it looked to Jackson like he had been asleep when they approached, though his jerky awakening felt too theatrical to be real. He ignored it for the time being, delightfully wallowing in his newly remembered pride.

"This the guy?" the officer asked as he rolled down his window. He visually scanned the man. "Looks kinda pathetic to me."

Even Jackson thought this comment unnecessary.

The man muttered something under his breath about pigs. If the officer in the squad car heard him, he didn't react to it.

"You wanna take him down?" Jackson asked, opening the back door of the cruiser. "I'll stay here with Evie."

"I'll radio for another car to swing by and take the both of you down. I'm almost done with my shift; might as well camp out here for the rest of it."

Jackson huffed.

If the officer was intent on sitting there and keeping an eye on Evie, he might try with his eyes actually open. Cops could be touchy on feedback, so he didn't want to make a federal case out of it, but the fact that this jabroni had dozed off while a ropey-armed stalker clambered up a fire escape and attacked Evie in bed didn't inspire confidence.

"Ya gonna stay awake for it?" Jackson asked, his cadence as joking as possible. "It looked like you were dead to the world when I got down here."

"I was resting my eyes for a second. Besides..." he visually scanned the man again, allowing a grotesque mask of disdain contort his features, "you got the fucker."

Jackson tried to hold his tongue but too much adrenaline still coursed through his veins. "Yeah, up in her apartment," he snarled.

The officer made a noncommittal shrug and radioed for another cruiser to swing by.

While he did, Jackson held the shivering man by the wrists. Now he was noticing what Evie had seen when he'd been busy subduing this guy; the battered clothing, the thin t-shirt, the skinny arms that were too weak to resist Jackson's hold at all. Years on the force, not to mention just living in the city, had taught him that there was no standard look to a criminal or a sicko or a rapist. Still, he was struck by the thought that this man seemed unlikely to be Evie's demented secret admirer.

"Where do you know Evie from?" he asked. He watched the muscles under the man's skin jump, sharp and involuntary quickness. "Ya live near her or something?"

"I dunno, pal. I just...saw her around."

"Just saw a cute girl and decided to start following her and breaking into her apartment to leave gifts?"

The man's face clenched in confusion then erupted in a violent cough, shaking his whole frail body with each hack. "Yeah, whatever."

From the half-closed window of the cruiser, the other officer chortled. When Jackson made eye contact with him, he shrugged as if he didn't understand his own reaction.

"I'm not sure I know what's funny about that." Jackson glared at the officer. *What was this guy's deal?*

The officer shook his head slowly. "Nothing, nothing. It's just amazing how easy it is for one of these pervs to get weird ideas, ya know?"

The backup squad car turned the corner and slowed to a crawl as it approached the motley crew in front of the building. There was only one cop, and he leaned across the console to talk to Jackson out the passenger side window.

"You're Jackson, right?"

"That's me. Badge is in my pocket if you need to see it."

"Nah, I know Jimbo over there in the look-out vehicle so if he says you're alright then you're good."

What a trusting group of folks, Jackson thought, the sarcasm dripping from every word. A growing tightness in his chest had him concerned; something felt wrong but he couldn't put his finger on it.

Jimbo, as he was called, got out of his car to stand around and oversee Jackson loading the man into the back seat of the cruiser.

He was watching everything with a performative intensity, acting like he had been ready to spring into action at the first sign of danger. Jackson convinced himself that the tension was from a personal dislike of a lazy cop who hadn't taken his job seriously enough and was now posturing once he had an audience.

"I gotta go back up and tell Evie I'm bringing this guy downtown," Jackson told the recently arrived cop. "Just give me a second, ok?"

"Yeah, yeah but don't take too long. My shift's wrapping up soon."

Jackson bolted up the stairs, taking two at a time as he got closer to the top. He knocked gently on the door, hoping it wouldn't startle her. "Evie? It's me."

"Me being Jackson, right?"

"Yeah, it's me."

The door cracked open, and one of Evie's eyes stared unblinking out through the seam. Harsh light from the hallway lit fire in the dark emerald of that iris, a singular point emerging from the blackness of the apartment. When it landed on his face, this disembodied fraction of the woman with whom he was falling in love swung the door the rest of the way open. Her expression wasn't exactly calm relief, but Jack saw for the first time since this all started that she felt safe; that she could be protected.

"Are they taking the guy...wherever cops take people they're arresting?" Evie managed a faint laugh. "Police officers don't actually say 'downtown' or anything like that, I'm sure."

"We most certainly do, and we most certainly are."

"We? Meaning you're going with them?"

Jackson nodded, and the expression of vague nausea returned to Evie's features. He had grown accustomed to it in some ways; it seemed more her true face than the one that *didn't* listen for lurkers in the dark corners in the middle of the night. The bend in her lip gave away that she wanted to say something, that she wanted to ask him to stay with her.

Jackson knew he would have if she needed it; if she truly felt like she couldn't be alone or with the other officer without her skin crawling and the walls closing in on her.

But she wasn't going to. In her typical Evie way, she accepted that he was going. Jackson could see the Mobius strip of affirmations running through her ever-active brain; they caught the man, there's another officer here, I am safe, I am not in any danger.

He knew full well that almost everyone living in a city had their own version of this; it was simply how people got through the day when crammed shoulder to shoulder with strangers they implicitly agreed to live with. His own version shifted throughout the years the longer he stayed on the force.

Evie stepped over the threshold of the apartment, her tired and drawn beauty viciously blasted with the flat lights from the hallway. She flinched once she was all the way out, dragged from the womb-like warmth and obscurity. There were goosebumps along her arms when she put them around Jackson's neck and kissed him.

"I'll be back as soon as I can get outta there," Jackson told her, the tips of his fingers reading the Braille on her skin. "You'll never even know I was gone."

"Well, that's a total lie but I appreciate it."

They unlocked from each other's grasp, and Jackson started back down the stairs. He listened for the sound of Evie closing the door then the firm, satisfying 'clunk' of the deadbolt slipping into place. The footfalls from his shoes reverberated without origin or direction as he got closer to the lobby, the only noise in the entire building.

The quiet lulled him into a false sense of security, and believing he was alone the way no one living in a city ever is, he hopped a few steps at a time, spinning in a slick circle when he hit the wide landing at the corner of the stairwell. Adrenaline still pumped, the nagging sensation he had outside that something wasn't quite right faded. Jackson let himself be happy and proud for one quick dance move on the echoey, empty stairs.

He hadn't seen the old woman hanging onto the banister and leaning over from the story just above his head. When he spotted her, he froze then laughed and lifted his hand in a stiff, formal wave.

"Sorry if we woke you up, ma'am," he said as he tried to pretend he wasn't letting the rushing chemicals in his brain get the better of him. "I'm with the NYPD. Everything's alright."

"What happened?" the old woman asked. She looked up through the winding boxes of steps as if there was still action to be seen.

"Just a routine B and E. Breaking and entering."

The woman brought her eyes down to him then started shuffling back to her apartment. Jackson was about to bolt down the rest of the stairs when he heard her tinny, gray voice call out to him.

"Officer?"

"Yes, ma'am?"

"Are you going to be staying around the building? What if there are more robbers that try to break in?"

"One of the squad cars out front is going to be here 'til I get back. I don't know if you can see them from your apartment, but they're out there."

"Yes, I can. I've been watching that one all night." She coughed, shaking her head rapidly like that would clear her throat. "I'd rather you were staying."

"I'll be back shortly. You're in good hands with the officer in the squad car."

The woman shook her head again, and Jackson realized she was disagreeing with him as silently and politely as an old New Yorker could. "I don't like him," she said as she creaked back to the door of her home. "Every time I looked outside, he was asleep."

Chapter Twenty-Four

The ride to the station was deathly quiet. Jackson asked the man a question or two but got little more than grunts in response.

The officer driving them glanced at their passenger in the rearview mirror. He narrowed his eyes before bringing them down to the road. "I dunno, Jack. This guy looks so familiar. I feel like me and Gifford dealt with him before, but I can't place it."

"Who's Gifford?" Jackson asked.

"The officer that stayed back there. Jimbo. I guess you never really worked with him, right? He had been on leave for something, and I think he started when you were, ya know, taking time off."

"How is he? Like, as a cop?"

The other officer shrugged. His face remained neutral. "He's fine. Nothing special but dependable. Why?"

"When I came down tonight, he was asleep. A woman who lives in the building said she could see him from her apartment, and he was asleep every time she looked out. Plus, I don't like the way he was dealing with the perp."

"The perp? The guy who's been terrorizing your little girlfriend? Ya feel bad for that piece of shit?" He made eye contact in the rearview mirror with the sad, shriveled looking man in the back seat. "Don't feel bad for any of them, Jack."

"I thought the way he acted was unprofessional. That's all."

They didn't speak the rest of the way to the station.

Jackson was more than happy to have a few moments to collect his thoughts. A misty rain had started a little after they left the apartment, and the black roads with their bright yellow garters were glistening, spitting up droplets as the tires sailed along them.

New York City was at its most beautiful on a rainy night. At least that's what Jackson always thought. Even if it wasn't so late that the noisemakers were chased off the streets, the city would clear out. A few brave souls might be seen sprinting between droplets, a vain attempt to get them to their destination without being completely soaked. The rain never lost that game, as Jackson knew all too well.

His first year or so as a cop, Jack worked nights. It was the shift given to the new guys and the rookies, pairing them up with an older officer looking forward to finally having a schedule that didn't demand he become nocturnal. Unlike the rest of them, Jackson liked working nights.

A city like New York with its tumultuous energy presented different faces of itself, and the longer Jack worked nights, the more of them he got to see. Caliginous streets, sidewalks, and alleyways allowed for both the strange and the sweet, in equal measure, to reveal itself. He helped a prostitute whose friend, a fellow sex worker, had been attacked by a man she refused to service. The one calling for help told Jackson she wasn't going to leave her friend behind, spitting that she'd never leave her in the hands of a cop.

"You either help her right here or move along," she said, unsuccessfully fighting the tears bubbling in her eyes. "I won't let you take her in."

Jackson assured the woman that nothing was going to happen to her friend. He gave them a ride to the emergency room and some money, hoping that would be worth it to them to take the night off. When he dropped them off and watched them walk inside, the wounded one leaning hard into her friend, he marveled at how much danger they were constantly surrounded by, and how fearlessly they protected each other. Neither of them looked back, eyes filled with overwhelming gratitude. They hardly even said thank you to him. The best he got was the unhurt one telling him he wasn't too bad for a cop.

"Ya could've made this night worse," she said after she helped her friend out of the cop car. "Most pigs would've loved to run us in."

It amazed him that in a stretch of hours where one of them had been beaten, there was still space for their night to get worse. He never mentioned the encounter to anyone, although once he became close with Wheeler, he knew she'd understand.

He had never seen the coldness so many people associated with this city. Even on those shifts where he thought the downfall of civilized society was imminent, and if he had any brains in his head, he would run from his job and his home as fast as he could and hide out in the woods. No matter how angry and disillusioned he felt about everything around him, he always saw a surprising amount of tenderness in that concrete jungle. People, ordinary and everyday people, were not just looking out for themselves; they saw each other, they helped each other.

One night when he was starting his shift, a shivering young man came in to make a police report about a mugging. It was the type of night Jackson loved; rainy and cold. Keeping everyone but the most discarded inside and off the streets. The young man was soaked from being outside, and when he sat in the hard plastic chair in front of Jackson's desk, puddles collected around the soles of his shoes.

"He didn't get everything," the young man said. "Just my watch."

"He didn't want your wallet?"

"Yeah, I mean, of course he did but before I could get it out, this little old lady came by and cracked him on the head with her umbrella. Or maybe her cane. I couldn't see that well." He wiped at the blood oozing into his left eye.

Jackson cocked his head to the side, unsure of what to say. The young man's teeth were chattering; his lips were starting to turn blue.

"A little old lady fended off your mugger?" He didn't mean for it to sound condescending and hoped the young man wouldn't take it as such.

The guy, no more than twenty, was too caught up in admiring his savior to be offended. "She hit him once really hard, and when he turned around, she maced him." The young man mimed the action. "She didn't speak English too good so she just waved the can in my face when the guy ran off screaming. Said something like, 'he blind. Go home.'"

Jackson wanted to laugh but managed to hold it together until the young man was done with his report and a ride to a safe location had been arranged for him. He gave Jackson a brief description of the old woman alongside that of the mugger, asking if there was any way to find her.

"I doubt it," Jackson told him. "We can't really send officers out looking for someone who didn't do anything wrong."

"I just want to tell her thank you," the young man explained.

"I'm sure she knows."

"But after she got the guy off me, I was still in shock. I didn't say anything to her at all, and then I let her walk home alone with God only knows who else on the street."

I think she's got a pretty good handle on that, Jackson thought but once again, he assured the young man that the woman knew how he felt, and that she was probably just happy he was safe.

Obviously, they never found the little old woman to pass along his thanks. Like so many other descriptions, Jackson read the one given to him and knew it fit most of the little old women in New York City. Sometimes, they'd pass a hunched and hurriedly walking senior citizen, and Jackson would briefly look at her face, wondering if that was the young man's savior. He told the young man before he left the station that the best thing he could do, since he probably wasn't going to find the old lady, was to pay it forward.

"Think about what she did for you, and do good for someone else," he said as the young man pulled a dry NYPD t-shirt over his head. "We all gotta look out for each other in this city."

As the young man was leaving, Jackson couldn't help but think about the running thread of affirmations this kid was going to have to hold in his head in order to walk down the street now. How many times would he continue to tell himself that he was alright, that he was safe? Several months later when the young man came in to follow up on the report, Jackson was taken aback by how well he looked.

"Ya know, it's the damnedest thing," the kid said in a good-natured accent that didn't sound like any of them Jackson knew from the Five Burroughs, "I was freaked out more than I ever had been in my life for, like, a week. Then one night I was sitting in my apartment, and all I wanted was a can of pop—"

Pop, Jackson thought to himself. *Midwest*. Somewhere corn fed and painfully wholesome. Iowa maybe. Or Kansas.

"... and I could see that the little general store at the corner was still open. At first I said to myself, 'Well, don't even think about it. It's nighttime. What if something happens?'" The young man put a finger in the air in the pantomime of an epiphany. "And now I just thought, "But something happened when I got mugged and someone rescued me. Someone for no reason whatsoever risked her life to help me."

"So next time you'll get the pop," Jackson finished.

"I'll get the pop." The young man smiled and crossed his arms over his chest. "People told me that no one in New York cares about anyone else but that's just not true, is it? You don't think it's true. I can tell."

He was right about that. Jackson had never thought that to be the case. All the stories he had heard about strangers stepping in when there was an emergency told him the citizens of that cold, heartless city were softer than they wanted the general public to know. 'New Yorkers,' Jack would say to anyone who would listen, 'want to be as heartless and cold as their reputation, but could never get there.'

The story intrigued Jackson and stuck with him to this day. It wasn't the fact that a healthy young man had been saved by a little old woman that tickled him; he wasn't laughing at someone who found himself at the ambushed mercy of a mugger. He was laughing that such a story even existed, that a woman who had spent a lifetime walking those nighttime streets didn't avert her eyes when she saw danger. He was laughing at how often he heard that New York was dangerous and hate-filled and everyone who lived there ignored what was happening around them and yet, here was a police report that said the exact opposite. Here was a written document of proof that said people in New York could also see each other as neighbors; they would protect each other if they had to.

Maybe it was this frame of mind that kept Jackson skeptical as they drove down to the station with the quiet, angry man in the backseat. At one point, Jackson glanced behind him to see the furrowed brow locked tight above sad eyes, and he didn't feel the anger he imagined he would once they caught the guy who had been terrorizing Evie.

He felt pity; he felt pain.

A clenching in his chest pushed down into his spine.

Evie, like almost every child in the world, was quick to blame things on her mother.

She kept the lights off in the apartment but started pawing through the canvases lining the hallway and the walls of the bedroom. When she got to one that looked interesting, she brought it into a shaft of light extended from the streetlamps outside the window. In their iconic yellow glow, Evie softened toward the woman who had raised her.

There was so much pain in her mother's work, so much fear and angst. Where Evie looked at a city filled with crime and homelessness, noise and chaos, and produced works of love and awe, her mother created darkness, rotted faces pitted by life and time.

One that looked partially done, although Evie could get the idea from what was there, reminded Evie of someone she knew. She pulled the canvas toward the light and propped it up in place so she could study it from a few steps back.

It was a child's face, pretty but plain. Beautiful the way most children are beautiful with their inherent innocence and glow. Evie recognized the flowered camisole the girl was wearing though it was splattered in blood from a gaping hole in her face where her other eye should have been. The one remaining eye was wide and bright, a stunning green color Evie knew well. She felt her legs go rubbery under her, and she sat down on the hardwood floor before she toppled over.

It was her.

No doubt in her mind. Her as a child, her maybe a year or two after they came to New York. Drawn from a photograph, Evie figured although she would have been terribly impressed if her mother was able to recall such fine detail from her memory. Not of my face, Evie thought as she scooted closer without standing up. Maybe of her own but never of mine.

The picture scared her, but she couldn't stop staring at it. Knowing her mother as she did, it was entirely possible the painting had been started years earlier, and she was either trying to finish it now or had pulled it out with the hopes of making it part of some show. Evie's mother had found success of her own, but her work was never lauded the way Evie's was. Her wry European manner helped the few sales she made, people loved hearing her accent and asking her questions about how much better France was than the United States, but only those who collected strange, macabre pieces were interested in hers.

"Zee Americans are as bad as zee British," Evie's mother told her one night, wine drunk after a gallery opening where a patron had told the show's curator that the paintings with the deformed faces were 'appalling,' and that he was tasteless for displaying them. "Zhey want zheir art to be simple and happy. No challenge, no questions."

But Evie had never seen this one before, and she wondered if her mother had stared the patron in the face and explained that this was a portrait of her daughter less than two years after they arrived in New York from Paris, then maybe there wouldn't have been a big ugly confrontation at the opening. Maybe people would have whispered about this highly unusual and tortured artist who painted the mangled face of the person she loved, or was supposed to love, the most in the world to show what life had dragged them through. What it was going to drag them through. Some of the faces were men but, Evie noticed as she rifled through the canvases, most of them were women. All she could remember from the few art openings she was allowed to attend were women too. Evie's sad, hurt mother painting sad, hurt women, and being told the very sight of them was appalling.

Naturally, Evie couldn't let her off the hook that easily. She knew enough about her own conception and birth to understand the cynicism that seemed to be constantly churning inside of her mother, but that didn't excuse the rest of it. It didn't excuse how she treated her, how tumultuous and frenetic Evie's childhood had been.

"If you didn't want to have me then you shouldn't have had me," Evie shouted at her mother during one of their teen years arguments. "Nobody asked you to give birth to me."

"Ah, listen to zhat. You are already American; not an original thought in zhat head."

"What are you talking about?"

"Zee French writers in the fifties were railing against zee injustice of having to be born, and teenagers have been spewing zhat tripe for God only knows."

Evie grew up assuming she had been unwanted, and that if her mother was given a chance, not to mention the benefit of hindsight, she would have never gone through with the pregnancy, and Evie wouldn't have ever existed. Studying that canvas, studying her own childhood face with its torn and empty eye socket, she knew she was in fact wanted.

Her mother felt pain and remorse and so many millions of emotions she couldn't properly articulate or understand, but this painting told Evie of the fear that existed within mothers since the dawn of time, and how helpless they all felt to watch their children step out into the world, knowing that protection and safety was a myth they told themselves as often as they told their kids.

Her mother was someone who claimed that she needed the suffering to create, and the older Evie got, the more she saw it as a defense mechanism. The suffering wasn't going anyway so what else could be done but to pretend it served a purpose? But maybe it was truer than Evie realized. Maybe, she wondered as she sat surrounded by the painted demons that once resided in her mother's head, her muse is suffering.

Evie's muse was the city, and the energy it fed her. Suffering seemed too easy, dare she say boring. The longer she worked on her Adonis and the more she watched it resemble Jackson, the more she wondered if maybe her muse was slipping.

Even then when she should have been thinking about how close she came to being at the mercy of some whacko who decided he loved her and vice versa, Evie was daydreaming about Jackson. She had the image in her head of him under her in her bed, his arms resting on the pillow under his head. It had taken a lot for her to admit how sexy she found him, and even more to admit how badly she wanted him. Right after they kissed for the first time, her brain cackled about what Rachel would think; how weird this all was, how he had barely known she'd existed before now.

Fortunately, she had been able to ignore the annoying voice that told her to stop, and from that day onward, her Adonis started to take a familiar shape.

There were few things Evie wished for the way she wished for her and her mother to be close. She wanted to discuss muses with a fellow artist; she wanted to ask questions about what art she had been drawn to as a child. Her mother was never interested in conversation topics beyond how ridiculous existence was and the amount she had to struggle just to get nowhere. By the time Evie was in college, those bad habits had rubbed off on her, and she loathed the classes in art school where she was forced to explain her work. People always seemed impressed with what she created; they always had more to say than she did.

Most of the time, she shrugged when someone presented a plausible theory about her process and meaning, and replied, 'If that's what you took from it, then sure.'

"I guess I wouldn't want to talk about it either, mom," she said into the hauntingly calm nighttime she refused to dispel from the apartment. "If this was what was inside my head, maybe I'd be inclined to keep it to myself too."

She stood up, and walked away from the canvas, leaving it propped where it was, off center in the living room. The one eye in the painting followed her even in the darkness. Evie bounced from one foot to the other as if trying to escape from its line of sight. The movement made her laugh, sudden and hysterical. It cut through the uncharacteristic city silence, and rattled hollow around the walls of the apartment. Evie was aware of being alone for the first time since Jackson left as her own panicked laugh returned to her in a dulled mimic.

An urge to smash everything her mother owned, starting with the portrait she had done of Evie and ending with anything else that held her image, curdled to thick, fetid chunks inside of her. She didn't know exactly what she was mad at right then, but if she was being honest, it didn't matter. She just needed to destroy something, and she liked the idea of it infuriating her mother angry. A fist through the canvas might prove a point she herself hadn't learned. Maybe line it up to take out that good green eye staring unblinkingly at her.

"After all, mom," Evie said, creeping closer to her own face, "the urge to destroy is indeed a creative urge."

She inspected the portrait for a weak spot to jab through then scoured her immediate vicinity for something sharp. If she didn't destroy this then maybe she could break a memento, one of the few trinkets her mother kept around the house. She could keep it simple and smash a bunch of glasses in the middle of the living room floor, leave the sparkling shards as a nasty surprise for when her mother returned, possibly well-praised but certainly full of malaise.

Whatever stayed Evie's hand from doing damage, she would be grateful for it later. Maybe it was guilt, or maybe the deafening ring of her mother's old rotary phone. She let it ring and ring, reminding her of childhood days gone by. The little girl in that fucked up painting used to love pretending to talk on that thing, shoving her tiny fingers into the holes and dialing, the satisfying click click click of them turning back toward her.

At the moment, thought the fight in her chest had dissipated, she wished she had the nerve to go through with it. Instead of smashing and destroying everything in sight, she sighed and settled onto the couch.

She was tired more than anything else. Going back to sleep didn't appear to be an option, and whenever she closed her eyes and tried to drift off, she couldn't get very far. It didn't matter that she was safe and Jackson had escorted the puny monster away. She still didn't feel ready to close her eyes and relax when there was no one else in the dark apartment but her and the empty-eyed portrait of her face. She convinced herself she'd sleep when Jackson got back, assuming he'd be gone an hour or so. She didn't know how long 'booking a perp' should take, but she was positive he wouldn't leave her by herself for long.

He knew what it meant to be scared; he knew what it meant to be alone.

A knock at the door jarred Evie out of her strange, meandering spiral. She waited, ears perked, hoping it was Jackson, and they could rest easy, curled up on the couch like a normal couple. This nightmare finally behind them.

Chapter Twenty-Five

"So that's him, huh?" Wheeler leaned against the darkened side of the two-way mirror. The man Jack had arrested sat in the uncomfortably bright room, his skinny wrists shackled to the metal tabletop in front of him. "Doesn't seem like much does he?"

"It's funny you say that because I felt the same way." Jackson moved next to her.

The man was glancing fearfully at the mirror then away, telling both of them he knew exactly how this whole thing worked. He pulled against the cuffs that attached him to the table. Not in a hard way, not like he was trying to break free. It looked to Jackson like he was feeling the weight of them, and that he was used to it being there.

Wheeler moved her face toward Jackson, her lips pressed tightly together. "You seem like a cop with a hunch," she said. "Care to share with the rest of us?"

"The rest of us? Ya mean you?"

"Who else do ya need?"

Jackson exhaled hard through his nose. As of yet, he wasn't sure what was wrong with this picture but he felt it, and the more he thought about it, the more he wanted to get back into the cruiser and back to Evie. He was having trouble convincing himself that it was alright to leave her; that the cop who had been sleeping when he was supposed to be on duty wouldn't make such an egregious error again. Nothing he told himself settled his mind, and how with Wheeler casting even more doubt on it, he wasn't sure what to say.

"I guess what I need to do is interrogate him," Jackson said. He still hadn't met her gaze. He stared straight ahead at the man who couldn't see him behind the smoked glass.

"Well, yeah, that's usually the first thing we do. I guess you have been on leave for too long if you're having trouble with that."

"No, that's not it. I mean, I need to know where he saw Evie for the first time, and how he came to be obsessed with her. It just doesn't..."

"It feels off. I get it."

"He doesn't seem like a guy who's big into art shows, ya know?"

Wheeler laughed and nodded. They were both thinking the same thing, but it didn't make sense yet to say it out loud.

How is this the right guy?

The man in the brightly lit room seemed like a junkie who got picked up every other week and went through the system so often that judges knew him by name. He looked like he had been sleeping on someone's floor when he was lucky enough not to sleep on the street; like a daily shower was a luxury he was rarely afforded.

The tale of the city that the newcomers heard was that danger lurked everywhere and people you have never seen before would try to hurt you. The sad reality Jackson had come to realize was that real danger usually came from someone close to the victim, someone the victim could pick out of a crowd.

"I gotta talk to him," Jackson said, heading toward the door.

"Whoa Adams." Wheeler put out a hand to block him. "You're not active."

"C'mon, you know I'll play by the book. I just need to get some answers."

"Playing by the book would be not going near my suspect."

"I'm not going in as a cop..."

Wheeler shook her head. "Victims' boyfriends aren't on roll call either. Let us handle this."

Jackson liked the surge of heat that went through his body at being called Evie's boyfriend, a strange new sensation from the last time he'd heard it. But it was the word 'victim' that made him push past Wheeler. "I'm not her boyfriend, I'm her security detail."

Either that was all the justification Wheeler needed or her own gut feeling made the decision for her. She stepped aside.

Ignoring the sinking sensation in his stomach and repeating to himself that Evie was fine, safe, in good hands, Jackson entered the interrogation room. The junkie greeted him with a sneer that belied the expression of terror already observed through the two-way mirror.

Jackson sat across from the man, tapping a finger on the metal tabletop as he did. He could still feel the goosebumps from Evie's arms on the pads of each one; he had read them like he was a blind man learning about her fear.

"So you know how this works, right?" Jackson asked. "You answer my questions without any problem, and we can all get through this with as little pain as possible."

"Pain, huh? Just like a pig to threaten with that."

"I'm not threatening ya. I meant that in a, uh, metaphorical way."

The man had stopped making eye contact, and Jackson ducked his head down to catch him. He tapped the table again, sitting back up to his full height. The man reluctantly looked in his direction. Every feature on his face was smaller, drawn.

Jackson could see Evie just as he left to bring this guy in, and he was struck by the similarities. *Maybe 'victim' is the right word*, he thought, picking through his mind for what to say. Neither of them looks like they're the one doing something wrong.

"You're wasting your time, pig," the man said. "I'm not saying a word without my lawyer."

"C'mon, don't do that. I'm not asking ya anything ya need a lawyer for. Alright? I promise. Swear to God."

"You expect me to trust the word of a fucking cop?"

Jackson sighed and dropped back against the hard metal bars of the chair. "Yeah, I do but, right, why would you?"

The man made a vulgar noise deep in his throat.

"That's why I'm not a cop."

The man's bloodshot eyes flew open and he recoiled in his seat. "You look like one."

"I'm... on leave."

"What kind of shit is this?" The man banged on the table and yelled toward the two-way mirror, "Hey, get me out of here!"

"Chill, man." Jackson put a hand out to calm the man. "Since I'm not here in an official capacity, nothing you say right now can be used against you."

The man relaxed. "Really?"

"Really."

The man fell silent and looked Jackson up and down.

Jackson could sense his trust slipping so he said, "Look, I'm not askin' about anything that'll get ya in trouble, ok? I just wanna know a few real simple things about how you met Evie."

"You want me to tell you about Evie?"

"No, I want you to tell me where you know her from. I want you to tell me the first time you saw her, maybe the first time you spoke with her. Think you can do that for me?"

The man shrugged. He stared past Jackson at the two-way mirror behind him. "How many cops are back there?" he asked. "I'll bet they're just waiting for your signal then they'll come in here and beat me up. Tell the DA some bullshit like I was resisting arrest."

"Ya got a bad perspective of us, I think."

In response to that, the man grinned a sickening, jack-o-lantern smile. Several of his teeth were missing; the ones that remained in his head weren't holding up particularly well either.

"I've had some bad experiences with you, I think," the man mocked. "Worse than you can imagine."

Jackson kept his voice even-keeled. He didn't doubt it. There were plenty of assholes and attitudes given badges and power. Friends of his in the military saw it, and so did he. He thought it was highly likely that this guy found himself in the hands of someone who wasn't going to put up with his smartass answers and landed a few good ones before anyone else got to the scene.

"There are some bad apples, I'll give ya that," Jackson said, leaning on his elbows. "Now, look, back to Evie—"

"Bad apples?! Brother, you don't even know who you've got on your force. You don't even know the types of men you're working next to every day."

"Alright!" Jackson snapped. The man visibly startled. "We're getting off track here."

Plenty of guys had sat in the same spot as this one and had run their mouth with the same vitriol, if not more, and Jackson had always managed to keep his cool. It didn't do any good to get all worked up. Besides, that's what they wanted. They loved it. He had seen the smug, satisfied face of soon to be convicts as officers screamed at them to talk, threatened them with every power they had under the sun.

It was a rush to get a cop all riled up. Honor on the streets.

This man didn't look smug, though. He wasn't gloating or smirking. Instead, he seemed scared. He seemed unsure of the information Jackson wanted. Even the mention of Evie's name elicited no response, almost as if he wasn't positive about whom Jackson was speaking.

"I'm not saying a word without my lawyer," the man repeated though it lacked the conviction of his earlier declaration. "You get me some representation and then we'll see how I feel." He cleared his throat. "Got it, pig?"

The final piece of the sentence came out like a struggle. That sinking feeling in Jackson's stomach got worse.

"Just tell me where ya saw Evie for the first time. That's all I wanna know."

"Around." The man's eyes flicked to the mirror. "By her apartment."

"By her apartment, huh? That one by the East River Esplanade?"

"Yeah, there and some other places. I seen her going for walks, decided she was cute, and followed her home. What? Isn't that what creeps like me do every day?"

By now, Jackson's stomach was beyond sinking; it had fully sunk. He felt like he had swallowed lead, but he couldn't be impulsive. Deciding that a mistake had been made and this guy had nothing to do with it would take more than some missed details in a story told by someone who may or may not be in his right state of mind.

Jackson told himself that it was entirely possible the man had gotten a glimpse of Evie when she was on her way to visit her mother or even spotted her when he was messed up on drugs and couldn't remember where exactly he had seen her. Memories were faulty among the best and the brightest. Someone who seemed as haggard and tired as this guy did could be cobbling together what he thought he knew as opposed to what he actually knew.

None of this put Jackson at ease but he pushed forward, hoping to land a piece of information that tied up the mess instead of adding to it. The man was staring at him, those victim's eyes blinking wetly. Jackson wanted to believe he was the stalker and since he had been caught, their problems were over. Yet, every second they sat there, it became less likely.

"Creeps like you, huh?" Jackson said, shifting his weight around in his seat. He was trying not to look uncomfortable, but the sinking feeling made that particular goal impossible. "You're telling me you're just a creep who started following some pretty girl around?"

"That's why you arrested me."

"No, I arrested you because you broke into an apartment in the middle of the night. If I was a betting man, I'd say that you've got a rap sheet. One as long as my arm."

The man gave Jackson another look at his grotesque jack-o-lantern grin. "Five to one, double or nothing. Place your bets, place your bets."

"I'm right, huh?"

The man shrugged.

Neither of them needed to hear the confirmation. Just by looking at him, Jackson knew this guy was in the system. His guess, what would be his real and actual bet, was that it had little to do with stalking, assault, or any other kind of power-based crime, and more with straightforward infractions. Petty theft, maybe. Drugs most likely.

"Can I get a glass of water?" the man asked, tugging on his restraints with a bored sigh. "And my lawyer."

"Why don't we finish talking first?"

The man gave a long, exasperated moan, tilting his head back so his fragile, naked throat was exposed. A vicious scar ran from below his jawline on one side of his neck to the bottom of the tendon on the other. When the tendons flexed against the skin, the scar went from a pale pink to a luminesce opal.

"I got nothing more to say!" the man shouted, slamming his shackled hands down to the tabletop. "Get me my lawyer, get me a drink of water! Unchain me and put me in a cage like you're going to fucking do anyway."

"Should we get your rap sheet in here?" Jackson asked.

"I don't see the God damned point but do whatever you want, pig."

"The point," Jack placed both hands flush to the table, "is that I think you've been arrested a bunch of times, and I just get this feeling that most of those times were for stuff like drugs. Maybe a smash and grab situation. Nothing nearly as advanced as stalking."

"Time for me to level up in the world," the man replied. He stared vacantly up to the ceiling the same way Evie had in the hospital; counting holes in the tile and wondering how much longer this was going to take.

"Alright, I can see I'm boring you. So, let's wrap this up." Jackson tapped the tabletop, his forehead wrinkling as if he was deep in thought. "Can you answer me one last thing? One little question and we'll call it a night?"

The man sighed and rolled his eyes. "Yeah, sure. Whatever."

"Where'd ya get the money to buy all those gifts for her? I'm curious as to how someone who doesn't seem to be a particularly good criminal successfully stalked and broke into a stranger's apartment, but something tells me ya won't answer that question. So how about the other one, alright? Those were some nice gifts, and I didn't see any of those theft prevention tags or holes from them being ripped off. Ya get me?"

Now the man let his gaze drop and settle on Jackson's. This was an expression Jack had seen before, an expression not of guilt but of capture. The frightened face of a mouse backed into a corner.

"I probably stole them," he answered after a long pause. His voice was shaky; Jackson saw his hands trembling. "Dirtbag like me."

There had been a few times in his career where Jackson experienced that unmistakable phenomenon of time slowing down. Right then, hearing the unconvincing excuse accentuated by the unsteadiness that appeared to be languidly moving through the rest of the man's body, Jackson saw the sides of the room bend back. A silence caused by hearing the spaces in between the noise gave his mind the first true break from processing it needed.

Since Marcus's death, it had either been on high alert or churning through the memories of that day, ripping the fabric of them to shreds more and more each time. With everything slowed to a crawl, including Jackson's own reaction of slamming his fist on the metal tabletop, he could hear what the sinking in his stomach was trying to tell him.

As the anxiety that had been whispering since before he loaded this guy into the back of the squad car rose to the surface, Jackson retracted his fist and hunched over the table.

"You're not the stalker," he said lowly almost like he was speaking to himself. "It's not you. You're just someone's patsy."

"Fucking pig. I want my lawyer."

The man jerked his wrists toward him, but his facade of righteous underworld anger had been eviscerated by Jackson's realization. His eyes watered, and he touched a fluttering hand to his mouth.

Jackson was on his feet and out the door before time had a chance to catch up with him. He couldn't afford for it to lag and trickle; to give him space between sounds and the closing of his eyelids for thinking problems through. Everything had to pick up the pace at this point. He had a plan to move at the speed of light.

"Hey," the junkie called from behind him, sounding far off in the distance to his hyper-focused brain, "If that counted as immunity, I got some other shit to talk about!"

Wheeler was coming out of the observation room as Jack entered the hallway. She pointed over her shoulder before Jackson could speak. "Go. Get back to her. I'll take care of him."

Jackson didn't bother to thank her. Not only was there no time, but in a superstitious way, he believed it bad luck. He'd always be able to tell her later because he kept reminding himself that he would be around later. Like everyone else in that city, he had his own clicking projector of affirmations. No need to say thanks now, Jack. There's always later, and you've got later.

Chapter Twenty-Six

The first knock on the door was easy for Evie to ignore. If it had been Jack or Rachel, they would have announced themselves. She figured it was too soon for it to be Jack, but it could be Rachel.

It didn't feel like enough time had passed since the call, but Rachel could light a fire under herself when she needed to. And she didn't know how long she'd been meandering down morose memory lane.

Evie wished she had looked at the clock once she got off the phone with her friend so she'd have a better idea of when she'd get there. Rachel had said, "give me twenty minutes," and Evie knew from experience that in an emergency, twenty minutes to Rachel was closer to ten.

"I'm coming over right now," Rachel had said when Evie called her. "Why didn't you call me sooner?"

Evie demurred, muttering something about just being relieved that it was done and she could stop living in fear. "Just get here when you get here," Evie told her.

"Yeah, and I said twenty minutes."

"It's not an emergency at this point. You can take your time and get dressed. Whatever you need to do. Oh, hey, actually is there anywhere by you still making sandwiches? Is there a chance you could grab some of them?"

The sound of Rachel tapping her tongue against her teeth was the only response Evie got. When Rachel finally did talk, it was clipped and pointed. "You're trying too hard to act casual."

"No, I'm not. You and Jackson have been great through all this, and I just know that sometimes people get locked into panic mode, but you don't have to be anymore. That's it, I swear."

"I'll still be over in twenty minutes."

Evie said bye and hung up the phone. Being casual was the wrong thing to do if she didn't want Rachel to freak out. If she had called in tears, Rachel's concern would have been tempered a bit but her attempt to sound like she felt safe and the danger was gone and all they were waiting for was Jackson to come back from the station only fanned the flames. Evie wasn't really good at asking for help or confiding her anxiety in people. At that point, she and Rachel were used to each other; many things could be figured out wordlessly.

As kids, there were a lot of aspects of Rachel's personality that drew Evie to her but the one she could never get her head around was Rachel's ability to be open with people. She didn't have the same iron layer over her emotions that Evie did; she didn't think of showing emotions and asking for help as a weakness. During a fight when they were in middle school, Evie told her she cried too much, and Rachel barked back, "because I'm human, Evie!"

Sitting on the couch, ignoring the first knock, Evie had already decided the conversation where she explained finding a warped childhood portrait of herself done by her mother was better suited for another day. Besides, she wasn't even sure what she wanted to say about it yet. She was sort of flattered; she was sort of touched. It was horrific and beautiful, and she couldn't believe her mother put her limited energy into a painting of the daughter she didn't care for much.

By then, she knew in her heart it wasn't Jackson or Rachel at the door; the odds of them knocking and not saying anything seemed low. The second knock came, and Evie moved off the couch, hoping to get a glimpse of who it was through the peephole.

She avoided getting close enough to cause a shift in light and shadows so whoever was outside would know someone was by the door. She had seen it in a movie one time then started paying attention to it in everyday life. It amazed her that she could tell when someone was looking out at her. Most of what she saw in the movies seemed like bullshit but that one worked.

With her head arched back, she was able to see a small, blurry image of a person. The image was overwhelming blue, and it took her a moment to figure it was a police officer in uniform. Jackson had been in plain clothes when he left, and she doubted he had gotten changed just to have some triumphant return to her.

Evie stepped backward to move stealthily away from the door. She toppled a bit and knocked into the wall, cringing as the noise bled through into the hallway.

A man cleared his throat; another assertive knock landed. "Ms. Hansen? Are you in there? It's officer Gifford."

Evie didn't know any officer Gifford. She kept quiet for what felt like a solid minute before he knocked again, repeating his introduction.

"Ok, you're officer Gifford," Evie finally answered, not opening the door. "What do you want?"

"Well, Jack radioed from the station and said he was going to be a bit longer than he thought so he asked me to come up and check on you."

"I'm okay. Thank you."

"Haha, yeah, I'm not sure that's what he had in mind, miss."

"Jackson knows me well. I'm sure if you went back down there and radioed him that I told you I was alright but didn't open the door, he'd be fine with it."

"Sure thing, miss. I'll do that. You sound tired. Sorry to bother you."

Through the peephole, she watched the mostly blue image turn away from the door and sharply turn back. Her breath caught in her throat. All she wanted was for him to leave. She had no rationale for why she was suddenly so scared, and she tried to tell herself that everything was fine, that she was safe, that Rachel was on her way. Another knock nearly caused her to jump out of her skin.

"What is it?!" she asked, a harsh and biting cadence turning each word into knives.

"Look, I'm so sorry to have to ask this but, truth is, I really need to use the little boy's room. I get that you're freaked out and everything, but I wouldn't ask if it wasn't an emergency."

Evie scoffed. *The fucking audacity*, she thought. "Just piss in the street or behind a car like everyone else in this city."

"It's a number two, miss."

Evie pressed her fingers into the temples on both sides of her head. When she applied too much pressure to the injured side, she flinched and dropped her arms to her sides. The absolute last thing she wanted to do was let a man into the apartment while she was alone, and certainly not to stink up the place.

Jackson's voice repeated in her mind, telling her not to let anyone but him inside.

"Look, I'm sorry to hear that but I'm not going to open the door just because you have to take a shit," Evie told him, one hand on the non-stitched side of her head. "I'm sure it sucks to crap in the gutter but homeless people do it every day, and they're fine. Ya know, relatively."

"Sure, yeah, sure. I get it. Safety first." Officer Gifford was quiet for a moment before continuing on. "That's a really scary thing to happen to you. I know it is. Something similar happened with my sister a few years back. She spent so much of her life living in fear afterwards. It was like she was never able to move past it and trust anyone again."

"Yeah, I can see how that would happen."

"Well, hey, if you don't want to open the door, you don't have to but if you wanna slide the key out from underneath and go lock yourself in the bedroom or something 'til I'm done, we can do that."

Evie sighed. Ignoring her cascading fear might actually be a step toward recovery; she might have a chance to not be paranoid for the rest of her life. Against her better instincts, Evie spun the deadbolt and listened to its small reverberation as it lugged itself out of the way. She opened the door but kept the chain across, peering out at the officer through the gap.

"Alright, I'll let you in but just... just got to the bathroom and leave."

"Fair enough," Officer Gifford said with the type of smile cops had when they were trying to put others at ease. It only succeeded in making Evie more tense than she already was. She hadn't expected him to be so big. He was probably Jackson's size. It should have made her feel safer, but it didn't.

She was about to close the door when his smile widened and he said, "Point the way, and I'll be out of your hair in no time."

Evie undid the chain, swung open the door, and stepped rapidly back as if she was expecting him to grab her the instant he got in. She stuck one finger out in the direction of the bathroom, shrinking into the dark living room, hoping he couldn't see her at all.

"That way," she muttered. "Show yourself out when you're done."

"Not a problem, miss. And thanks again."

Evie sat in the chair farthest away from the door and turned it to face the entryway head on. She heard a scrape along the hardwood floor as she maneuvered the clunky club chair but she ignored it. Ignoring things was a skill at which she was getting better, she noticed.

From behind the closed door of the bathroom, the toilet flushed. Evie listened for the running water of the tap to rush then shut off. A few more seconds, and officer Gifford would be leaving. Another thing she had to keep telling herself: he's going to leave, he's going to leave, he'll just be another minute then he's going to leave.

Officer Gifford opened the bathroom door and paused when he got to the entryway. Evie was certain he could see her in her chair in the corner, keeping as far away from him as possible.

"Much appreciated, Ms. Hansen. I won't take up any more of your time."

"Okay. You're welcome."

As he turned to leave, officer Gifford's eyes rested on the portrait of Evie as a child. Evie hoped he had the good sense to continue on his way, but she knew from his inquisitive expression that another conversation was about to start.

"That's a great painting," he said, stepping away from the door and toward the picture. "Did you do it?"

"No," Evie replied curtly.

"Yeah, I guess not. Doesn't look like one of yours."

Evie's entire body shuddered as she watched officer Gifford approach the painting and crouch down in front of it.

At a glacial pace, she crawled out of the low-slung club chair until she was standing upright. Her hands moved behind her, searching for a weapon of any kind.

God, if you get me out of this, I'll never ignore my instincts again.

Rachel was on her way, but she still could be another twenty minutes, more if she had decided Evie's request for sandwiches was in earnest. Evie knew all too well that it didn't take that long to crush someone's windpipe. If Rachel was outside the apartment at that very moment, maybe then she'd have a shot at stopping whatever officer Gifford intended to do, but Evie suspected that unlikely.

How long would it take to rape her? How long would it take for him to knock her out and drag her off and squirrel her away to some terrifying location where she was at his mercy?

"What do you mean, 'One of yours?'" Evie asked, her hand still searching wildly behind her for anything she could use to fight him off.

As soon as she said it, she knew it had been the wrong move. She should have waited. Damn her always needing to be in control of a situation.

"Well, uh, you're an artist, right?" Officer Gifford tried the smile again, the cop smile that was supposed to put people at ease. "Pretty sure Jackson told me you were."

"Yeah, but just because you know I'm an artist doesn't mean you've seen my work."

Officer Gifford chortled to himself, looked down at the floor between his feet, then stood to his full height and set his shoulders back. He wasn't trying to put her at ease anymore.

By this point, he didn't care if she was frightened, at ease, or screaming bloody murder. Evie could see in his face exactly what he was thinking; 'You shouldn't have let me in, girl."

Should have made you shit in the gutter, Evie thought.

"Evie, baby, I don't know why you're doing this." Officer Gifford took a step toward her, his massive and callused hands outstretched. "All I ever tried to do was show you how much I appreciate you. How special I think you are."

"Don't come any closer," Evie warned. Her fingers closed around a wrought iron candle holder her mother had touted as being not only French but one of a kind. She brandished it in front of her. "I swear to God, I'll hit you in the fucking head and watch you bleed out."

The officer chortled again; it rang in Evie's ears. He wasn't scared of her, and her weapon would be useless the moment he knocked it out of her hands. They both knew it. His mocking laughter said so.

"Why are you acting like this, baby?" He paused where he was, both hands pressed into his chest like Evie had stabbed him in the heart.

"You broke into my house. Twice! You threw a brick through my window."

"After everything I did for you. After everything I forgave you for."

"Forgave me for?"

Officer Gifford slid quickly toward her. A startled scream bloomed then died on Evie's lips. He hadn't touched her but he had come close. Close enough to grab the candle holder. Close enough to pull her right into him.

"You shouldn't have had another man over," he told her, reaching out to slap her makeshift weapon away like a cat batting a toy. "What kind of cheating slut would do something like that right in front of me?"

"You're sick," Evie said though her throat ran dry. "You're fucking demented."

"Evie, baby, stop acting like you're scared." Officer Gifford took another step toward her. "I'm here now. We can be together. Everything is going to be okay now."

Despite Evie's overly casual tone, Rachel thought it pertinent to hurry. She didn't love the idea of Evie being by herself, and if she knew her friend as well as she thought she did, Evie would be sitting in the dark, sinking into a spiral of freaky thoughts. Rachel had long since accepted her friend's sometimes weird behavior as part and parcel for being an artist. On the other hand, every good artist needed a friend to yank them away from the pits of despair when they were enjoying too much time. wallowing there. Evie never quite agreed with that assessment, reminding Rachel that more often than not, famous artists were alone and unhappy for the majority of their lives.

"Yeah, well, maybe if they had a friend who took them shopping every once in a while, they would have been fine," Rachel retorted. The suffering creative trope had worn thin on her years back. She wasn't about to let Evie resign herself to such a dull, trite existence.

When she'd made it outside, the night turned wetter and colder than she expected. Autumn in New York liked throwing curveballs. For a moment, she considered running back inside and getting another layer but the cab she had called arrived just as she fished her keys out of her pocket, and she thought it better to get to Evie as soon as she could.

Unlike the street, the inside of the cab was too warm. Rachel dabbed at the sweat forming along her hairline and upper lip after only a few moments in the tropical climate. The heat made it stuffy too. She felt as if she was having trouble breathing but she gulped down a few mouthfuls of air and calmed herself.

Evie was alone, and Rachel was worried about her. The stress of it made her feel like everything was too much; too cold, too hot, too much to handle.

The ten-minute cab ride stretched longer than it should have. Rachel checked her watch and sighed loudly. In the rearview mirror, the driver made eye contact with her.

"You goin' somewhere important?" he asked. "Seem like you're in kind of a hurry."

"I'm going to a friend's place, and I'd just thought it would be faster than this."

"Faster than this? Lady, with traffic this drive could take almost a half hour. How much faster did you expect it to go?"

Rachel moved forward so she was sitting on the edge of the seat, her fingers poking through the grating that separated them. "Yes, with traffic it could take a half hour but I don't see any traffic, do you? It's two in the morning. We've seen one other car since you've picked me up. I've done this drive before and it usually takes about ten minutes."

"Done this drive, yeah? The two in the morning crosstown drive?" The driver winked at her in the mirror before looking back at the road. "I know a booty call when I see one."

"Oh Jesus Christ," Rachel muttered, sliding back into the seat. "Just get me there and try to do it before dawn, will ya?"

"Yeah, yeah, keep your pants on. Or don't. Wouldn't be the first time."

Rachel tented her hands and pressed her fingers to the tip of her nose. She had done this a lot as a child when her family still pretended to go to church. To her, it felt like praying, and in a way she couldn't explain, it relaxed her. The more pressure she applied, the better she felt.

Right now, though, it wasn't doing much of anything. Panic had started to rise in her chest, and she wished she had left sooner. Cursing herself for taking time to get properly dressed, Rachel took another deep breath and stared out the window as the city crawled by, shiny and wet and bigger than her imagination.

She would call back if something was wrong, Rachel told herself, right before some sinister voice deeper in her head added, *if she can*.

Chapter Twenty-Seven

"Out of my way! Get out of my way!"

Jackson sailed through an intersection, sirens blaring. He hadn't bothered to check that no one was coming the other way. He got lucky that it was so early in the morning, few people were on the roads. There were a few cabs and one oblivious motorist who didn't understand to pull off to the side when a cop car was behind him with flashing lights. Finally, Jackson was able to turn onto a side street and scream toward the upper east side.

"Maybe I'm being crazy," Jackson said out loud to himself as he cut a corner too close and his tires rolled up onto the curb. "Maybe the junkie really is the guy and Gifford will be asleep in his car when I get there."

At that moment, the only proof he had that an officer of the law was Evie's stalker was his gut. He knew he couldn't make an arrest on instincts alone, but he could at least be with her. Protect her.

Gifford had been the one to suggest Jackson take the intruder downtown; otherwise, he would have been more than happy to stay put.

"Being crazy, Jack. Being crazy." He slammed his hand on the steering wheel. "Why the hell did I listen to him, huh? Why the hell did I trust him?"

There was no sense in calming himself down, which didn't really seem possible at that time anyway. Jackson knew he worked better when he focused his rage, even though so much of it was directed at himself.

He was furious that he hadn't insisted on staying, furious that he hadn't told Gifford to take a hike. When he saw an on-duty officer sleeping in his car, especially when that same officer was trusted with watching over Evie, he should have made a stink. He should have told Gifford to drive the perp down to the station and knock off, give him some line about how he seems tired and should get some rest.

He rounded the corner and saw the straight shot that he had to cover to get to Evie's mother's place. To get to Evie. To lock the door and climb into bed with her, and sleep in late and rub their bodies together as they were gently roused from slumber. *All those things and more,* he thought as he sped through another stoplight. *We'll have all those things and more once I'm there.*

Jackson threw the car in park, lights still flashing, and ran toward Gifford's car. He wanted for all the world to catch the officer sleeping, to bang on the hood and scare the shit out of him. To call Wheeler once he was inside with Evie and get the man put back on leave, or worse.

But the cruiser was empty.

Jackson inhaled and exhaled, telling himself that that could mean any number of things. It didn't mean Gifford was the guy or that anything horrible was happening.

"I already know he's a shitty cop," Jackson said as he bolted toward the apartment building.

Please let him be around back with a working girl.

Even as he tried to reassure himself, Jackson couldn't shake that feeling that something was wrong. He took the stairs two at a time and didn't slow down once.

Evie held the candle holder above her head then out in front of her again. It was a terrible weapon, but she felt safer with it in front of her. Neither way mattered to Gifford. He was shaking his head and smiling as he stepped toward her, closing in. Her back almost touched the wall. She could feel it every time she breathed.

"I went to your show," he told her, steady and self-assured. "I fell completely in love with your work." He banged a hand on the small table beside the couch. "Bam! Just like that."

"Then buy a piece like everyone else and leave me alone."

"If I did that, I'd be ignoring all those details you put in it for me. All those little signs and messages."

Evie dropped the candle holder by her side, her heart pounding against her ribcage like a bucket drummer in Washington Square. "What the hell are you talking about?" she exclaimed, her expression twisting from frightened to downright angry. "Messages? To you? I've never even seen you before!"

"That one painting with the cops," the officer continued. "It started there. That pastry shop you painted is one of my favorites. Then, I started looking around at the rest of your work, paying close attention, and you know what I saw? So many of my favorite locations. So many parts of the city that I love, too."

"You've got to be kidding me," Evie said, her voice hollow. "Jesus Christ, you're out of your mind."

"Then, of course, I saw you. Do you know how beautiful you looked that night? Your hair, that dress. You smiled at me when I complimented your work, and I knew that was special because you didn't smile a lot during the whole show. For most of the night, you looked too anxious to smile." He touched his chest, his hand resting above his heart. "But you smiled at me."

"Listen, officer," Evie said, hoping to remind this freak of his badge and responsibilities. *Didn't he have to swear some oath?* "I think you've got this twisted up, ok? I don't even remember seeing you at the gallery opening. I'm sorry, but I saw so many people there."

Evie couldn't believe she just apologized to her stalker. Everything her mother, and years of city living, had taught her completely fled her mind. She had to regain control before this thing ended badly.

Officer Gifford's shoulders relaxed at her apology and she knew she was right. He thought things were going his way.

He inched closer. "I went out of my way to find those gifts for you, and you didn't even say thank you. In fact, you went right out and found another man. You brought him into your bed as if I didn't matter at all."

The sticky sweet cop smile had vanished. His eyes went dead then flared with anger.

Evie had seen that look before, on her park masturbator's face. That man had been older, hunched over and twisted up with his demons. But Gifford's eyes now had the same desperate, out of touch look in them, like he couldn't control the urges raging inside him much longer.

Evie stared past him toward the door, hoping to God that someone, anyone would come running in. She thought about trying to break past him, wondered if she could get the door open and scream so loud everyone on the floor would hear her.

They might be pissed off at first and come out just to chide whoever made that ungodly noise at two in the morning, but they wouldn't leave her in the hands of this lunatic. If nothing else, someone would call the cops.

It was a terrible idea, but her only chance.

Every second she waited, Officer Gifford closed the gap between them, narrowed the passageway through which she planned to escape.

Maybe I should just start screaming now, she thought, noticing that the chain for the door dangled longways down the molding. Door's unlocked. If I scream with all I've got, someone's bound to hear me.

"You're thinking about screaming, aren't you?" Gifford reached out to grab her arm. "I know you so well."

Evie swung the candle holder and landed a blow directly on his knuckles.

"Shit!" He clasped his struck hand against his body and glared at her. "You try to scream and I'll choke the life out of you."

"So what do you want from me?" Evie asked, still plotting her break for the door. "What? You want to date me? You want us to be boyfriend and girlfriend?"

"I would have considered that before I saw what a slut you are," Gifford spat.

"You're crazy!"

"You're a whore. You took my presents and wore them for another man. You didn't give a shit about what it did to me. As long as Jackson got his dick wet, right?"

Now or never.

Evie couldn't stand to hear any more of this man's deluded fantasies, and the longer she waited, the closer he got.

Without warning, she sprinted forward, breaking past him and reaching the door just as he turned to chase her.

I can't believe that fucking worked.

But when the door opened, his fingers wrapped through her curls. He yanked her backward into his arms. He pressed his face against her neck, inhaling deeply.

If there had been any doubt left in her mind, it was gone now.

"Leave me alone, you fucking creep," Evie said, throwing an elbow as well as she could with his arms around her.

"You remember that night you caught me?" he whispered, his tone too playful for his depravity. "You let me smell your hair."

"I didn't let you do anything!"

"You didn't stop me though."

Evie struggled but made no progress. Gifford held her, watching her twist to get away from him and knowing she couldn't. They both knew he couldn't.

He threw her violently down to the couch. Evie's stitches connected with the armrest, and she saw stars for one long agonizing moment. When her vision cleared, Gifford was on top of her, his hands roaming and his breathing heavy.

"Help me! Please, somebody help me!"

His hand clamped down over her mouth. "You keep quiet, understand? I don't want to hurt you, but I will if you make me."

Gifford pinned Evie's arms above her head, and Evie squeezed her eyes closed. She hoped it would be over quickly and he'd leave her alone. Deep down, she knew that wouldn't be the case.

His eyes had gone black, vacant. Nothing she could say would make a difference now.

Evie kicked as hard as she could, bucking and jerking to wrestle free. But every time she gained an inch, he closed himself around her like a snake.

"God, yeah," he grunted in her ear. "I knew you were a fighter."

Evie felt his eagerness pressing against her sweats.

She only had one shot left. When he let go of her to gain access, she had to be ready.

Suddenly, Gifford stopped. He released Evie's arms and slowly inclined with his hands above his head.

"Don't make me hurt you," Evie heard Jackson say though she couldn't see him. "I want to very much, and I will."

"Figured that out pretty quickly, Jacky," Gifford said with a blank look on his face. "I didn't expect to see you back here so fast."

"Get off her. On your feet."

Gifford stood up, leaving a wide-eyed Evie trembling on the couch. Jackson's gun was resting on Gifford's back the entire time until he turned around. Then Jackson pressed it into his chest.

"You figured that out on instinct, did you?" Gifford sneered. "You'd be a good cop if you weren't such a pussy."

"Your fall guy gave you away," Jackson told him. "Next time, hire an actor. Not a junky."

Gifford laughed. "Not enough method actors these days. Hard to find someone dedicated enough for a B and E." He shrugged and slowly climbed off Evie.

Jackson jerked the gun toward the far wall, signaling for Gifford to shut up and move.

Evie curled up in the corner of the couch, covering her bare legs with her shirt.

She'd barely gotten away from Gifford when, with two quick movements, he knocked Jackson's gun away and hit him right in the throat.

Jackson stumbled back, coughing, as Gifford slammed the door shut and threw him to the ground.

"I'll kill you, and your little girlfriend if I have to," he threatened, climbing on top of Jackson and wrapping his fingers around his neck. "If you had just stayed down there. If you had just stayed at the station."

Evie didn't want to think about the implication in that sentence. What would have happened seconds from now if Jackson hadn't come back for her. Or worse, when Gifford was done with her and she posed a threat to him.

Jackson, even with the other cop's large hands around his throat, managed a menacing growl. It reminded Evie of a wild animal giving one last warning before battle. It must have had the same effect on Gifford because he reared back, losing his grip.

In a split second, Jackson flipped them over and his hands went around Gifford's neck.

Evie didn't want to look but couldn't stop herself from staring at the deranged smile on her attacker's face, even while being throttled. He stared back at her as his face went red.

Jackson made as sound as if trying to speak, but his voice broke. He coughed and cleared his throat before yelling, "Evie, Find my gun!"

Evie tore herself away from the scene of them on her mother's musty beige carpet, from those piercing, soulless eyes, and scanned the living room. "I think it went this way," she said, heading toward the dining area.

Her attention had only been off them for a second when Jackson gasped in pain. When she turned back, Gifford was back on top. He punched Jackson in the chest and Evie felt her own heartbeat lurch in response. Then Gifford's meaty hands went back to Jackson's throat.

One of Jackson's hands pushed into Gifford's face, wedging itself under his chin, while the other reached overhead. The outstretched fingers crunched into a fist, clutching at nothing. Evie could see his eyes starting to bulge, a purple red hue was spreading from his forehead to his cheekbones.

Gifford was a much larger man than Jackson, and both of them had the same training as cops. Jackson had kept in markedly better shape, but he was helpless now that he was pinned. Evie knew Gifford's weight was immovable.

She caught her own breath, still faint and shaky, and scanned the room for a weapon. She was positive Jackson had come in the door gun in hand, but it had been knocked out of sight, and she couldn't find it.

Jackson let out a rasping sound.

Time was up.

Evie raised her mother's painting of her and swung the corner down into the back of Gifford's neck. The frame snapped and splintered, and Gifford released Jackson, his hands going to the injured spot.

"What the fuck? You stupid bitch!" he roared. His voice was so loud Evie didn't hear Jackson's panicked, desperate breath as he sucked air hungrily into his lungs.

"Don't you touch him! You hear me?" Evie swung the broken frame as Gifford turned toward her. "I'll kill you; I swear to God."

Gifford twisted his face into a sneer. "Kill me? How exactly, dear sweet Evie?"

"However I have to."

Gifford knocked the painting away. "Looks like you're out of weapons."

As he got closer, Evie rested a hand on the old rotary phone on her mother's end table next to the couch.

For years, Evie along with any man her mother dated, tried to convince the woman to update to something a bit more modern but she had always resisted. She told Evie she liked the weight of the older phones, that they sat in her palm with a heft the newer cordless phones didn't. Bringing it up silently behind her back, Evie found her and her mother in rare agreement.

This time, it was Evie who took a step forward.

Gifford froze, watching her intently. But, like the man that he was, his attentions weren't on her hands.

Evie cleared her dry throat, which made him finally look her in the eyes.

"If you've done your homework like a good little stalker, you'll know I grew up in this city. I know how to turn everything into a weapon."

She swung the phone wide, striking him square in the jaw.

"Asshole."

His teeth jutted outward. His eyes crossed. It was too dark to be sure but Evie thought she saw a trickle of blood running out of the corner of his mouth.

She dropped the phone at her feet as Jackson tackled Gifford from behind and held him to the floor.

There was little struggle left in him. To Evie, his eyes still look unfocused; she wondered if he was seeing stars.

One time after falling out of a tree as a kid, her vision went to a black gauze decorated by splashes of color spraying their tendrils in all directions. It had been a moment of pain that fascinated her to no end, and from then on, she understood the phrase she had heard so many times before.

Gifford was muttering, his voice sounding syrupy and thick.

Jackson weighed him down and yanked both his arms behind him. Evie noticed he looked like he had something on his mind, like he was suddenly very far away.

"What is it?" she asked.

"I don't have handcuffs," he told her.

"Maybe they flew off when he knocked your gun away."

"They're still on the junky."

Evie held a finger in the air and sprinted into her mother's room. She wasn't proud of what was about to happen, but considering Jackson was holding her hopefully concussed assailant to the floor with no way of restraining him, this was a necessary evil.

Next to her mother's bed was a table with a tiny drawer. When she yanked it open, she saw exactly what she knew she would.

Back out in the living room, she presented Jackson with a pair of handcuffs. Not pink and frilly ones, fuzzy with the playfulness of marital bondage, but real metal handcuffs. There was no safety catch, no release aside from the key rattling around somewhere in the drawer. Evie didn't care to look for it.

"They're my mother's," Evie said when Jackson took them from her with a quizzical expression involuntarily wrenching his features.

"Evie, I can't use novelty handcuffs to keep this guy restrained."

"They're not fake," Evie told him with a sigh that suggested she didn't want to talk about this. "Trust me."

Chapter Twenty-Eight

Jackson clicked one handcuff to Gifford's wrist and the other to the old radiator pipe jutting out of the wall. Gifford's head rolled from side to side, and he blinked as his eyes focused. He tugged his arm roughly, trying to grab Jackson while he struggled to free himself like an animal trapped in a snare.

"Let me out of here, Jack," Gifford warned, cool and even. He stopped thrashing and stared right into Jackson's eyes. "You don't want to fucking do this."

Jackson crossed his arms over his chest. "You have the right to remain silent. Anything you say can be held against you in a court of law—"

Gifford bellowed again, stretching one arm out in a futile attempt to bring Jackson down to his level. Jackson dodged the grab easily and continued with the spiel. He had considered just knocking Gifford out and telling the next cops on the scene that he went through the Miranda rights just as he was supposed to.

This piece of shit doesn't deserve rights, he had thought, but dismissed the idea before he gave it much attention. A slip-up like that was all it would take for Gifford to walk free, and then he'd be out on the streets again, angry about being rejected and knowing far too much about Evie for either of them to ever sleep soundly again.

"You have the right to an attorney. If you cannot—"

"You're a disgrace, Jack," Gifford snarled, glowering at his captor. "You're a fucking joke, and the whole force knows it."

Jackson struggled to ignore that jab but he kept on, unaware that Evie had ripped the old phone out of the wall and was crossing the room as calmly as if she was going to open the drapes to let in some sunshine.

Until it was too late.

Evie cracked Gifford in the face again, and he slumped silently to one side. A dark bruise immediately began to swell on his cheek. His eye split where she had landed the blow.

He looked so sad and helpless by then. This man who had terrified her, broken into her home and shattered her sense of peace, now lay discarded like a ragdoll. The phone clattered to Evie's feet she lowered herself to the ground.

Jackson went to her. "Evie, why did you do that?" he asked, gently. "Don't you understand that he can claim I abused him in custody? That I didn't get through his rights?"

Evie shrugged but didn't even glance in his direction. "Only the three of us know. It'll be our word against his."

Jackson couldn't believe what he was hearing. It had to be shock. She was in shock and not in control of her actions.

He pulled her into him. "Evie, that's lying, okay? That's not what I do. Not what we do. We're better than him."

Evie made a rattling noise in her throat, tossing her hands in the air then letting them drop heavily against the floor. When they connected, a dull echo leaked up to them from the apartment below. Walls in cities could never be thick enough to keep neighbors out of each other's space; there was always a sound or a smell or some annoyance that wriggled through the seams, the insulation, the gritty white plaster.

"You can do it this time, Jackson," Evie snapped at him. "You don't always have to be such a boy scout."

There was a pounding on the door that caused the two of them to freeze. In the struggle, the door had been slammed shut. When they didn't answer, the pounding continued.

"It could be my back-up," Jackson said. He slowly stood, looking around for his weapon.

"Are you expecting back-up?" Evie stayed on the floor beside Gifford.

Jackson wanted to move her, get her far away from him, but another knock interrupted that thought.

Evie gasped this time and looked to him for the answers. For protection.

"I tore out of the station so quickly. I don't know what I'm expecting. Wheeler probably sent someone."

"Cops usually announce themselves, right?"

Jackson nodded, and neither of them moved.

Finally, a voice they didn't recognize started to introduce itself through the door. "It's your neighbor," the voice told them. "We're just checking to make sure everything's alright. We thought we heard fighting."

Evie burst out laughing, and Jackson sighed through a smile. He bent over and kissed the top of Evie's head.

"Ya think they're used to hearing your mom fighting with people?" he asked as he straightened up and walked toward the door.

"God only knows what they hear from that woman."

Jackson pulled his badge out of his pocket and opened the door at the same time. A couple in their fifties was standing in the hallway, the man with a baseball bat nestled over his shoulder.

"Everything alright in there?" He tried to look past Jackson at Evie sitting hunched and laughing on the floor. "We heard some, uh, interesting noises."

"Sounded like you two were beating the shit out of each other," the woman said. She was doing the same dance as her husband; craning her head this way and that to get a glimpse of the action.

Jackson flashed his badge, holding it long in the light so they could see it clearly. "NYPD. I just subdued a predator that was attacking the young woman in here."

"No kidding," the man said, peering at the badge like he was checking for the mistake that would give away an obvious fake. "You need us to, uh, call anyone for you?"

"Yes," Evie said from out of sight. "The phone in here isn't working for some reason."

This made her burst into laughter again, and even Jackson broke a little before pulling himself together.

"If it makes you feel better," he told them, "then you should absolutely call the police. You don't have to trust me just because I have a badge."

The man and woman exchanged looks, and she nodded. "Ok, we're going to do that. No offense, ya see. We just don't want to walk away after hearing noises like that."

"Please do," Jackson said. "Tell them Officer Jackson Adams has subdued the assailant." Then, almost to himself he added, "And they're not gonna believe who it is."

"Well, now, that doesn't sound real at all," the man said as they walked back to their apartment. He lowered the bat right before he went inside, narrowing his eyes at Jackson. Not in a hateful way, more perplexed than anything.

Jackson didn't blame him. He was starting to feel pretty slap happy himself.

"Oh God," Evie said once the door was closed, and the apartment was returned to darkness.

"What? What is it? What's the matter?"

Jackson flicked a lamp on, fearing to see Gifford either awake and grabbing her or convulsing in a death rattle from head trauma. After all this, he wasn't about to let Evie get brought up on charges for killing a cop. Even if he was a psycho who stalked her, that could be a hard charge to fight.

But nothing was happening.

Evie knelt in the same spot except now the splintered frame of the portrait captivated her attention. Jackson watched as her eyes went cloudy then cleared. She got to her feet and stood over the wrecked piece with a weighted breath.

"My mother is going to kill me."

This was more than Jackson could take.

Response to traumas and emergencies were different from person to person. He was painfully aware of that as he had been since Marcus died, but the fact that Evie cared about anything at that moment, least of all a broken frame of a grotesque picture, throbbed the veins in his head.

He yanked her up toward him, closing his arms around her tighter than he meant to. Like a child hugging a puppy that had been lost, Jackson clutched Evie against him. Both their hearts pounded against every part of their bodies.

"You don't know how terrified I was," he said, his hand resting on the curls of the back of her head. "I was in the station with this sinking feeling in my stomach, and when it finally came to me..." He trailed off, cleared his throat like he was going to keep talking, yet stayed silent.

Evie nodded her curls against his chest. "I didn't want to let him in, Jack," she told him.

"It can be hard to say no to cops."

"Even as I was doing it, I felt like I was doing something wrong. Like I was making a mistake."

Jackson released her, cupping her face in his hands. "You didn't make any mistakes. You were doing the best you knew."

Evie leaned forward and kissed him.

At first, Jackson didn't quite kiss back. He seemed frozen, stock still and unsure of what the protocol was. As his lips softened to hers, Evie felt him shift gears.

"You don't have to be a cop right now, or a bodyguard, or anything else," she told him. "For the first time since we've been together, you can just be Jackson."

"Oh my, Evie. I didn't know we were 'together.'" He moved as if pulling away, an over dramatic look of concern on his face.

Evie slapped his shoulder, limp wristed.

Parts of her were on fire, powered by adrenaline and the manic thrill of survival. Her brain splashed images of Jackson's body prone on her bed, his wrists handcuffed in place, her mouth closing around the head of his cock, their hips connecting as she sank onto him like he was driving a sword into her.

She tried to pull herself away from the spiral but that didn't do any good. The more she tried not to think about fucking Jackson, about earlier that day when he fit so perfectly and smoothly inside her ass, the more images her mind's eye showed her.

For what it was worth, Jackson seemed to be having the same trouble. "I wonder how unethical it would be for us to fuck while we waited for the back-up to get here," he mused, his fingers creeping under Evie's shirt. "Maybe that couple called the cops, and we'll be interrupted by officers who have no idea what's going on here."

"What? Like they've never seen an unconscious, beaten man handcuffed to a radiator while a couple has sex right next to him?"

Jackson grimaced. "Dear God, you perv. I was at least going to suggest the bedroom."

He pressed his lips to her neck, and Evie exhaled loud through her nose. Her fingers pressed into his shoulder blades; she crushed her body into his. She tried to fill the space between them. Then she stepped away so abruptly that Jackson almost stumbled forward.

"Rachel's on her way over. If she isn't already here."

"When did you call her?"

"A little before this asshole started attacking me. She said she'd be here in twenty minutes, and when it comes to 911 situations, your sister can motor."

Jackson snorted and shook his head, then moved his hand in front of his bulge self-consciously. "You're kidding me."

"You don't think so?" Evie swatted his hand away and traced the outline with her fingernail.

"I guess I've never seen her in an emergency," Jackson said through a loud exhale. "Anytime I'm waiting for her to show up somewhere it's just for fun, and she's always thirty minutes late." He stepped forward, pushing them both toward her room.

Evie kissed him, hard, but pulled her hand away. "That's so she can make an appearance."

As she moved to give Jackson space to fix himself, she caught sight of Gifford's blood on the floor.

Then, without warning, Evie felt like Alice in Wonderland, the apartment shrinking around her as her pulse thundered in her ears. The apartment spun; the floor rushed away from her, then nearer.

"Ya ok?" Jackson asked, sounding very far away.

Evie put a hand on his shoulder and let him lead her out into the hallway. The first blare of lights washed the world into a florid glare but the cool dark wood and fading yellow bulbs of the stairwell soothed them both. From Evie's shaky perspective, the hall lights had blasted everything so strongly that it went flat; the stairwell brought back the dimension.

"I think it just occurred to me that I was standing next to the man I hit in the face with a phone," Evie said, leaning her forehead against the polished wood banister. "Being in that apartment felt impossible."

"Can I ask you a question?"

"Sure." Evie shrugged. She hadn't quite regained control of her body so the motion felt slow and thick.

"Where did your mother get real police quality handcuffs from?"

Evie faced him, incredulous. "That's what you want to know? Not why she had them? Just where she got them from?"

"Oh, Evie, c'mon. I'm not a child." He lifted his shoulders, grinning sheepishly and knocking his foot into hers. "I know why she had them."

"Control issues run in the family, I suppose."

"Do you think she wants to be in control or out of it?" Jackson asked, his foot knocking into hers again. "She could be kind of a switch like you."

"I'm nothing like my mother. And you're gonna traumatize me worse than the stalker if you don't stop."

Jackson brought Evie's hand to his face, kissing the back of it then touching the red knuckles, raw from battle. "I should go down to the squad car and actually make sure that back-up is coming. Or at least tell Wheeler that we're okay."

"You can do that in a minute," Evie said, draping her leg over his thigh. "Sit with me for a bit more. Wait with me until Rachel comes."

They leaned their foreheads together. Jackson pressed her hands in his. "You don't have to stay here, ya know. You can sit in the squad car."

"The idea of standing up and walking down stairs is impossible right now. I think I forgot how to do either of those things."

"I'll carry you. All the way down to the street."

Evie sat back from him, her expression soft. She nodded, not bothering to say anything beyond that. Jackson slid his arms under her and lifted her to his chest. Instinctively, her arms went around his neck, and she had to roll her eyes at the whole scene.

"What?" Jackson asked.

"Nothing. It's just... what a cliché, right?"

"Evie, trust me, nothing about you is cliché."

He went steadily, and Evie tried not to worry about how many flights they had to go down, how many more steps, how heavy she was getting to him. Her mind leapt between flashes of Jackson emerging from the bathroom in a towel, certainly strong enough to carry her for miles, with flares of anxiety.

How long had she been insisting she was fine on her own? How many years had she managed to make it? And now she was being carried down the stairs?

Oh shut up, she told her brain when the ticking concern started. *Just let me enjoy this.*

"I feel like I'm high," Jackson said with a soft giggle as they got closer to the lobby. "Like I'm just sort of floating along."

"But officer Adams, how could you possibly know what it's like to be high?"

Jackson smirked at her then pinched her wherever he could get his fingers together. Evie shrieked, reflexively folding inward.

"I'm not that much of a boy scout," Jackson said, catching his own eye as the yellowed mirror came into view. The memory of the last time he passed the distorted image burned into his mind. He'd ignored his gut and put Evie in danger. "I've done some bad things here and there."

"I'll bet."

Crossing the lobby this time, Jackson was struck by the oddest sense of déjà vu. Not that it was the same as it was when he was leading the handcuffed patsy out to the waiting squad car where the man who set him up slept. Or pretended to.

Jackson realized now that the sensation he experienced when he thought he had won the game wasn't relief that this was over but the feeling he got from being satiated, collapsing in orgasm or watching a playmate twist in their own.

Other arrests, high stakes or not, he felt the animation of adrenaline; felt himself being powered by a fuel his body released to push him further. He saw it in the speed freaks and coke users they brought in; he understood that specific urge more than he cared to admit.

If he was feeling adrenaline, it was quieter than it had been in the past. Mainly, he felt a calming breeze flow down his face, drying the sweat that collected where Evie's wrists met the skin of his neck. Whether it was a draft from the glass paneled front door or a catharsis Jackson couldn't put into words didn't matter to him. Evie grew faintly heavy in his arms, and he was calmed by the sight of rain shimmery on the street.

"It's such a beautiful night," he said, lowering Evie to her feet as they got to the door. "Can you walk?"

"Yeah, thanks."

They stepped outside, and Evie gave a contented sigh, as if she knew what he meant right away. Beautiful nights don't happen like beautiful days. It was chilly and rainy and the golden echo of streetlights danced on every surface.

"Beautiful," he repeated.

"Beautiful," Evie agreed.

Jackson reached for the non-existent collar of a jacket he wasn't wearing. He froze with his hands tugging by his ears and shook his head. "I can't believe I didn't bring a coat from the station."

"I guess you were in a hurry."

"If I had taken my shoes off, I'd be barefoot right now."

He sprinted down the steps toward the squad card, leaving Evie alone in the alcove under the overhang.

The stone awning caused irregular streams of rain to form, and they blew across Evie's vision like scratches on a filmstrip. She started to shiver but hardly noticed; the golden shimmering night was too intriguing for her to feel the cold.

Jackson emerged from the driver's side of the squad card and sprinted back up the stairs with something in his hand. He tossed it at Evie as he got closer.

"What's this?" she asked. She held the item up, and it fluttered in the wind like a flag.

"Pants. Sweatpants. Probably someone's workout pants. They were bunched up on the floor of the car."

"Oh, dear God." She lowered the pants to her side. "Of all the indignities I've suffered tonight—"

"Shut up and put 'em on. Wheeler's gonna kill me if a cruiser rolls in and you're standing there in a t-shirt and panties."

"Just tell her we were fucking so hard we didn't notice when they got here."

Jackson gave her a look out of the side of his eye, running his tongue over his teeth and shaking his head. "Don't tempt me, woman," he said. He raked his eyes over her still bare legs. "I'll bend you over this banister and knock your knees apart so quickly…"

Evie looped a finger into the waistband of his pants and pulled him toward her. "Oh yeah, officer? That's what you're going to do with the poor victim in your custody?" She made her voice as sickeningly sweet and faux innocent as she could, pouting her lips.

"You nasty girl."

They came together again, one of Evie's small, tight fists clenching the pants to keep from grabbing his cock right there. Her legs were turning to rubber under her, and Jackson's large hot hand slipped under the inner part of her thigh just in time to feel the tremor.

"We probably shouldn't," Evie whispered as she wrapped a leg around him. "It's not a good idea."

"Then why are you rubbing your cunt on me like you're marking your territory?"

"Because that's exactly what I'm doing."

Their mouths connected, pulse points pounding in sync. Only moments ago the cold encroached but now, under the stone awning rivering raindrops into streams, they pressed into each other and gave off steam. Neither gave a shit about the city street life buzzing around them.

Chapter Twenty-Nine

A sense of timing was probably Rachel's best feature, though at that very moment, she wondered if it was more of a curse than a blessing. The cabbie had ignored her for most of the ride unless he was telling her that she must not know the city that well.

"Or maybe this is just a new guy's house," he remarked, eye contact in the rearview mirror. Rachel refused to look away, staring right back at him expressionlessly. A few years in a city teaches someone how to deal with every situation imaginable, and Rachel had encountered plenty of guys who tried to get a rise out of her. Any reaction suited them except for stony silence.

They rounded the corner to the block the apartment was on. Rachel told the cabbie to slow down and head toward the haphazardly parked police cruiser. There were a few lights on in the building; Rachel hoped that was a good sign.

"Ok, you can drop me off right by the cop car," she said, handing him a fistful of bills. She hadn't looked at the meter; she knew she was probably overpaying but she wanted to get out of this cab and find Evie as soon as possible.

"What kinda trouble you in?" the cabbie asked. Rachel ignored him again, pushing the money against his shoulder. "'Drop me off at the cop car', she says. I had you pegged from the start." He didn't call her anything vulgar but his tone said enough.

"I'm not asking you to stick around or anything. Just drop me off and take the money and go find your next victim."

"I hope he's worth it," the cab driver sneered, snatching the money from her fingers. "Or I hope he's still alive."

The rain wasn't coming down very hard but it was steady, silvery. Rachel pulled her jacket over her head and ran toward the building. There were people on the stoop; she could see the shape of them but not who it was.

Oh God, please be Evie, she thought as her feet splashed water up on the back of her knees. And Jackson. Oh God, please be Evie and Jackson.

Upon the figures on the stoop coming clear, Rachel skidded to a halt. She stood on the glittering sidewalk staring up at them, her jacket tented overhead in her two index fingers and sending the collection of droplets down the sides of her wrists. Once again, her infallible sense of timing had led her to bear witness to her brother and best friend making out, one of them being sans pants. If she hadn't been so whiplashed, going from anxious to repulsed in a heartbeat, she might have actually found it all funny.

"Ugh, is this what I'm going to have to get used to?" Rachel crowed, dropping her tented fingers and scampering up the steps. "Look, I'll agree to you guys dating if you promise never to, like, have sex or anything."

"Scout's honor," Jackson said as Evie dropped her leg, and he put his arm chastely around her. "Evie said you were gonna be here in twenty minutes."

"I think she made it in nineteen," Evie said.

Rachel brushed her wet hair off her face then held her hands out as if trying to touch both of them but not getting close enough. "Does somebody want to tell me what happened or why you two are down here in the rain in what some might say is inadequate clothing?"

"Don't be such a prude." Evie held up the sweats, wrinkled and moist from the rain. "I've got pants."

"We'll talk about it later," Jackson told her.

"But everything's okay?"

"Yeah, everything's okay." He and Evie smiled at each other. Evie raised her eyebrows rapidly. "Everything's great."

"God, this feels weird," Rachel said but she dropped it after that. None of them knew what else to say anyway.

Evie slipped her feet through the elastic around the ankles of the sweatpants. The very bottom of the cuff was already wet, and she knew this wouldn't do much good in the way of keeping her warm. Her body rested against Jackson's; any chill she had felt was gone. He was a better source of heat anyway.

Above them, through the uneven drone of rain, Evie and Jackson heard the neighbors talking back and forth. Their voices flowed down the stairwells, out the windows. Beyond that, sirens shrieked their arrival, far away yet but growing. Their lights were thrown further in the slick, reflective city, and the tsunami of blue and red could be seen from blocks away.

Evie wriggled her bare feet onto the cold stone of the stoop as the squad cars approached. The muscles in her shoulders sank deeper into her back; her lungs lifted as if they were being pushed upwards from below.

It had been so long since she had been able to exhale; to breathe normally. The damp air was a torrent into her chest; she tasted the rain across her tongue.

Filled with a sense of calm, Evie lifted her head and kissed Jackson. A long, determined kiss that she hoped said everything she would probably never be able to put into words. He pulled her to him, their entire bodies pressed to each other, their connection more than just crotch to crotch.

She wasn't sure how long they kissed, standing there out in the open on the rain-soaked stoop, but Jackson eventually leaned back, kissed her on the forehead, and gathered her in a warm hug.

"It's a beautiful night," Jackson whispered in her ear as their last moments of solitude were broken by the sirens and the tires slicing through water.

Evie inhaled and exhaled the moisture again. She wrapped her arms around her very own Adonis and sighed again.

"It really is," she agreed. "It would make a great painting. Maybe I'll call it *Beginnings*."

Thank You for Your Time

I truly hope you've enjoyed my story. I can promise you I had a lot of fun writing it. If you could, please consider leaving a review on Amazon, Goodreads, Bookbub, or your own blog. I'd love to feature any reviews or comments.

Reviews go a long way toward helping authors get noticed and your feedback is very important to me.

Remember to check out these other titles…

And join my newsletter to be notified of our new releases every month! www.sendfox.com/hardmoonpress1

Printed in Great Britain
by Amazon